As he stared, a doorway on the opposite side of the chamber opened, and a group of seemingly normal humans burst in. One of them sprinted frantically for a control board which, Jason was coldly certain, contained a self-destruction switch.

"Stop him!" Jason yelled.

But even as he spoke, another IDRF squad emerged from the far door and proceeded to blast down the Transhumanists they had been pursuing. One man, not content to have killed the running technician, fired a second plasma bolt into the control board, which fairly exploded in a shower of sparks and a cloud of smoke.

"Cease firing!" Jason called out. "We want to take all this stuff intact."

"That's affirmative," said Major Rojas, who had just entered the chamber. She walked across the stage looking around curiously, and stepped up to Jason. They both removed the hoodlike flexible helmets of their combat environment suits and took deep breaths of the ozone-shot air.

"Everything under control, Major?" asked Jason, running a hand through his sweat-drenched hair.

"Pretty much. We're mopping up. A good thing surprise was total. As it is, we lost too many men. And some of the things we lost them to . . ." The major couldn't continue. She was a hardened combat veteran, but she was also, inescapably, a product of her culture.

"Yeah, I know. I saw." Jason hoped the medics, following along behind the advancing squads, had gotten to Wei in time. "But take my word: it was worth it."

"So we've all been told."

Baen Books by Steve White

The Jason Thanou Series:
Blood of the Heroes
Sunset of the Gods
Pirates of the Timestream
Ghosts of Time
Soldiers Out of Time

The Prometheus Project
Demon's Gate
Forge of the Titans
Eagle Against the Stars
Wolf Among the Stars
Prince of Sunset
The Disinherited
Legacy
Debt of Ages
St. Antony's Fire

The Starfire Series:
by David Weber & Steve White
Crusade
In Death Ground
The Stars at War
Insurrection
The Shiva Option
The Stars at War II

by Steve White & Shirley Meier
Exodus

by Steve White & Charles E. Gannon
Extremis
Imperative

To purchase these and all Baen Book titles in e-book format, please go to www.baen.com.

SOLDIERS OUT OF TIME

STEVE WHITE

SOLDIERS OUT OF TIME

Copyright © 2015 by Steve White

A Baen Books Original

Baen Publishing Enterprises
P.O. Box 1403
Riverdale, NY 10471
www.baen.com

ISBN: 978-1-4767-8173-0

Cover art by Don Maitz

First Baen mass market printing, August 2016

Distributed by Simon & Schuster
1230 Avenue of the Americas
New York, NY 10020

Library of Congress Cataloging-in-Publication Data:
2015017029

Printed in the United States of America

10 9 8 7 6 5 4 3 2 1

SOLDIERS
OUT OF TIME

CHAPTER ONE

✧✧✧

In the claustrophobic confines of the subterranean tunnel, the sound was deafening as the near-fusion-temperature discharge from the Mark XI plasma gun roared down its laser guide beam. And the star-like glare would have been blinding had the faceplate of Jason Thanou's combat environment suit not automatically polarized. That suit also protected him from being roasted alive by the backwash of superheated air—not that his tingling skin felt particularly protected.

He had, by virtue of his brain implant, detected the presence of functioning bionics just before the cyborg had appeared around a corner from a side-tunnel with superhuman suddenness, bringing a rocket launcher into line. That small edge had enabled Jason to fire off a snap-shot. Thus it was that he lived while the cyborg was enveloped in flame and incinerated. Its screams (Jason would not allow the thing the pronoun "his") were

1

inaudible in the general hellish noise. Now Jason proceeded on, motioning his squad to follow.

His unaided strength would barely have sufficed to lift the plasma gun off the floor. But his form-fitting suit, while lacking the servo-boosted myoelectronic "muscles" of the space marines' golemlike powered combat armor, was more sophisticated. It had an inner lining of pressure sensors that allowed its nanofabric, with its microscopic electric motors, to not only duplicate the wearer's movements as if the suit wasn't there but also amplify his strength by a factor of almost two. It was the kind of application of nanotechnology that could pass muster under the Human Integrity Act, for it had a legitimate purpose and it did not blur the sacrosanct distinctions between life and non-life, between man and machine, between brain and computer. And it represented the cutting edge of late twenty-fourth-century military equipment.

Thus it was that Jason hefted a weapon that used a battery of tiny converging lasers to heat a superconductor-suspended hydrogen pellet to a plasma state and expel it through a magnetically focused field along the laser beam that drilled a tube of vacuum through the air. It wasn't a subtle weapon, even by the standards of today's military firepower. But this wasn't a time for subtlety. And even at this moment, in the midst of this firefight, he took an instant to reflect that it was a far cry from what he was accustomed to.

For example, the black-powder percussion-ignition Minié rifles and front-loading revolvers of the American Civil War, on his last mission. Or the muzzle-loading smoothbore muskets and flintlock pistols of the piratical seventeenth-century Caribbean, on the mission before that. Not to mention assorted swords, spears, maces, axes and so forth in the course of his career as head of the Special Operations Section of the Temporal Service, the enforcement arm of the Temporal Regulatory Authority which oversaw all lawful time travel.

That word "lawful" was, of course, the rub. And it was precisely why Jason was here, on a mission in his own native time, somewhat outside his usual jurisdiction. Indeed, he was the cause of that mission.

The Transhuman Dispensation had had three generations of absolute power, beginning in the early twenty-second century, to try to remake Earth in their own twisted image. They had made full use of the time, employing genetic engineering, bionics and perverted nanotech to generate distorted travesties of humanity—specialized castes ruled by an elite of genetically enhanced supermen. But then the descendants of the colonists who had fled the hell Earth was becoming had returned to the homeworld on the wings of the faster-than-light drive they had invented. The revolt they had sparked had taken another four decades, but by 2270, the year of the Human Integrity Act, Earth had been washed clean by a torrent of blood.

Or so everyone had thought until Jason had returned from Classical Greece with the horrifying truth. The Transhumanist leadership, foreseeing defeat well in advance, had secretly prepared for it, carefully establishing a large, lavishly financed and very well equipped underground organization that was alive and well in the shadowy places of Jason's own era, still pursuing its mad dream of a self-created evolutionary step beyond *Homo sapiens*.

Nor was that the worst of it. At some point after 2310, when Weintraub had discovered the theoretical basis for time travel, but before he and Fujiwara had perfected the temporal displacer two decades later, the Transhumanists had stolen Weintraub's work. And they had discovered a flaw in Weintraub's math that was still sticking like a thorn in the heel of the Authority's time-travel technology; only a titanic installation, requiring an energy expenditure that would have been beyond the capacity of any civilization that had not harnessed the power of matter/antimatter reactions, could overcome it by brute force. The Transhumanists' displacer, suffering from no such handicaps, was compact and energy-efficient enough to be concealable. And they were using it in an ongoing campaign to subvert the past.

And it got even worse. The time-traveling Tranhumanists had made contact with the Teloi aliens who, as Jason had previously discovered, had created the human species and continued to meddle as best they could. Contacts between the two were fitful, but should they ever manage to effectively combine forces, the consequences did not bear contemplating.

It was because of all of this that the Special Operations Section had been formed, under Jason's command. It had foiled a number of the Transhumanists' plots and on two occasions aborted their attempts to exploit Teloi contacts. But, as Jason had known only too well, he was struggling in the dark with only the vaguest intelligence concerning his enemies.

Then on Jason's last mission, to the final months of the American Civil War, a real break had finally come. Amid the flaming chaos of Richmond's fall, he had obtained a certain Transhumanist data chip. It had not provided the one item the Authority—and Earth's entire law enforcement community—most desperately wanted to get: the date known as *The Day*, when the Transhuman nightmare was due to rise again. But it had been a goldmine of other information about the underground organization, including the second most-desired item: the location of the illicit temporal displacer.

Intelligence analysts had been skeptical at first, wary as always of cleverly planted disinformation. At the same time, in case it *was* genuine, the data had been tested out in ways that would not reveal the Authority's possession of it, for Jason had assured them that the Transhumanists had no way of knowing the data chip hadn't simply been left in the ashes of Richmond's "Burnt District." Repeated, careful probing of unimportant targets had finally convinced the skeptics. Only then had this assault been authorized.

It was, of necessity, a military or at least quasimilitary operation. But Jason had been assigned to it at his own request, as the Authority's liaison and for his extensive and often sanguinary experience in dealing with the Transhumanists. Thus he had been aboard one of the six GV-73 armed personnel carriers, heavily modified for enhanced stealth and other purposes, that had unobtrusively rendezvoused at a point on the barren eastern coast of Patagonia just south of the Rio Chico, at fifty degrees south latitude. It had been early southern hemisphere spring, and they had had just enough time to thank whatever gods they worshipped that it was not winter, as they endured the bleakness of a seacoast only a hundred and fifty miles north of the Straits of Magellan. But then the prearranged time had arrived, and Major Rojas of the Internal Defense and Response Force had given the order.

They had set out by night, westward up the valley of the Rio Chico and then turning slightly to port and following the tributary that led to Lake Viedma, in the foothills of the Patagonian Andes near their southernmost end. Skimming the lake, they had continued on over the mountains on the wings of grav repulsion, following gorges flanked by conifer-covered slopes and granite cliffs, keeping to the undetectably low altitude permitted by terrain-following radar and other sensors, under computer control. No one had been in the mood to admire the scenery by the gathered starlight of passive IR imaging.

Beyond the crest, the Andes had sloped steeply toward the Pacific coast—a fjord coast of labyrinthine waterways and islands, the mountainous chasms choked with immemorial glacier ice. Beyond the glacier, the fjord they had sought had snaked its way westward, past Saumarez Island where there was some human habitation. But their objective lay before that, and Jason and the other men had grasped handholds to steady themselves as the carriers had surged ahead and simultaneously banked hard to starboard, toward a huge but well-camouflaged entrance in the almost sheer cliff-face bounding the fjord to the north.

That cliff, they had known, was honeycombed with sensors and defenses—but most of these had a westward orientation, expecting any attack to come from the Pacific, beyond the maze of mountainous islands. So the Transhumanists had been caught flat-footed when the formation of carriers had wheeled and the lead two units—the ones that had been fitted with hardpoints for missile launchers of a sort usually reserved for spacecraft—had fired a rapid volley of two Firebird missiles each at the entrance.

This had not been an occasion for subtlety, especially given the lack of nearby human habitation. Nevertheless, the Firebirds' "dial-a-yield" laser-triggered deuterium-fusion warheads had been set at their lowest yield—about 0.0001 kiloton of the traditional measure of TNT. It had proven adequate. The four simultaneous detonations had merged into a single momentary artificial sunburst that had blasted in the massive sliding doors. After riding out the shock wave, all six carriers had surged forward through the jagged opening, their plasma repeaters—larger, rapid-fire versions of the portable versions—firing through the smoke into the interior, clearing the way by indiscriminately destroying anything and everyone inside.

They had settled down on the floor of a cavernous space, now littered with wreckage and incinerated bodies and smoldering with scattered fires. The side panels of the GV-73s had fallen away and the IDRF raiders had sprung forth. Even though Jason's captured data had led them to expect this extensive grav-vehicle hangar, its size had still been a shock. Only lavish application of nanotechnology could have permitted the hollowing out of such a volume under the Andes unnoticed, even in this godforsaken near-Antarctic region.

And this was only the vestibule, as it were, of the installation. At once, according to prearranged plan, the squads had fanned out, blasting down the few surviving Transhumanist personnel in the hangar, and headed for the hatchways that led into the bowels of the beast.

As a kind of liaison officer and consultant, Jason wouldn't normally have been leading one of the IDRF squads. But he had a couple of special qualifications.

For one thing, he held the rank of commander in the Hesperian Colonial Rangers, the paramilitary constabulary of his native world. (Coincidentally, it was the same rank-title he bore in the Special Operations Section.) So he was not unfamiliar with military-grade firepower, however rarely he had ever had to use it. But more importantly, his rank and duties entitled him to a neurally interfaced computer implant of the sort that flew directly in the face of the Human Integrity Act but for which exceptions were grudgingly made for certain military and law enforcement officers. Among its many other functions, the implant projected directly onto his optic nerve a map of his surroundings, as long as those were programmed into it. Major Rojas, who had a very limited number of subordinates possessing such implants, had put Jason in command of one of the squads converging through separate tunnels on their common objective.

Now he quickly consulted the ghostly map display that

seemed to float in front of his eyes, with the tiny red dots that showed the location of the other squad leaders' implants. At first those dots had seemed to exist in the near-limbo of a very partial floor plan. But now the map display was growing in complexity as the tiny but very sophisticated computer in his skull was swiftly adding details as it absorbed visual input. *So far so good*, he thought. Just ahead, a ramp led up to a right turn in the passageway . . .

A small sphere came sailing out from beyond that corner, hit the wall with a *pling*, and rolled down the ramp.

Jason acted without pausing for thought. "Grenade!" he yelled, as he stepped forward and kicked the thing back up the ramp, and then instantly joined the rest of the squad in flattening himself against the walls.

There was none of the shattering explosion he had expected. Indeed, there was little more than a loud *pop* near the top of the ramp, and a spray of a viscous fluid. But then the walls and floor in that area began to lose their texture, dissolving into a gray goo. Spots of the same dissolution of matter sprouted down the ramp toward the squad as the fluid spattered.

Jason's gorge rose as the invisible cloud of nanobots did their work of breaking down the molecular structure of matter. Corporal Wei clutched his arm and screamed as the microscopic agents of destruction ate through the nanofabric of the combat environment suit and into muscle and bone.

Mere possession of the stuff was a felony, use of it on humans a capital felony. But, Jason knew, the nanobots only remained active for thirty seconds. As he counted down those seconds, a second grenade came from around the corner. He fired at a range of only a few yards, blasting the thing into its component atoms in mid-air. Even inside his suit, his body was instantly bathed in sweat and he was sure he could feel blisters rising. But, ignoring the intolerable heat, he sprang forward, splashing through the partially dissolved floor, and swung around the corner, plasma gun leveled.

He faced an improvised barricade. The three defenders behind it made his gorge rise even more than the nanoweapon had.

The Transhumanists he had encountered on extratemporal expeditions had, of course, been ones who could pass unnoticed in earlier epochs. Some had been genetically tailored for extreme good looks, others for mere ordinariness, but all were of normal human semblance. But here, there was no need to blend. These were cyborgs of the soldier castes, grotesquely squat and muscular, and no attempt had been made to conceal or soften the obscene coupling of flesh and machinery. One of them raised an artificial left arm incorporating an integral weapon, and the air crackled as a stream of electromagnetically accelerated flechettes went supersonic. Jason went to his right knee just in time; someone behind him screamed briefly. But then other members of the squad piled around the corner, and a fusillade of plasma bolts reduced the cyborgs to charred flesh and melted metal.

"Almost there!" Jason called out, and led what was left of his squad through the shattered barricade. Ahead, a large doorway loomed. Beyond, they found themselves in a large open space, its walls lined with instrument panels and most of its floor occupied by a flat stage.

That stage was larger than that of the Authority's installation in Australia. But that, Jason knew, was deceptive. This required no massive supporting equipment, and it was powered by an ordinary micro-fusion reactor.

As he stared, a doorway on the opposite side of the chamber opened, and a group of seemingly normal humans—technicians, by the look of them—burst in. One of them sprinted frantically for a control board which, Jason was coldly certain, contained a self-destruction switch.

"Stop him!" Jason yelled.

But even as he spoke, another IDRF squad emerged from the far door and proceeded to blast down the Transhumanists they had been pursuing. One man, not content to have killed the running technician, fired a second plasma bolt into the control board, which fairly exploded in a shower of sparks and a cloud of smoke.

"Cease firing!" Jason called out. "We want to take all this stuff intact."

"That's affirmative," said Major Rojas, who had just entered the chamber. She walked across the stage looking around curiously, and stepped up to Jason. They both removed the hoodlike flexible helmets of their combat environment suits and took deep breaths of the ozone-shot air.

"Everything under control, Major?" asked Jason, running a hand through his sweat-drenched hair.

"Pretty much. We're mopping up. A good thing

surprise was total. As it is, we lost too many men. And some of the things we lost them to . . ." The major couldn't continue. She was a hardened combat veteran, but she was also, inescapably, a product of her culture.

"Yeah, I know. I saw." Jason hoped the medics, following along behind the advancing squads, had gotten to Wei in time. "But take my word: it was worth it."

"So we've all been told." Rojas looked around the chamber again. "So this is it?"

"Yes. This is the Transhumanists' temporal displacer."

CHAPTER TWO

"Well," said Kyle Rutherford, gusting a sigh of relief and leaning back in his chair with a smile, "that's that!"

"Is it?" asked Jason expressionlessly.

Rutherford's brows knitted, and he gave the three people across his desk a sharp look.

They sat in Rutherford's office, deep in the Temporal Regulatory Authority's vast displacer facility in Australia's Great Sandy Desert. The Authority was a quasi-public agency, and its organizational structure was corporate; Rutherford, as its operations director, was the equivalent of its chief executive officer, reporting to the governing council that answered to a board of directors. As such, he rated a large office, although he kept (and actually preferred) a smaller one on the other side of the globe, in Athens practically in the shadow of the Acropolis. But his inner sanctum was less opulent than most people expected, largely bare of ornamentation that might have distracted the eye from the display case along the wall behind the desk and the literally priceless objects from the past that it contained. It was against this backdrop that Rutherford now sat, stroking his neat gray Van Dyke, not in his usual insufferably self-satisfied manner but in a nervous way that suggested reawakened worry.

"Whatever do you mean, Jason? You've made a report favorable on all points. Yes, I know," he hastily added, raising a hand against interruptions. "There are still many Transhumanist cells to be located and rooted out. Indeed, the evidence turned up after the raid suggests that their top leadership is still at large. But now it is just a matter for ordinary law enforcement. We've taken their temporal displacer, so the past is secure from their subversion."

"Can we be certain of that?" asked Superintendent Alexandre Mondrago, Jason's second-in-command in the Special Operations Section. Like a number of Special Ops personnel, he was an ex-mercenary, and Jason could amply attest to his deadliness. Indeed, it almost lay in his genes, for he was a Corsican who came of a long and violent tradition—*not* necessarily always a criminal one, as he was at pains to point out. He had once told Jason that he numbered among his ancestors a member of the "Action Service" of the French Secret Service— predominantly Corsican, and with shadowy links to the *Union Corse*—in the mid-twentieth-century when the French state had been in a fight for its life against the extreme right-wing terrorists of the "Secret Army Organization." He had said it as though it meant something, and Jason was fairly sure it did; he was hazy on the details of the vicious underground war that had raged in France, but he had a pretty good idea that some highly unorthodox measures had been required.

Rutherford gave the short, dark, wiry Mondrago a sharp look. "Of course we can be certain, Superintendent. We've taken their displacer intact. So now they can send no more expeditions back in time, and as for the expeditions they have already dispatched, we can capture them as they are retrieved."

Any object, living or non-living, that had its "temporal energy potential" cancelled by the Fujiwara-Weintraub Temporal Displacer or its Transhumanist counterpart and sent into the past (at least three hundred years, due to the uncontrollable initial energy surge required) was there until the temporal energy potential was restored. This was almost effortless, for temporal displacement was such a profoundly unnatural condition that a "temporal retrieval device" or TRD no larger than a small pea could do the job. Whereupon the time traveler snapped back to the displacer stage from which he had departed, after the same elapsed time spent in the past—the "linear present" as it was called. There had been some theoretical speculation as to what would have become of Transhumanists awaiting retrieval if their displacer had been destroyed. But no one had wanted to do that, for it was still being studied intently. And it had been unnecessary. Now the stage under the Andes was constantly ringed by shifts of non-lethally-armed guards prepared to paralyze anyone who popped into existence on that stage.

Already, Jason knew, one group, dressed in somber

frock coats and long female dresses had been bagged in this manner. That they had yielded no information was disappointing but not surprising. The pointlessness of interrogating Transhumanist prisoners was well-established. The personnel of the security-obsessed Underground were equipped—knowingly or otherwise—with implants that automatically destroyed their brains at the touch of any kind of probing, or any attempt to surgically remove them. However, the internal evidence of certain objects in that group's possession had yielded a particular year and location, and a Special Operations team had been sent back to the sooty Manchester of the First Industrial Revolution to ferret out whatever long-germinating devilment might have been planted.

"That's true, Director," Mondrago nodded. "Things seem to be under control since we captured their displacer." He shot Jason a sour side-glance, which Jason ignored. The Corsican was still pouting about having been denied permission to participate in the raid. The argument that *both* of the top people in the Special Operations Section's chain of command shouldn't be simultaneously put in the line of fire had failed to impress him. "But how can we be sure it's their *only* displacer?"

A dead silence fell. It was not a consideration that came naturally to anyone. The stupendous cost of the Authority's displacer had always seemed to render it impossible as a practical matter to build more than one, even though there was no theoretical objection to it. But the Transhumanist underground could build them on the cheap . . .

"We can't be absolutely sure," admitted Rutherford.

"But remember," he added with the air of a man grasping at a life preserver, "we have no evidence that any of the Transhumanist expeditions you've encountered in the past originated from any point further in the future than the present time. Isn't that so, Chantal?"

The small, slightly built woman sitting on the far side of Mondrago from Jason wore the look of studious concentration that seemed to sit naturally on her pale, regular features. She spoke in her always-quiet tones. "Just so, Director. We have no evidence for that—or against it, for that matter. And what of Transhumanist expeditions that Commander Thanou and the Special Operations Section have *not* encountered?"

The silence returned, more gloomy than before.

Chantal Frey had been part of Jason's research expedition to the Athens of the Battle of Marathon. It had been then that he had discovered the existence of the Transhumanist underground and its efforts to plant the seeds of an eventual Transhumanist triumph in the blank spaces of the human past, outside the range of the "Observer Effect" that precluded changing recorded history. And she had been seduced by the Transhumanist leader, genetically upgraded into a kind of charisma to which she had been peculiarly vulnerable.

Jason had saved her from being cast adrift in the fifth century B.C., and thanks to him she was the first time traveler ever to have been returned to her own time after having her TRD cut out of her body. (And without doubt the last one, given the Authority's horrified aversion to deviations from established procedures.) Since then she had lived in a kind of limbo, distrusted as a former defector but valued for the insights she could offer about the Transhumanists among whom she had for a time dwelt. Recently, the value had finally overcome the distrust sufficiently for her to be allowed on another extratemporal expedition. She had accompanied Jason and Mondrago briefly to seventeenth-century Jamaica, where Jason had loose ends to tie together with respect to Zenobia, a she-pirate and Transhumanist renegade of his previous acquaintance. The expedition had ended in tragedy amid the cataclysm of earthquake-shattered Port Royal. Zenobia had died as the Observer Effect required, and Jason had learned—or, rather, relearned—the futility of trying to fight it. But his inner wound had been, if not healed, at least salved when he had subsequently learned that she had lived long enough to bear his child. He had, in fact, learned it from one of his own remote descendants.

As for Chantal, she had justified the Authority's trust, and was now in somewhat better graces. And what they had gone through in Port Royal had had yet another consequence, intimations of which Jason had noticed while they had been there. Now he noticed it again, as he saw her eyes briefly meet Mondrago's, and fleeting smiles cross both their lips.

I know what they say about opposites attracting, thought Jason with a rueful mental headshake. *But there must be limits!*

"Well," said Rutherford after a moment, a little too briskly, "you have undoubtedly raised a disturbing—albeit entirely speculative—point, which I shall certainly bring to the attention of the council when it meets tomorrow. By the way, Jason, I'd like you to accompany me to that meeting, in your capacity as head of the Special Operations Section."

Jason wasn't sure he liked the sound of that.

The governing council's meeting room was a good deal more ornate than Rutherford's office, in the mannered style of elaborate, history-infused formality typical of an Earth still self-consciously seeking to reestablish the roots that had nearly been torn up by the Transhuman Dispensation of the previous century. Some would have characterized it as elegant. Jason preferred words like "pompous" and "affected."

Which, come to think of it, makes it a perfect setting for this bunch, he reflected as he sat beside Rutherford at one end of the long, gleaming-topped table, lined with a quorum of the council. At the other end, Alastair Kung, who currently held the rotating chairmanship, overflowed his chair and peered through small eyes almost hidden between rolls of flesh as Rutherford concluded his report.

"So, Director," Kung addressed Rutherford in his unexpectedly high-pitched voice, "now that the threat of Transhumanist meddling with the past is over—"

"That's not precisely what I said," Rutherford gently reproved. "I remind you of the concerns raised by Superintendent Mondrago and Dr. Frey."

"Ah, yes: Dr. Frey." Alcide Martiletto's sneer exceeded even his usual capacity for superciliousness. He had opposed Jason's rescue of Chantal from the fifth century B.C., and his distrust of her was still unabated. Snickers and mutters from certain other councilors suggested that he was not alone.

Helene De Tredville spoke in a voice as tight as the bun into which her white hair was pulled. "These 'concerns' belong to the realm of the imagination. Commander Thanou, is there any actual evidence that the Transhumanist underground has a second temporal displacer?"

"No," Jason admitted.

"And," Jadoukh Kubischev rumbled, leaning forward massively, "did the data you retrieved on your last expedition mention such a displacer?"

"Again, the answer is no. But given the underground's mania for security and compartmentalized information—"

"That will be sufficient, thank you, Commander. We must deal with facts, not speculation."

"And the fact is," chimed in Serena Razmani, a newcomer to the council and relatively young by the standards of this near-gerontocracy, "that there is no proof that any Transhumanist expedition into the past came from our own future." She stopped with a puzzled look. Tenses could be baffling in discussions of time travel.

"Just so," Kung stated with an emphatic nod that compressed his chins into even greater multiplicity. "Director Rutherford said as much. And now I have heard all I need to hear." He inflated himself, toadlike. "I initially had deep, yes, deep reservations about the creation of the Special Operations Section of the Temporal Service. Nevertheless, I reluctantly consented to it when Commander Thanou discovered the existence of the Transhumanist underground and its illicit extratemporal activities. Since then, my reservations have been reinforced by the Section's frequently rash and unorthodox methods—"

Which have frequently saved your bacon, thought Jason, although he held his peace, hoping Rutherford would speak up to the same effect.

"—not to mention some of the personnel Commander Thanou has recruited for it." Kung oozed distaste. "Some of them little better than common toughs! Not to mention . . ." Kung's eyes met Jason's briefly, and he left it hanging.

Not to mention outworlders, Jason—a native of the colony planet of Hesperia, Psi 5 Aurigae III—mentally finished for him. Over the years, he had become inured to the snobbery of Earth's bureaucratized intelligentsia.

"Nevertheless," Kung resumed, "I have tolerated it as a necessary evil . . . the necessity for which has now ceased. In light of Director Rutherford's report, I propose that we can now dispense with the Special Operations Section."

A moment passed before it even registered on Jason. Then he waited for Rutherford to speak up. When the older man finally did, it was in tones of hesitant diffidence. "Ah . . . Mr. Chairman, I believe this decision needs to be deeply pondered. I suggest we solicit Commander Thanou's thoughts on the matter."

Jason took a deep breath. "Even if we discount the possibility of one or more remaining Transhumnist displacers, the need for the Special Operations Section is as great as ever. We have absolutely no reason to suppose that there are not now—in terms of the linear present, of course—previously dispatched Transhumanist expeditions still at work in the past. Furthermore, we have no way of knowing how many of their previously laid projects in the past are still in operation."

Razmani wore a perplexed look. "I've never understood this. The Transhumanists *can't* change history. The Observer Effect won't let them. So what are we worried about?"

By a supreme effort, Jason refrained from screaming and smashing the furniture. He noticed exasperated eye-rolling even on the faces of some of the councilors. He drew another, even deeper breath and spoke slowly in what he hoped were not insultingly elementary terms.

"Perhaps, Ms. Razmani, as a new member of this council you have not yet had the opportunity to familiarize yourself with these matters. The Observer Effect rules out changes in *observed* history that would create the kind of paradoxes people speculated about when time travel was merely a fictional device. Something will prevent you from going back in time and killing, say, Hitler . . . or one of your own ancestors." *Or saving the life of someone who is known to have died*, he thought with a small, dull pain of remembrance that would never go away. "But there are vast 'blank spaces' in the past. The Transhumanists are operating in the shadows: founding cults and secret societies, planting retroactive viruses and delayed-action nanobots, and so forth. All these sociological, biological and nanotechnological time-bombs are due to simultaneously come to fruition like a time-on-target salvo." Jason saw from Razmani's blank look that she didn't know what that term meant. But he pressed on. "This is due to happen on what they call *The Day*, which obviously lies sometime in our future. And," he concluded, with a hard look down the table at Kung, "we still don't know when The Day is going to be."

"Yes," said Kung with ponderous heaviness. "I am aware of your failure to obtain that very important datum. But now that Transhumanist extratemporal activity has been curtailed, that can be left to the normal law enforcement agencies, with military support when required. So it is no longer necessary for the Authority to act in concert with those agencies."

And this, Jason suddenly realized, was the crux of the matter with mentalities like Kung's. The Authority's sacrosanct independent status was all, and now that Kung glimpsed an opportunity to restore it he wasn't about to let such trivialities as facts stand in his way.

"So," Kung continued, "the Temporal Service can now stop, er, playing soldiers and revert to its proper function."

Nursemaiding parties of ivory-tower academic historians through the most violent eras of Old Earth's blood-drenched history, keeping them alive while they search for evidence to support their pet theories, Jason mentally translated. Aloud: "And what if, in the course of that 'proper function,' evidence of Transhumanist activity in the past is turned up, as it has been on several occasions?"

"Then," said Kung in what was probably his best attempt at a mollifying tone, "I am confident that the Temporal Service can deal with it within the context of its traditional, tried-and-true operating procedures. Since the problem has been cut off at its source, all that remains now is cleaning up whatever mischief the Transhumanists may have already planted in Earth's past—whatever 'already' may mean in the context of time travel."

From the affirmative-sounding muttering that ran around the table, Jason knew Kung had a majority with him. There was skeptical silence from some, but for the most part this was what these people wanted to believe. He looked at Rutherford for support, but none was forthcoming. Desperately, he spoke up himself.

"But—"

"Thank you, Commander Thanou," Kung cut him off. "You have answered our questions." He left off the obvious corollary: Jason had no business speaking in this august company except to answer questions—and wouldn't have even if he had had the good taste to be born on Earth. "And now, as to the personnel of the Special Operations Section. We are naturally appreciative of their past services, and after it is disbanded all of them—including and especially you, Commander Thanou—will be given the opportunity to revert to positions within the normal organizational structure of the Temporal Service, if they so desire."

Jason rose to his feet, occasioning a certain muttering around the table. He looked down at Rutherford with a glare that eloquently expressed his thoughts: *Thanks, Kyle. You've been a tower of jello.* Then, council member or no, he spoke, causing a rise in the decibel level of the muttering.

"That will not be necessary in my case. Effective immediately, I tender my resignation from the Temporal Service. I intend to return to my homeworld, very far from Earth—on which I hope there is a God to have mercy."

And he turned on his heel and strode out of the room, trailing a wake of scandalized twitters at the impropriety of it all.

CHAPTER THREE

✧✧✧

As Jason watched, leaning on the balustrade of the observation deck, an interstellar liner bearing the insignia of the Olympian Line swooped lightly down with a low-pitched hum and settled its tens of thousands of tons of mass to earth, the grav surface effect raising a momentary cloud of dust off the Ukrainian steppe.

The use of grav repulsion as a secondary form of propulsion for atmospheric maneuvering had long ago put an end to the annoying dichotomy between deep-space ships and surface-to-orbit shuttles—at least for ships that so used it. Military capital ships were still orbit-to-orbit, for their designers had no mass to waste on such fripperies as the ability to land on a planet. But paying passengers did not appreciate the inconvenience—or cargo carriers the expense—of having to make connections in orbit. Thus it was that the vast expanse of the spaceport, over

27

which Jason gazed from the roof of the terminal building, was dotted with the great interstellar liners and freighters. As he watched, one rose and swooped away into the cloud-fleeced sky. His eyes followed it until it reached the altitude where the efficiency of its grav repulsors' lateral movement capability fell away (although they could still provide lift) and a reaction drive was required, and its stern lit up with the blue-white glare of the photon thrusters that would propel it past escape velocity.

He would have preferred to depart directly from Australia. But Olympian was the only line with direct service to the Psi 5 Aurigae system, practically at the periphery of the roughly fifty-light-year-radius sphere of human settlement. And it operated out of Pontic Spaceport. So here he was, shivering in the chill just north of the Black Sea and smiling to himself as always at the conscious archaism of the spaceport's name, so typical of today's Earth. It was one of the many things he didn't expect to miss.

A gust of wind whistled across the steppes. Jason, drawing his coat more tightly around himself, turned to go inside and seek out a bar, where there ought to be time for a drink or three. He descended by grav tube to the main concourse . . . and stopped short at the sight of three figures, two men and one woman.

"Hello, Commander," said Alexandre Mondrago with a smile that almost—not quite—banished his ugliness. "I suppose it's still all right to call you that."

"Yes, it is." Coincidentally, it was also Jason's rank in the Hesperian Colonial Rangers, which, like the soon-to-be-defunct Special Operations Section, used a streamlined version of the old London Metropolitan Police system of titles. "But you don't have to. After all, you're not in the Rangers."

"Yes. Well, aside from just saying goodbye, that's one reason we hoped to catch you here." Mondrago reached a hand behind him. Chantal Frey stepped forward to stand beside him and take his hand. "You're planning to resume your commission in the Rangers, right?"

"Right." Jason had always been on a kind of ill-defined loan to the Temporal Service.

"Well," Mondrago began, and then hesitated. Chantal grasped his hand tighter and he seemed to draw strength from her frail self. He began again. "Well, Commander, I was wondering if, maybe, the Rangers might have an opening for somebody with a good letter of reference."

Jason stared at him. Then he turned his stare on Chantal. He knew that the protective custody in which the Authority had been holding her had been lifted. But . . . "I sort of thought you'd be going back to your homeworld of Arcadia, in the Zeta Draconis system."

"I had sort of thought that too," she said with a smile.

Whither thou goest, I shall go. Jason turned back to Mondrago. "Alexandre, you don't have to quit the Temporal Service just because the Special Operations Section is being disbanded. In fact, with your record you have a great future in it."

"Yeah. Well, after some of the things we went through in Special Ops, I think I might find it a little dull. And besides . . ." Mondrago suddenly wore an uncharacteristic look of embarrassment. "And besides, you wouldn't be there."

Rather than replying, Jason turned to the third figure. "You too, Angus?"

Angus Aiken flushed as red as his hair. The young Scot had accompanied Jason to Civil War North America, a mere constable on his second extratemporal expedition. Chance had thrown him on his own for months, and he had acquitted himself so well as to earn accelerated promotion to sergeant and bring himself into notice. "No, sir. I'm staying in the Service—"

"Very wise," nodded Jason. "They'll need good people."

"—but I wanted to say goodbye . . . and tell you it has been an honor to know you."

Again, Jason didn't trust himself to speak. So he addressed Mondrago instead, with unconvincing gruffness. "Well, Alexandre, the Rangers certainly accept naturalized Hesperians—they include quite a few of them, in fact. They also include a certain number of insubordinate smartasses—"

"No one would ever have guessed it," Chantal interjected, deadpan.

"—so you ought to fit right in," Jason finished, ignoring her. "And I suppose I might be able to bring myself to write you a favorable recommendation. I'll set everything up when I arrive there, and get word back to you."

"Is it too late to book passage aboard your ship?"

"*What?* You mean . . . *now?*"

By way of answer, Mondrago pointed at the floor behind them. Jason hadn't noticed the pile of luggage.

"I gave them a ride," Aiken explained.

At first, Jason was at a loss for a response. Then he grasped Mondrago's hand and with his other arm gave Chantal a quick hug. "All right, you lunatics. It probably *is* too late. But let's go see if—"

"Commander Thanou! I'm *so* glad I found you in time!"

At the sound of that nasal voice, Jason froze into incredulous immobility. Then, very slowly, as if hoping his ears had deceived him but unwilling to put that hope to the test of his eyes, he turned and stared into the beaming, vaguely rabbitlike face of Irving Nesbit.

"I came with great haste," continued Nesbit, who had made something of a career of being a bearer of ill tidings . . . to Jason, in particular. "Director Rutherford was most concerned that you might have already departed before—"

"NO!" bellowed Jason, drawing glances from passersby. "You can't do it to me this time, Irving! This time I'm not just going on leave. I've resigned from the Service—absolutely, permanently and irrevocably. And don't quote me any well-hidden 'emergency reactivation clause' or any of that crap! I'll fight it in court! I'll fight Rutherford and the entire Authority!"

"Director Rutherford said to remind you that the Special Operations Section of the Temporal Service has not yet been officially disbanded. And he thought you might be interested in an unforeseen contingency which has now arisen."

"Ha! 'Unforeseen contingency' my left one! Don't tell me, let me guess: Rutherford has learned that there's another Transhumanist displacer. Well, it *wasn't* unforeseen! We warned him of the possibility, but he wouldn't listen—or he didn't want to rock the boat by telling those smug fatheads on the council anything they didn't want to hear. And now he wants me to pull his chestnuts out of the fire. Well, you tell that dried-up, self-conceited old fart that he can—"

"As yet, no evidence has come to light of any such displacer on Earth," Nesbit interrupted.

"What?" Something in Nesbit's tone—steadiness overlaying strain—belatedly reminded Jason that the man had more to him than the spineless bureaucrat Jason had once thought him. They had gone through hell together in the seventeenth-century Caribbean, and afterwards Nesbit had stood up to Kung and others of his ilk by defending Jason's often highly unorthodox actions, leaving everyone concerned thunderstruck. "I don't understand. What's the problem if there isn't a second displacer?"

"I said *on Earth*," Nesbit corrected him. And now the strain was uppermost.

For several heartbeats, neither Jason nor any of his three companions spoke.

"Irving," Jason finally said, "if you're saying what I think you're saying, then . . ." He looked around at the passing crowds. "Then maybe we'd better find a less public place to talk. Preferably a nice, quiet bar."

It was a bedrock theoretical absolute that temporal displacement only worked within, and in relation to, a gravity field of planetary magnitude. Einstein had been right about relativity. There was no such thing as an "absolute location."

This was a wonderful thing from the standpoint of time travelers. Otherwise, someone temporally displaced from Earth's surface to such an "absolute location" in the past would have found himself floating in space, attempting to breathe vacuum while enjoying (if possible) the spectacle of Earth receding from him at over eighteen miles per second as it orbited around Sol. Except that he wouldn't have been able to watch it, because Sol itself, with its planets in tow, was revolving around the center of the galaxy at a velocity that was of interest only to astronomers. And the galaxy was . . . but at that point imagination failed.

So as a practical matter a temporal displacer had to be emplaced on a planet. And there had always been an unspoken assumption that *on a planet* meant *on Earth*. Not that there was any theoretical objection to any other planet of reasonable mass (the exact lower limit of the gravity field was still a matter of learned dispute), but what would be the *point*? Only Earth had a history, with questions to be answered and controversies to be settled and mysteries to be resolved. On a planet like Jason's homeworld of Hesperia, still in the process of terraforming, who would want to go back in time a few centuries and contemplate oceans whose microbial life was only just starting to encroach on continents of stone and sand? There were, of course, colony worlds with more interesting life forms than that. But not interesting enough to justify the colossal expense of building and operating a Fujiwara-Weintraub installation, a strain even on Old Earth's budgetary resources. The political economics just weren't there.

Still, if one *did* have a good enough reason, and possessed Transhumanist time-travel technology . . .

"You realize," Nesbit temporized, "that my information is vague to the point of virtual nonexistence, given my lack of a need to know."

They had managed to find a relatively uncrowded bar. The five of them sat hunched over a table in a corner booth, with much-needed drinks. Nesbit paused and fortified himself with a sip of a concoction based on the rum for which he had acquired a taste among the buccaneers of the Spanish Main.

"Understood," nodded Jason. "But I gather you *do* know that there's reason to think the Transhumanist underground is engaging in time travel on some planet other than Earth."

"Not exactly," Nesbit cautioned. "As I understand it, there is conclusive evidence that they are engaging in some form of extrasolar operations—"

"Which is a first in itself," Mondrago interjected grimly. "At least as far as we know."

"—and considerably more tenuous indications that these operations might involve illicit time travel. The mere possibility of the latter was, of course, enough to arouse a sense of urgency in the Authority."

"No doubt," muttered Jason absently, as he contemplated the implications.

"But *why?*" wondered Aiken, taking a pull on his (of course) Scotch. "What can they hope to gain? Even if they can operate undercover on the colony planets—and it's hard to see how—they can't go back and do anything to prevent the establishment of the settlements. The Observer Effect would prevent it."

"They could," suggested Mondrago, "go back before colonization, when everything was one big 'blank space' in history, and plant some of their delayed-action biological and nanotech nastiness, timed to cause disruption and social paralysis on those planets on The Day."

"But it hardly seems worth the trouble and expense," objected Nesbit. Then he shot an alarmed look at Jason and Chantal, colonials both. "Oh, I *am* sorry! I didn't mean to imply—"

"Forget it," said Jason with a dismissive wave. "Anyway, you're right. It has to be something else. Do you happen to know which of the colony planets these 'tenuous indications' point to?"

"Actually, none of them." Nesbit hesitated a moment. "As I understand, the information had its source in the Zirankhu system."

They all stared at him.

"But that's crazy!" blurted Aiken. "How could the Transhumanists operate clandestinely? They wouldn't exactly blend!"

"They might," Chantal cautioned. "Remember, there are a fair number of humans there. Diplomats, business people—"

"—And, since the rebellion started, more and more gun smugglers and mercs," Mondrago finished for her. They often finished each other's sentences. "I know that from some old acquaintances. But even if they could somehow build a temporal displacer there without anyone noticing, what would be the point of all the trouble and expense? Why should they be interested in subverting the past of a nonhuman civilization?"

"It raises some disturbing philosophical implications involving the Observer Effect," mused Chantal, studying her Chablis rather than drinking it. "We all know that observed history can't be changed, although the past can be, after which the change will *always* have been part of the past. But . . . *whose* observed history? Everyone's? Not just humans?"

There was an uncomfortable silence, for this was something no one liked to consider—especially as it might apply to the fanatically militaristic remnant of the Teloi race that had still been prowling the spaceways with the patience of near-immortality at least as recently as the seventeenth-century, and for all anyone knew might still be abroad.

"Well," Jason finally said, "that's not something we need to concern ourselves with just yet. Irving, I'll go with you to Australia to see Rutherford—"

"Actually, he's relatively nearby, at his Athens office."

"Very well. But mind you, I've resigned! I'm only going as a . . . consultant."

Chantal looked at Mondrago and spoke with the quiet underlying firmness that so often surprised people. "I think perhaps we all should."

CHAPTER FOUR

"All right, Kyle, what's the story?"

Rutherford gave Jason a sour look. The younger man had taken the time to change into the quasi-military service dress uniform of the Hesperian Colonial Rangers—field gray, faced with silver-edged dark green. He had always found this to be an infallible way of irritating Rutherford, and he had yet to forgive the operations director for his invertebrate performance before the council.

They sat in Rutherford's Athens office, with its breathtaking (albeit virtual) view of the Acropolis, serene in the unnatural clarity of the temporal stasis field that protected it from the unintended side-effects of modern civilization. Rutherford had made no objections to the presence of Mondrago and Chantal. There had been a certain amount of huffing and puffing about Aiken's junior rank, but Jason had insisted and Rutherford hadn't thought the point worth contesting. So they all sat across the wide desk, facing Rutherford and the display case behind him with its items snatched from the past, some of which even Jason could never look at without gooseflesh.

Now Jason forced himself to avert his eyes from those items and concentrate on the matter at hand. "Why are we here, Kyle?" he prompted anew. "What makes you think the Transhumanists are engaged in illicit time travel off-world—and on Zirankhu, of all places?"

"Actually," Rutherford admitted, "we have no proof of off-world time travel on their part. But we have compelling evidence that they are active in the Zirankhu system. And since their machinations that we *do* know about have involved time travel, we thought it advisable to call in you and your colleagues here, so that we could draw on your unique expertise in these matters."

Jason ignored Rutherford's as-always-inept efforts to stroke him. "And as to this 'compelling evidence'?"

"You must understand that the current rebellion on Zirankhu has placed our government in a somewhat delicate position—"

"So I've heard."

"—and therefore the intelligence branch of the Internal Defense and Response Force has been called in . . . without undue publicity, inasmuch as it is somewhat outside their usual jurisdiction."

"Somewhat," echoed Jason drily.

The government—by courtesy so called—of the Confederal Republic of Earth had arisen from the rubble of the war of liberation from the Transhuman

Dispensation. Like the revolutions of the sixteenth-century seven provinces of the Netherlands or of the eighteenth-century North American colonies, that war had been in the truest sense a conservative revolution. So the resultant confederation had been cobbled together from the old nations, however uncomfortable a fit they had been with the demographic, economic and ethnic realities of the late twenty-third century. Now, a hundred years later, they were still jealous of their sovereignty, their jealousy reinforced by the general archaism that permeated Earth's culture. In particular, the resources for large-scale military action were still under the control of the few nations that could afford them, with all the resultant duplication of effort and divided command. The Deep-Space Fleet was an administrative abstraction; there was no such thing as a unified "space navy." Any major coordinated action practically required negotiation preceded by sealed bids.

The quasi-military IDRF, however, had been permitted by a human race still very much attuned to the dangers of internal subversion. As the one instrumentality that the Confederal Republic could employ without cumbersome consultation with its members, it tended to be employed in ways that pushed the envelope of its strictly defined legal powers.

"Certain of their agents on Zirankhu possess brain implants like yours," Rutherford continued. Like most contemporary people, however urbane, he was unable to keep a faint distaste out of his voice at the mention of such things. "By chance, one of them detected functioning bionics."

"That was luck," said Jason. The sensor feature was very short-ranged.

"Indeed. Our natural assumption of a Transhumanist presence was confirmed by subsequent investigation. Unfortunately, the Transhumanists seem to have become aware of the attention they were drawing, and have grown more circumspect. As a result, the trail has largely gone cold."

"Not surprising," Mondrago remarked, and Jason nodded. The Tranhsumanist underground had been practicing and refining secrecy for a century, growing ever more obsessive about it.

"Now, however, the IDRF is sending a new officer to Zirankhu to take charge of the investigation. An officer with intelligence training in addition to considerable combat experience—including some experience in dealing with Transhumanists. In fact, she is here now. You and she are already acquainted, Jason." Rutherford spoke into his interoffice communicator grill. "Send her in."

A side door opened and a thirtyish woman in the dark blue service dress uniform of the IDRF entered.

"Major Rojas!" Jason rose halfway to his feet and extended a hand. "Good to see you again."

"Likewise, Commander," said Elena Rojas, the Peruvian IDRF officer who had led the raid on the Transhumanist temporal displacer facility. She shook Jason's hand, but her features barely softened from their usual severity. Those features, with their high cheekbones and curved nose, together with her coppery coloring, suggested more Indian blood than Castilian. But she was exceptionally tall and slim for that heritage, and obviously in an extreme state of physical fitness. Her straight black hair was gathered into a practical braid at the back of her head. "But I haven't met your colleagues here."

Jason made introductions. Rojas acknowledged Aiken with noncommittal courtesy. She was civil enough to Mondrago, although something ambivalent in her expression suggested to Jason that she knew of his mercenary background. But when the introductions came to Chantal she ceased to have any expression at all. Her face became an immobile mask of chill control, and her eyes narrowed and froze into black ice.

Yes, thought Jason, *she knows more about my "colleagues" than she admits.*

"Since you've undoubtedly been briefed on the situation on Zirankhu," he said aloud, "I was hoping that you would be able to fill us in on the findings of your investigators before they came to a dead end."

"Certainly." Rojas took a seat, apparently willing to change the subject. But first she turned to Rutherford. "Director, may I assume that *everyone* here is cleared, and has a need to know?" This was accompanied by a pointed glance at Chantal.

"You may, as your own superiors will confirm if you insist."

"That won't be necessary." Rojas still looked skeptical. But she addressed Jason. "How much have you already been told?"

"Only the manner in which your people became aware of the previously unsuspected presence of Transhumanists on Zirankhu."

"Then you know it was a lucky break. We could hardly

expect any more such breaks, and we certainly haven't gotten them." Rojas didn't add *as of my most recent information*. That always went without saying. In the absence of any sort of instantaneous interstellar "radio," messages had to be carried by ship, as they once had been carried across the oceans of Earth. Information was chronically out of date. "We never dreamed there were Transhumanists there; that wasn't what our people were there for." She paused. "How much do you know about the situation there?"

"It's a little outside my field," Jason admitted. "I know our merchants and diplomatic representatives there are in an awkward position as a result of the rebellion against the ruling Manziru Empire."

"That's putting it mildly. We're walking a tightrope. The Dazh'pinkh rebels have asked for our aid, saying that we're natural allies, since they claim they're inspired by ideals we humans have introduced to their race's ossified culture. We can't even acknowledge receipt of these requests."

Aiken wore a look of youthful perplexity. "I've never understood why that is. With our help the rebels would make short work of the rotten, corrupt Manziru Empire. And from everything I've read, a Dazh'pinkh regime would *have* to be an improvement."

"Don't be so sure," Rojas cautioned grimly. "Part of the problem is that a lot of bleeding hearts on Earth and other human worlds have convinced themselves that the Dazh'pinkh really are believers in democracy, pluralism, free-market economics and all the rest. But in fact they've just memorized the right slogans. They've completely misinterpreted everything, and they've turned the areas they control into a hell of mismanagement by a bunch of leaders who are really nothing but bandits and warlords. No, our policy is to continue to officially recognize the Manziru Empire as the legitimate planetary government, even though dealing with them is a nightmare, given their unrealistic arrogance."

"Which is not unreasonable from their perspective," said Chantal mildly. "That is precisely what they claim to be, even though there are large fringe areas they've never really controlled. In fact, Zirankh'shi political theory is based on the idea that there can be only one source of legitimate political authority—and, in fact, of civilization. There are parallels from human history, although none of them ever came anywhere near as close to making their pretensions as real on Earth as the Manziru have on Zirankhu."

Rojas shot her a look in which the previous frosty expression-lessness was only slightly thawed by the realization that Chantal had been doing her homework. "True. None of which makes it any easier for us. So our team was sent there to provide our diplomatic people with as accurate intelligence as possible. When we happened to detect bionics, we simply didn't know what to make of it at first."

"There are certainly no bionics among the Zirankh'shi," Jason nodded.

"After the shock wore off, our people realized it could only mean Transhumanist involvement. So they traced every possible lead as far as they could until the leads dried up. And they were able to get an indication of what the Transhumanists were up to." Rojas paused, then spoke in the tones of one dreading the reaction she expected. "They were buying large quantities of food."

"Food?" was Jason's incredulous echo.

"Well," Chantal said thoughtfully, "the biochemistry of Zirankhu is sufficiently similar to Earth's that humans and Zirankh'shi can consume each other's food. Of course, neither can live on it exclusively; certain dietary supplements are required on both sides. But still, it can be consumed without harm. I've heard some items are quite tasty."

"But," Mondrago demanded of her, "why would the Transhumanists go all the way out to the periphery of human-explored space—slightly over fifty light-years, isn't it?—to buy *food*?"

"I can't think of a reason in the world," Chantal admitted. "In *any* world," she added with a rueful smile.

"Neither could we," said Rojas grimly. "Nor could we think of any reason for their purchase of various basic raw materials that our investigation subsequently revealed before it hit a dead end." She seemed to become belatedly aware that she had slipped and agreed with Chantal, and glared on general principles.

"Well," said Jason after a moment, "this is all very intriguing. But I gather that you don't have any direct evidence of extrasolar time travel by the Transhumanists."

"No, we don't. But we know they have been heavily involved in it. And since there doesn't seem to be any conventional explanation . . ."

"Precisely," said Rutherford reasserting his authority.

"It is for this reason that the decision has been reached, through consultation between the Authority and the IDRF, that when you go to Zirankhu to take charge of the investigation you will be accompanied by a Temporal Service team to advise you on time travel-related matters. Commander Thanou will head the team. Superintendent Mondrago will assist him; given the gravity of this situation we must send our 'first team,' as people say."

Rutherford had, Jason reflected sourly, not bothered to obtain his consent to the arrangement, despite his currently somewhat ambiguous status with the Temporal Service. But he decided not to make an issue of it. And Mondrago, as always, clearly had no objections to being put in the way of killing Transhumanists.

Rojas, Jason noted, gave him a carefully neutral sidelong look. He was fairly sure what was going through her mind. The IDRF made no bones about using a traditional military rank structure, so any attempt to determine which of them outranked the other would be like comparing apples and oranges. He decided he'd better put a certain amount of effort into reassuring Rojas that she was unequivocally in charge.

"Also," Rutherford continued, "Dr. Frey will accompany the party, to provide the benefit of her . . . unique perspective on Transhumanist-related matters. Also, her professional qualifications in the field of intelligent nonhuman life should prove helpful on Zirankhu."

Rojas froze into a sculpture entitled *Hostility*, and did not meet Chantal's eyes. "Is that necessary, Director? I point out that Dr. Frey is . . ." She paused and searched for something acceptable to say. "Dr. Frey is a *civilian*. We would be responsible for assuring her safety."

"The decision has been made, Major," said Rutherford firmly. "If you wish to obtain confirmation from your superiors—"

"Again, that won't be necessary." But not an atom of Rojas softened.

Oh, yes, Jason sighed to himself, as he often had before upon meeting the personnel of extratemporal expeditions. *This trip is going to be a gas.*

CHAPTER FIVE

✦✦✦

The government courier vessel soared starward under photon thrusters, out to the "Primary Limit" (about thirteen thousand miles from planetary center in Earth's case) where the local gravity field was less than 0.1 G. There the negative mass drive could alter the properties of space, reducing normal gravity ahead of the ship to produce an effective thrust of a couple of hundred Gs— fortunately imperceptible to its occupants, who would have been in free-fall weightlessness save for the ship's artificial gravity—and Earth dropped rapidly astern. Under such a furious acceleration, it took relatively little time to reach the "Secondary Limit," just short of the asteroid belt. There, with Sol's gravity less than 0.0001 G, the drive could not merely fold space but wrap it around the ship, forming a field of negative energy to create a bubble in space-time that moved faster than the rest of

47

space-time with the ship being dragged along within that bubble. Thus a way had been found around the sacrosanct velocity of light. (*Not* "through" it, as the theoretical physicists, still in denial after a century and a half, never tired of insisting.)

The drive's efficiency was more or less directly proportional to the percentage of a ship's mass that was devoted to generators and powerplant versus everything else, so ship designs always involved a tradeoff. Since time was of the essence, the ship they rode was a *Comet* class courier, built for speed (or *pseudo*-speed, as the theoretical physicists always primly corrected for the edification of anyone who would listen) and little else. To be sure, it incorporated certain features that were sometimes handy in specialized roles and did not add significant mass, such as state of the art sensors and a very sophisticated stealth suite. But it was certainly not designed for luxury. An interstellar liner that *was* designed for luxury would have required about three weeks to reach the Zirankhu system; they would be enroute for less than half that.

Still, they had eleven and a half of the standard days of Old Earth in which to endure the *Comet*'s passenger accommodations, and each other.

Those accommodations consisted of two two-person staterooms, by courtesy so called. In order to observe the proprieties of a culture whose conservatism in certain matters would have surprised the people of three or four centuries back, Jason and Mondrago took one of them, Chantal and Rojas the other. But Jason, who had less concern for the proprieties than some, arranged at various times to absent himself and let Mondrago receive Chantal as a guest. At such times, he kept to what Starways Shipbuilding, which produced the *Comet* class, was pleased to call the passengers' lounge. There he sometimes socialized with members of the two-person crew. But it also sometimes brought him into Rojas' company, and he made as much use of these opportunities as possible.

This proved not quite as difficult as he had anticipated. Rojas clearly had little regard for the Temporal Service, even its quasi-military Special Operations Section. But she had a certain qualified respect for him, based on his overall reputation as well as her own observation of his performance, and his apprehension of professional jealousy on her part proved unfounded, for Rutherford as well as her own superiors had assured her that she was the ranking officer in charge of the investigation. And he had been pleased to discover that she shared his taste for Scotch, of which they had both been able to bring along a small private stock. Still, even with that lubricant, she was not exactly given to light, bantering conversation.

Nevertheless, there was one subject he felt he must broach with her, after some of the things he had heard from Mondrago.

He did so one "day" when they were alone in the lounge and both crew members were occupied elsewhere. The lounge at least offered ample facilities for interactive electronic entertainment. But at the moment they were both simply sipping Scotch. "So, Major," he asked with careful casualness, "how are you and Dr. Frey holding up?"

"I'm holding up quite well," she relied expressionlessly. "As for Dr. Frey, you'll have to ask her."

"Oh. I thought you, being in such close quarters with her, might be able to shed some light." Actually, Jason hadn't thought anything of the sort. Mondrago had told him that Rojas hadn't uttered an unnecessary syllable to Chantal during the entire voyage. "And she is, after all, at least partially my responsibility, since I represent the Authority, which sent her."

"Yes, I know they did." Rojas' opinion of the Authority's decision could hardly have been clearer.

Jason decided to cut to the chase. "You don't like her, do you?"

Rojas didn't even blink. "I am aware of her background," she replied, somewhat obliquely but gaining Jason's respect by not attempting any hypocritically indignant denials.

"Then you will also be aware that the Authority now regards her as having regained their trust, even to the extent of having once again sent her on an extratemporal expedition."

"Yes, I know." Once again, Rojas barely troubled to conceal her skepticism concerning the Authority's judgment. But then her curiosity won out over her disdain. "I understand that you were her mission leader when she . . . ah . . ."

"Defected," Jason finished for her helpfully. "Yes. We went back to 490 B.C. to observe the Battle of Marathon and determine if any Teloi survivals were still passing themselves off as Olympian 'gods.' We got more than we bargained for. It was then that we discovered the existence of the Tranhumanist underground and its program of subverting the past."

"In alliance with the surviving Teloi, from what I've read," said Rojas.

"Right, although the two groups ended up having a lethal falling-out. We'd brought Dr. Frey along as an expert on alien life-forms. And she was intrigued by the Transhumanists." Seeing Rojas' look of uncomprehending contempt, Jason decided he'd better explain Chantal's cultural background. "She's from Arcadia, Zeta Draconis A II. As you may know, that planet was one of those settled early, during the slower-than-light colonization era. But at thirty-five light-years it was much further out than any of the others; those people wanted to be *really* isolated. And they succeeded in taking a holiday from history. Contact with them was reestablished only after the Transhuman Dispensation had been overthrown. They missed out on all that horror—to them it's just dry history. So she was particularly vulnerable to the leader of the Transhumanist expedition, who was one of the castes genetically and bionically enhanced for charisma. You might say she lacked the cultural antibodies you and I have." He chuckled. "That changed when he betrayed her."

"I understand they cut out her implanted temporal retrieval device . . . and that you brought her back to the present anyway." Rojas gave him a perplexed look. "I'm no expert on time travel, but I had always been under the impression that that was impossible."

"Ordinarily, that's true. If you don't have your TRD to restore your temporal energy potential and return you to the linear present to which you're inseparably linked, you're stuck in the past. However the same 'physical contact' principle which enables the TRD to bring whatever or whoever it is attached to back to the linear present also means—for imperfectly understood reasons—that you can bring back whatever you can conveniently carry . . . like the items in Rutherford's display case. I did that with Dr. Frey, who is a small woman. The Authority's governing council almost had a collective stroke." Jason smiled at the pleasurable recollection. "But the point is that in the end she saw the Transhumanists in their true colors. Ever since then, she's been more than happy to put her knowledge of them at the disposal of the Authority and Earth's law enforcement agencies, for the purpose of ramming it to them as hard and as often as possible. She detests them at least as much as you or I do."

"Are you absolutely certain of that, Commander?" Rojas' eyes grew very hard.

"Are you perhaps suggesting that I was allowed to bring her back, so she could act as a mole?" Jason, knowing he would need to maintain a working relationship with the IDRF major, restrained himself from using loaded words like *paranoia.* "If you knew the circumstances of her retrieval, you'd know there's not the slightest chance of that. Not even Mondrago, who tends to be security happy, has ever entertained such a far-fetched notion."

"Superintendent Mondrago is not exactly objective in this matter," Rojas sniffed. "But even granting that she is not a conscious tool in a deliberate Transhumanist ploy, is it not possible that she may still cherish a latent attachment to them? I have known of such cases among supposedly returned defectors."

Jason held onto his temper with both hands. "I remind you that the Authority—an organization never noted for lack of caution—deemed her reliable enough to be sent on an extratemporal expedition. I was the mission leader, and I can assure you that nothing in her behavior gave the Authority reason to regret that trust."

"Yes, I read the report: an expedition to Port Royal, Jamaica, in 1692. But that wasn't really a test of her loyalties, was it? Correct me if I'm wrong, but to my knowledge that expedition never came into conflict with the Transhumanists. According to the report, the only Transhumanist encountered was a deserter from their ranks and therefore not likely to arouse any . . ." Something Rojas saw in Jason's face caused her to trail to an awkward halt.

For all at once he was once again in the flower-burdened, cicada-singing warmth of Jamaica, blind to all save the magnificent black she-pirate and Transhumanist renegade Zenobia. *Yes, blind to all,* he thought with bitter self-reproach. *Including the Observer Effect. I tried to fight it, knowing it cannot be fought. I tried to prevent her from dying, as I knew history required that she die. And precisely as a result of my folly, she died. That became part of the past . . . indeed,* had always been *part of the past. The Observer Effect won. It always does.*

But not before she and I had done something that also became part of the past.

He had learned that from his great, great, great grandson, in 1865, across the James River from the smoldering ruins of Richmond, Virginia. And now he could never look at any North Americans or West Indians of obviously African descent without wondering if his own genes slumbered within them.

He returned to the here-and-now, and saw Rojas' quizzical look. He saw no pressing need to enlighten her.

"Well," he sighed, standing up, "I'll take your concerns under advisement. But unless you can give me any specific, concrete reasons to doubt Dr. Frey's loyalty—and so far you haven't—I'm inclined to give her the benefit of the doubt. And, as I mentioned before, she's my responsibility in my capacity as ranking representative of the Temporal Regulatory Authority."

Rojas also rose to her feet. Her eyes squarely met his—she was very nearly his height—and while they held no overt hostility they were equally devoid of any flexibility. "I must beg to differ, Commander. I remind you that this is an IDRF investigation, of which I am in charge. *All* of its personnel are my responsibility. And it is my duty to be suspicious. I am disinclined to give *anyone* the benefit of the doubt."

Jason met her eyes for a perceptible instant, then relaxed into the insouciance he had always found to be the best way of irritating Rutherford. "Well, then, Major, I suppose Dr. Frey will just have to rely on your objectivity and fair-mindedness, which of *course* will prevent your judgment from being clouded by either preconceptions or personal animosity."

Rojas, unable to come up with an acceptable response to that beyond a muttered echo of Jason's "Of course," tossed off her Scotch and stalked from the lounge.

✧✧✧

Thus matters stood when a Sol-like G0v star in the constellation of Serpens waxed in the forward viewports until it passed the ill-defined dividing line between "star" and "sun," and the *Comet*'s drive field switched off as they passed the Secondary Limit of the Zirankhu system.

CHAPTER SIX

Strictly speaking, the star's astronomical designation was HC-4 9701 III, but of course no one ever called it that. And the system had a ready-made name, courtesy of its inhabitants, for it was home to that great rarity, a nonhuman civilization.

Only a tiny minority of planets were of the "Goldilocks" variety capable of giving birth to life, and not all of those were old enough to have done so yet. But, as had become clear even as early as the turn of the twenty-first century, there were a *lot* of planets. So, in absolute numbers though not in percentages, quite a few worlds were life-bearing. Many of those, like Jason's native Hesperia, were too young for life to have evolved much beyond the level of seaweed. But that still left a significant number of planets with highly developed biospheres, some of which included tool-using animals whose "intelligence" (to the extent that quality could be defined and measured) was comparable to that of humans.

Civilization, though, was a freak. Most tool-using species made do without it. Their lack of cities sometimes made it difficult for humans to recognize such species as intelligent, until such time as they demonstrated their intelligence by turning captured weapons against colonizers from Earth with a disconcerting degree of tactical cunning, providing employment opportunities for mercenary free companies. Or unless they lived contentedly among the crumbling, vegetation-overgrown ruins of a *former* civilization's cities.

Why this was so—or, to put it another way, why humans *had* developed civilization and kept it—was a subject of learned dispute. Traditionally, the prevailing view had held that intelligent beings lock themselves into civilized states only under pressure. To put it simplistically, the Near East had dried up with the retreat of the glaciers, the game had gone away, and agriculture had required widespread well-organized irrigation. Then the discovery that the Teloi had genetically engineered *Homo sapiens* a hundred thousand years ago in the southwest Asian/northeast African region as a slave race, which had subsequently rebelled and been taught the arts of civilization by the crew of a crashed warship of the Teloi's Nagommo enemies in the Persian Gulf, had forced a rethinking. Perhaps such a background had preconditioned humans to civilization. (Of course, this merely begged the question of why the Teloi and the Nagommo had risen to civilization on their own.) And afterwards, humans seemed to have avoided the various ways civilizations had of dying from their own toxic sociological by-products. As the former slaves had spread outward from the core area, escaping slavery and differentiating into the racial varieties of modern humanity, a variety of civilizations had grown up . . . and many had almost succumbed to the common fate, as though civilization was, as the twentieth-century cynic Mencken had called it, "a self-limiting disease." But the diversity of civilized societies had been the saving grace; one, the Western society, had by various fortunate happenstances escaped all the pitfalls and set in motion the dynamics of continued advancement.

One of those happenstances, it was generally agreed, was that gunpowder weapons had appeared in the West amid a chaos of competing sovereignties, and therefore set off an ongoing, self-regenerating "arms race" that drove technological innovation. Introduced into a society's universal empire, such weapons merely froze that society into a stasis by making the empire invincible. Earth had seen the beginnings of this often enough—in China and India and others—before the arrival of the Western ferment.

And this, it appeared, had happened on Zirankhu, HC-4 9701 III. Thousands of years before, the Manziru Empire had established unchallengeable hegemony over the entire planet, aided by its geography. (This was a less massive planet than Earth, with extensive but landlocked seas rather than island-continents in a world-ocean.) The other cultures of the Zirankh'shi had continued to exist, but forced into unnatural Manziru patterns—a "pseudomorphosis," as a human historian named Spengler had once called it. And the empire had settled into the normal state of unchallenged empires: an extravagant, degenerate imperial court; a fossilized bureaucracy whose corruption was no longer even perceived as corruption; an intellectual establishment mired in pedantic worship of an approved version of the past; and all the rest.

Then the humans had arrived. And the resulting social dissolution had been as Karl Marx, in the mid-nineteenth century, had once described the opening of China to the West: a long-buried mummy in a hermetically sealed tomb suddenly exposed to the open air.

They landed at the spaceport that the imperial court had grudgingly allowed by treaty on the outskirts of the city of Khankhazh, about a thousand miles south of the capital city of Shandu.

"We're still negotiating to get a permanent embassy established at Shandu," said Evan Orsini, the young staffer who had come from the Earth legation to meet them, as he led them across the tarmac to his glide car. "But they're resisting it every step of the way, by every tactic of diplomatic delay and obstruction they can think of, because the whole idea of recognizing another sovereignty is repugnant to them. As far as they're concerned, there's the Manziru Empire and there are savages—period."

"But," ventured Chantal, "can't they see that we're civilized, and far more powerful than themselves? Surely our technological superiority speaks for itself."

"If only in the form of our advanced weapons," added Mondrago. "Which they've seen in action in a couple of punitive expeditions."

"If a robber steals your money because he's got a deadly weapon and you haven't, does that make him your social equal?" Orsini looked tired and harried. "Anyway, the emperor and his courtiers and officials don't have to face the facts. They're isolated from the world in that enormous palace complex in Shandu, living in a world of the lies their bureaucratic sycophants tell them, never talking to anyone else, out of touch with reality. You simply have no idea of their blind, self-satisfied complacency!"

"I think I might," said Jason, chuckling inwardly as he recalled the Council.

They passed through the terminal, walking with a springy step in Zirankhu's 0.72 G gravity but growing slightly out of breath, not having had time to adjust to air that was thinner and less oxygen-rich than Earth's though within the limits of human breathability. Outside, their car waited. A solidly built Eurasian man leaning against it stood up straight as they approached.

"Captain Janos Chang, Major," he greeted Rojas. Both were in civilian clothes, so no salutes were exchanged. Instead, Rojas extended her hand first, as was proper. Chang showed no sign of resentment at being relieved of command of the local IDRF team; if anything, he seemed relieved.

Rojas introduced the Authority people while their luggage was loaded into the trunk by half a dozen native Zirankh'shi workers—considerably more than was necessary, even though this was not a physically strong species. Another Zirankh'shi did nothing more than supervise . . . and "supervision" seemed to consist of nothing more than standing there and lending the presence of an extremely low-ranking member of the all-pervasive bureaucracy, without which practically no act in the Manziru Empire was supposed to be performed. Afterwards, he would write a report which would vanish, unread by anyone, into the cavernous storehouses that held the suffocating weight of millions and billions of such reports.

Jason watched curiously, never having seen Zirankh'shi in the flesh before. They were bilaterally symmetrical, as was almost invariably the case with tool-using species; an active animal profits from having a definite front end. Almost as typically, they had four limbs and had liberated the forward pair for tool-using by evolving a more or less erect posture. The result was an upright biped a little less than five feet tall, gracile by human standards, covered with fur ranging from cream-colored to deep yellow. The stature was mostly flexible torso and long neck, for the legs were short—considerably shorter than the arms. Both pairs of limbs ended in appendages of six digits, in sets of three. These had evolved into mutually opposable sets of three fingers in the case of the hands, allowing a manual dexterity in some ways superior to that of humanity's four fingers and one opposable thumb. The face was dominated by enormous greenish or amber eyes that seemed ill-adapted to the light of a Sol-like G0v star until one noticed the nictitating membranes that protected them. The jaw was delicate, tapering to a narrow snout which made the guttural sounds of their language seem incongruous, for irrelevant anthropocentric reasons. And while convention dictated the use of masculine pronouns for them, they were in fact fully functional hermaphrodites. (Which, Jason had read, contributed to the empire's stability by simplifying the succession.)

Given their fur covering, and the lack of seasonal variations on a planet with very little axial tilt, they had no need for clothing, especially in these near-equatorial latitudes. Whatever they wore, hung from a kind of harness, was purely ornamental, and minimal in the case of the workers. The "supervisor" had a tiny medallion which meant much in the equally tiny but all-important gradations of Manziru officialdom.

The loading took several times as long as it had to, but Jason noted that Orsini and Chang didn't fidget. Evidently, one cultivated patience on Zirankhu. Finally they got underway, the car's fixed-altitude grav repulsion leaving a trail of swirling dust from its surface effect. Beyond the spacefield was the city, where monumental public buildings with the local architecture's characteristic profusion of domes rose over the teeming streets and low hovels. They proceeded along those streets on the way to the legation compound, their eyes and ears and noses filled with the unfamiliar and exotic to the point of sensory overload, too overwhelming to fully register.

Jason, child of a raw young planet, had often been struck by the layers of history that lay like geological strata in Earth's ancient cities. The effect was even more noticeable here, where a millennial empire's overburden had simply grown and grown. Even to newly arrived eyes, it was obvious that the empire's rigid social order, ordained by the ages, was nothing more than a pompous façade behind which seethed a cauldron of picturesque squalor—a cauldron of whose existence the imperial court was blissfully ignorant, if Orsini was to be believed.

And not far from here, as planetary distances went, was the region controlled by the Dazh'Pinkh rebels, where even now they and the imperial army were busily slaughtering each other and most of the local population. Not even the emperor and his creatures could ignore that, floating about in the cloud-cuckoo land of the court though they were.

There were seemingly incongruous elements in the sights of the city. Although human imports like the one they rode were rare, there were numerous rubber-tired wheeled vehicles, heavy and overornamented but functional. Jason, who had visited twentieth-century Earth, smelled none of the miasma of gasoline fumes and carbon monoxide he remembered from its cities. Coal smoke, yes; these automobiles were steam-powered, burning powdered coal. So were the rigid balloons he saw overhead, whose hydrogen gas was slightly less hazardous in this less oxygen-rich atmosphere.

All of this Jason had learned in his orientation. The scientific method had never occurred to anyone here. But by a gradual accretion of rule-of-thumb engineering, the Manziru Empire had over millennia reached a steam-age technological level very roughly equivalent to that of nineteenth-century Earth—but "spotty," and far less diffused among the general populace, being largely monopolized by the official class. There were a lot more carts pulled by draft animals (or lowest-class Zirankh'shi workers) than steam cars.

As they neared the legation, they began to see occasional humans in the streets, bulking above the Zirankh'shi. Most of these were presumably business people, although some had an unmistakably disreputable look. And others . . .

"Mercs," declared Mondrago flatly.

These grew more numerous in the immediate vicinity of the walls surrounding the legation that were the imperial bureaucracy's unavailing attempt to contain the contaminating alien influence. One group in particular was armed, and sorting itself out in rough-and-ready military fashion. Mondrago peered curiously at their weapons.

"Good old nitrocellulose-burning slugthrowers, with caseless ammunition," he pronounced. "Mid-twenty-first-century vintage design—what they called 'advanced combat rifles' in those days."

Orsini, who was doing the driving, nodded while keeping most of his attention on maneuvering through the chaotic congestion of the streets. "That's the most advanced stuff they're allowed. And it can do no harm if it falls into local hands, given the total impossibility of Zirankh'shi industry reproducing the rifles or the ammunition for them. Of course, the imperial government would *like* really up-to-date weaponry, even though that would be in direct contravention of the treaty restrictions on high-technology imports that they themselves insisted on. And the Dazh'Pinkh have asked for the same thing, through their *sub rosa* contacts with us. But the Confederal Republic government is adamant."

"And I've heard that all the colonial governments have

gone along, thus closing our usual loophole," added Mondrago, unconsciously referring to the mercenaries in the first person out of old habit. It was a Freudian slip that drew a sharp look from Rojas.

Jason had heard the same thing. The *laissez-faire* attitude of human governments toward the free companies had certain limits. When their clients were human colonists, they could use essentially anything they could buy, up to and including "dial-a-yield" tactical nuclear weapons. But in the very rare cases—such as this one—where they were inserted into the internecine wars of low-technology nonhumans, they were denied the use of the utterly destabilizing products of state-of-the-art twenty-fourth-century military science. It was all very subjective, but the rule of thumb was to exclude anything so advanced as to fall under the well-known law of the sage Clarke.

"Actually," Chang put in, "some of the local weapons are nastier than you might expect. Their firearms are nothing much; they're limited to black powder, and to muzzle loading for the heavy artillery. But they have a kind of crude flamethrower using liquid-fuel incendiaries. By atomizing that fuel, and compressing it and fine coal dust into a cylinder with steam-driven pumps, they've actually produced a primitive fuel-air explosive. Makes quite a big bang, I can tell you! A really large barrel of it, rolled down a hill toward a rebel-held city, leveled a good part of the city."

"Still," Rojas put in, "I gather that the imperials are more and more dependent on our mercenaries."

"Right. The army is as rotten as everything else in the

Manziru Empire. The troops are as likely as not to desert, and the officers to sell out. Any general who's too successful is distrusted as a potential usurper and eventually falls victim to murderous court intrigues. Sooner or later, some talented and ambitious human mercenary leader is going to take advantage of that and get himself put in command of the imperial army."

"Right," Mondrago nodded. "He *can't* be a usurper, since he can't possibly be a threat to the imperial succession."

"Precisely. And that will be the end of the rebellion."

"And he'll be the power behind the throne," Rojas observed.

"Which will make our position here even more delicate," said Orsini morosely.

"And then," said Jason, steering the conversation toward the reason for his own presence, "there's also the little matter of the Transhumanists."

"Who possess the capability of time travel," Chantal added. "With all that implies."

Neither Orsini nor Chang had any comment to make that might have lightened the general depression, as they entered the compound, with its modern structures, leaving the great alien hive of Khankhazh behind.

CHAPTER SEVEN

"Actually," said Narendra Patel with a smile, "the title they've fastened on me is 'Legate.' I have to handle our affairs from here in this treaty port. We're still trying to pressure the imperial court into letting us establish a formal embassy up in Shandu, against bitter resistance. They'd prefer to pretend we don't exist, and they don't want a constant reminder that we do."

"So your Mr. Orsini told us," said Rojas.

They sat in Patel's office—Rojas, the Authority team, and Chang—as a Zirankh'shi servant finished providing them with drinks. Officially, imperial subjects weren't allowed to take employment in the sink of cultural contamination that was the Earth legation. In practice, as usual, the decrees of the imperial government were disregarded at the local level in exchange for the most perfunctory bribes. And often not even that was necessary; it was simpler to bypass the bureaucrats and deal directly with the underworld of criminal organizations, secret societies and kinship groups that dominated the slums, unnoticed and unacknowledged by higher officialdom. So the legation had a full native staff of low-level workers . . . and, Jason suspected, was a sieve of security leaks.

Patel sank back in his chair and sighed. The expression on his round face, the color of fairly well-creamed coffee, turned wry. "So our government considers this legation a temporary expedient—which is why we're chronically underfunded, hence understaffed, including our IDRF unit. We're very glad to have you, Major Rojas."

"Especially," said Jason, determined to keep the meeting focused, "in light of the discovery of Transhumanist activity here."

"Umm . . . yes. That came as a shock to us all." Patel clearly felt he already had quite enough problems. He turned to Jason for reassurance that there wasn't still more to complicate his life. "But, Commander, we don't really *know* there are Transhumanists here, do we? All we know for certain is that someone on this planet—in this city, in fact—has unauthorized bionic enhancements."

"That sort of narrows it down," Jason pointed out, "when you consider how tightly controlled and restricted such things are. Only law enforcement officers like myself and Captain Chang are allowed things like my brain implant—and even we have to demonstrate a legitimate need for them. In point of fact, the prohibition is so absolute—and enforced by social mores as much as by the Human Integrity Act and its enabling legislation—that the

Transhumanist underground are the *only* people with illicit bionics we've ever encountered."

"But there's no actual evidence that whatever they are up to here involves time travel. Is there?"

"That's what we're here to try to ascertain." Jason turned to Chang. "I'd be very interested to know how you found out about them in the first place. Was it pure, blind chance that your implant detected their bionics?"

"Well, not altogether. We had gotten a lead on some kind of suspicious activity through an intelligence source of ours—a human mercenary. In fact, he's organizing a new free company." Chang turned to Mondrago. "Those were men of his you saw earlier, outside the compound. We've been cultivating him for his contacts among the native underworld. You see, he has a sort of varied past."

Patel's normally mild features took on a look of icy disapproval. "That's one way to put it."

"In point of fact," Chang admitted, "he was at one point facing the prospect of a rather serious criminal charge. He turned informer for us in exchange for immunity. But he's proven reliable, and sometimes very useful—as in this case."

"I'd like very much to meet this individual," said Rojas.

"That can be arranged. But there's some danger involved. He lives in a highly disreputable part of the city."

"I'll take my chances."

"So will I," said Jason. "I'd also like to talk to him. Alexandre, you come too—you and he may have some acquaintances in common. Chantal . . . maybe you'd better stay here in the compound."

✦✦✦

The interiors of Zirankh'shi living accommodations involved a lot of stooping and crouching and bending for humans. Mario McGillicuddy was less bothered by this than most, for he was short as well as wiry. It went with his hyperactive mannerisms and flashing black eyes.

To Jason, he was a familiar type, characteristic of the adventurers, drifters and occasional out-and-out rogues to be found on the outer frontier of human interstellar expansion. In his experience, such men were often closet idealists whose idealism was not incompatible with an eye to the main chance. It soon became apparent that McGillicuddy was of that breed.

"Yes, I started out believing in the Dazh'Pinkh movement," he admitted as they reclined on cushions around a low table in his quarters in the warrens of Khankhazh's criminal district—which, of course, officially did not exist, but whose status was generally recognized and confirmed by a well-established schedule of bribes. The room was redolent of the—to modern human eyes— almost pathological overelaboration of decorative motifs and oddly contrasted colors that characterized Zirankh'shi interiors. They sipped cups of the mildly stimulating herbal beverage called *tchova*, and smelled the disturbingly ambiguous delightful/repulsive aromas that clung to all Zirankh'shi residences, as McGillicuddy continued.

"I thought they had really caught on to concepts like freedom and democracy. I thought they were going to kick this decomposing corpse of an empire apart and set up something along modern lines—something we could do business with. And think of the opportunities that would open up! You have no idea of the potential of this planet, if the Manziru Empire could just be swept out of the way! I was determined to help them . . . even to the extent of a little gunrunning." Catching sight of Rojas' glare, he hastened to explain. "Hey, nothing *really* up to date—no plasma guns or anything of that sort. Just gauss rifles and electromagnetic grenade launchers and such. What do you think I am?"

Rojas' continued glare gave that question all the answer it required.

"Well, anyway," McGillicuddy hastened on, "I got caught in a little indiscretion, but the good Captain Chang here was willing to overlook it in exchange for my cooperation in certain matters. And besides . . ." All at once his eyes turned inward and his expression turned grim. "By that time I had seen the Dazh'Pinkh from the inside out, in the territories they control. And I knew I had been wrong. They've learned a bunch of the right slogans, but that's just a way of sucking in gullible humans . . . like me," he admitted ruefully. "Mind you, they may have had some worthwhile ideals at first. But now everybody in their territory except the leaders of the movement are slaves, herded into forced labor compounds—that's how they interpret 'democracy'— while the leaders live like the emperor, and everyone who protests is exterminated. And everyone who doesn't get slaughtered is dying of famine, thanks to their mismanagement of everything."

"In short, a typical revolutionary movement," said Jason, who had observed twentieth-century Earth and its assorted "liberators."

"The one thing about the Dazh'Pinkh that works," McGillicuddy went on, "is the army. You can be sure *they* get enough to eat, and whenever they're not terrorizing the civilian population—which keeps it too terrified to even think about resisting—their discipline is brutal. And they've got some competent generals. The imperial army is bigger and better armed, but it's useless—a festering mass of demoralized troops and corrupt officers, commanded by court favorites who aren't fit to dig latrines."

"So you think the Dazh'Pinkh are going to win?" Mondrago querried.

"No. You see, I'm not going to let them."

For a moment McGillicuddy's listeners were silent in the face of sublime certitude.

"You?" Jason finally managed.

"That's right. I'm organizing a mercenary company that will work under an exclusive contract with the imperial government. And once we start scoring some victories, the other free companies will stop offering themselves to either side. Nothing succeeds like success! Just wait; I'll bring them all into an umbrella organization."

"Won't this 'exclusive contract' make you, except by a lawyer's quibble, simply part of the imperial army?" Mondrago wanted to know. "And won't that violate Earth's position of neutrality?"

"Ah, but I won't be working for the Earth government! So their hands will be clean. Even a fuddy-duddy like Patel understands that." Chang, who had been maintaining scrupulous expressionlessness, allowed his eyes to narrow and his lips to thin into a hard line of disapproval. But McGillicuddy, now in full tilt, was oblivious. Jason was not surprised, for he had known too many similar cases. Typically, the next stage beyond idealism was a disillusioned idealist who had seen the light and switched sides. "And anyway, I've got what counts: the financial backing of some of the most important human merchants with a stake out here. They know I'm their best bet to restore stability on this planet. They also know that after I've cleaned out the Dazh'Pinkh I'll have a lot of influence; I'll be in a position to make it easier for our people to do business here without interference."

Either this character is madder than a hatter, thought Jason, *or else he's the mercenary leader we were speculating about. Or, possibly, both.* Out of the corner of his eye, he noted that Chang was looking very serious indeed.

"In the meantime," he said aloud, "I gather that it was while working for the IDRF that you found out about the Transhumanists."

"Well, yes, although that's giving me too much credit. All I discovered was that *some* humans were buying large supplies of food. We mercs naturally obtain the bulk of our own supplies locally, you know."

"Naturally," Jason echoed. Except for low-volume, high-value luxury items and novelties, and required dietary supplements, no one transported foodstuffs across interstellar distances—certainly not in bulk. It just wasn't a paying proposition.

"So I have contacts in the local high-volume food markets. And I began to hear that other humans were buying so much as to drive the prices up."

"That must have been distressing," said Rojas drily.

"You bet." McGillicuddy, like most of his ilk, was clearly impervious to irony. "I brought it to Captain Chang's attention, of course. The IDRF likes to keep tabs on the humans doing business here—they're a mixed lot, and I'm afraid that lately we've been getting a questionable element." His listeners carefully kept straight faces. "And my men I'd sent to watch the markets spotted some humans who were unfamiliar to us but somehow didn't quite seem to fit the usual riffraff profile."

"So," Chang took up the narrative, "I looked into it personally, just doing surveillance around the markets. I never dreamed that my implant would come into play."

"But after that," Rojas prompted, "you never got another lead."

"No. Everything dried up after that one contact."

"But," McGillicuddy put in, "*someone* is still doing the buying, because the prices are still going up."

"Presumably," said Chang, "they're doing it through go-betweens among the . . . riffraff. So many layers of them that we can't trace it."

"Well," said Rojas to McGillicuddy, "thank you for your help." With a few more mumbled pleasantries, the group took its leave, standing up carefully to avoid bumped heads. As they emerged from the door, Jason halted, snapped his fingers and swore.

"Damn it, I forgot something! I'll be right back." Before anyone could ask any questions, he ducked back inside the house, where McGillicuddy was still reclining and sipping his *tchova*.

"Unless I'm mistaken," Jason stated without preamble, "you know more than you're telling the IDRF people."

"Well," the mercenary drawled, "a man must protect his confidential sources, mustn't he?"

"Of course. But remember, I work for the Temporal Regulatory Authority, which doesn't give a damn about your . . . business associates here on Zirankhu. My colleagues and I are here for a limited time, and for a limited purpose which involves only the Transhumanists. And whatever the Transhumanists are up to here, it can't be good news for you."

That last obviously made an impression. McGillicuddy's expression showed that the word "Transhumanists" had the same effect on him as it did on almost all twenty-fourth-century humans. "Will you keep any information I give you secret from Major Rojas and Captain Chang?"

"You know I can't promise that. But I'll conceal its source."

McGillicuddy reached a decision. "There's a Zirankh'shi of my acquaintance who knows what's going on if anyone does. Come back here after dark, alone."

"Can I bring Superintendent Mondrago?"

"All right, all right. But no IDRF people."

"Agreed."

CHAPTER EIGHT
✦✦✦

Khankhazh's main thoroughfares had gas-burning street lamps, many of which often worked. But the system did not extend into the precincts where McGillicuddy had his lodgings, and Jason and Mondrago hadn't wanted to request light-gathering optics from the IDRF people and thereby arouse Rojas' curiosity about what they were up to. And Zirankhu had no moon. So they had only the aid of flashlights as they picked their way through noisome streets and alleys lit only by oil lamps flickering inside windows and occasionally festooning the porches of eating places. There was, however, a glow to the west, for the criminal district of Khankhazh was close to the spaceport.

Jason was sure they were in no particular danger. The Zirankh'shi had learned the inadvisability of molesting humans, and McGillicuddy—who knew the way well enough to require no flashlight—was well known here, and occasionally exchanged greetings with acquaintances whose disreputability was unmistakable even across the gulf of race and culture. Jason was not qualified to say how good the mercenary's command of the local language was—human vocal apparatus couldn't form its sounds any better than the Zirankh'shi could manage Standard International English, if that. Still, he seemed to be able to make himself understood.

"So, Mario," said Jason as they turned down a more-than-usually uninviting alley, "tell me about this individual you're taking us to see."

"Well, he's something of an odd duck. Almost *sui generis*, you might say. He's extremely old, and used to be an imperial official—quite a high-ranking one, in fact. But he got in trouble, partly as a result of drinking—alcohol affects the Zirankh'shi nervous system in the same way it does the human one, you understand—but mostly because he could never restrain himself from expressing his opinion of the brain-dead bureaucracy. However, they could never come up with grounds to actually expel him, given his eminence. He still retains his rank—it's just that his services were never required again. So he's set up shop as a . . . there's really no way to describe it. 'Private investigator' doesn't cover it. A sort of solver of problems for people who don't want to go through official channels . . . which nobody ever does, if they can help it, what with all the bribery and red tape it entails."

"Of course," Jason nodded. It was a familiar pattern.

They turned into a narrow, winding alley, stepping gingerly over the prevailing filth with the aid of their flashlights. The only other illumination was the flickering lamplight in the windows of a sagging shack at the alley's end. This proved to be their destination, somewhat to Jason's discomfiture. But McGillicuddy banged on the door unhesitatingly. The Zirankh'shi who opened it was clearly young, to anyone who knew the indicia. He was also the most physically formidable specimen of his race that Jason had yet seen—not extraordinarily tall but broad-framed and heavily muscled to such an extent as to deviate from this species' norm as much as a champion professional wrestler or weightlifter did from that of *Homo sapiens*. Jason got the impression that, at least in this his native gravity field, he would be a match for the average human.

He exchanged a few words with McGillicuddy, who turned to Jason. "This is Luzho'Yuzho—a typical peasant name, which is exactly what he is. He's an assistant to the individual we're here to see, and has been for a couple of years. He tells me that his master is meditating, which means he's drunk. So this may take a while." He shouldered his way in despite Luzho'Yuzho's protests, ducked his head, and led the way through an interior that reeked of sour *dugugkh*, the Zirankh'shi wine that was still the staple for those who could not afford the new human imports. They passed through an inner doorway that required even deeper stooping. In the room beyond was a raised pallet where a Zirankh'shi lay on a filthy, stinking mattress, seemingly dead except that he was giving off surprisingly humanlike snores. Studying him, Jason recognized the signs of extreme old age: his fur was whitening, and had taken on a coarse, bristly texture quite unlike the smooth silkiness of youth, and his frame—tiny even for this species—had grown brittle.

McGillicuddy gestured to Luzho'Yuzho, who resignedly approached the sleeper and shook him. The huge eyes, dim and rheumy, opened slowly. The mouth opened several times in vain attempts to speak before croaking one clearly understandable word: "*Dugugkh!*"

"Oh, no you don't!" McGillicuddy reached into his pocket and withdrew a pneumospray hypo. "I had a feeling I'd need this," he explained in an aside to Jason and Mondrago. "Sober-Jolt works as well for Zirankh'shi as for humans. In fact, it works faster due to the lesser body mass." Luzho'Yuzho looked resigned as McGillicuddy applied the hypo—Jason had a feeling this had happened before—and the supine oldster jerked spasmodically. Then, with a wheezing sigh, he slowly sat up, shivering and holding his head tightly.

McGillicuddy spoke formally. "Allow me to present Lizh'Ku, formerly sixth degree official of the Imperial Inspectorate." He turned to the blearily staring Lizh'Ku and continued to speak in Standard International English. "And this is Commander Jason Thanou, and his associate Superintendent Mondrago. They represent the Temporal Regulatory Authority," he added hastily. "*Not* the IDRF."

"Ah, the Temporal Regulatory Authority," said Lizh'Ku in the same language. "I have heard that your race, among its other marvelous achievements, has the ability to travel into the past, despite the philosophical difficulties that would seem to pose." He gave a tittering sound that Jason supposed—correctly—was Zirankh'shi laughter. "Even if we had the capability, I am sure its use would be forbidden. The scholars would be terrified that it might upset the approved version of our history, as set forth in the classics. It makes one wonder if they are really as confident of the truth of those classics as they claim to be."

"That mentality isn't entirely unknown among us," Jason admitted. Inwardly, he was marveling at Lizh'Ku's fluency in Standard International English, a language he couldn't possibly have learned before being well along in years, given the short time humans had been on this planet. Zrankh'shi vocal apparatus combined with old age and *dugugkh* to give his speech a decidedly odd quality, compounded of a croak and a rasp, but it could be understood.

"I asked Lizh'Ku to look into the food-buying," McGillicuddy explained. "He knows everybody around here, and has sources of information my men couldn't even come close to. He helped point us in the right direction. But, as you know, the trail ran cold after the IDRF began looking into it and detected the use of bionics."

"Yes," said Lizh'Ku with a nod—something he must have picked up from humans along with the language. "Regrettably, the IDRF investigation put the Transhumanists, as you call them, on alert and they vanished from sight." He paused, clearly too tactful to express his opinion of the IDRF investigation. Besides which, Jason doubted that even his command of Standard International English extended to the ancient term *Keystone Cops*. "However, my curiosity was aroused, and I continued to draw on my somewhat unorthodox sources of information. "

"What have you learned?" asked Jason.

"The Transhumanists have continued their purchasing, but are now doing it through impenetrable layers of human go-betweens."

"Yes, so the IDRF has surmised."

"And I am even less able to trace the linkages upward through those layers than the IDRF, lacking as I do human sources. So I directed my inquiries downward instead, through the Zirankh'shi workers at the spaceport. The imperial government officially disapproves of their employment there, so naturally they are under the control of the criminal organizations, among which I *do* have certain sources. And I have been able to ascertain the destination to which the purchased items are taken."

McGillicuddy leaned forward. This was obviously news to him. "The IDRF says they've gone to great lengths to conceal that."

"So they have. In an out-of-the-way corner of the spaceport there is a hangar which the Transhumanists—indirectly, of course—have leased, and for which they have purchased a high degree of privacy. There they keep a small flying craft, to which the deliveries are made."

"If it's so small, it can't carry much in the way of bulk items," Mondrago objected.

"True. But it makes frequent trips, often returning after only a few hours."

Jason and Mondrago stared at each other. "A surface-to-orbit shuttle," said the latter.

"It has to be," Jason nodded. "But . . . *why?*"

It was a good question. In fact, the Transhumanists seemed to be inexplicably reverting to past history. Given the grav repulsion that allowed them to land on planetary surfaces, today's cargo carriers no longer had to deal with the tedious business of surface-to-orbit interface via shuttles.

"I'd like very much to get a look at this craft," Jason mused.

"Why not?" Lizh'Ku's ancient eyes twinkled. "It's not far—on the outskirts of the spacefield." Before Jason could recover from his surprise, he stood erect with unexpected spryness and motioned to Luzho'Yuzho, who walked over to the pallet and turned his back to it.

Jason hadn't noticed that the typical Zirankh'shi utility harness that Luzho'Yuzho wore over his youthful bright-yellow pelt had a couple of pocketlike pouches at waist level. Lizh'Ku inserted his feet in these as he hopped onto the brawny young assistant's back. "I'm not as quick on my feet as I used to be," he explained. "Now, follow me!" The three humans could only follow as Luzho'Yuzho trotted out, effortlessly carrying his almost-weightless burden.

"I can see how they make a good team," Mondrago remarked to Jason in an undertone.

They proceeded toward the westward glow of the spaceport, barely needing the flashlights given Lizh'Ku's intimate knowledge of this congested urban labyrinth. Presently they came to an area where the shanties thinned out and finally came to an end. Ahead was a cleared area, terminating in a drainage ditch, beyond which was the spacefield.

Reaching the edge of the ditch, they saw that at this season it held nothing but mud and a trickle of water.

Splashing through this, they reached an embankment on the other side, where they went prone and peered at the spacefield, on a slightly lower level and stretching away to the west beyond a narrow stretch of marshland. At this hour, there was not much activity; floodlights illuminated some areas, near warehouses, depots and machine shops, with grounded ships casting long shadows. The rest of the field—including most of this fringe area—was in darkness.

"Look!" hissed Lizh'Ku, pointing to the right toward an isolated hangar which, unlike most of this fringe of the spacefield, was floodlit. "The small craft is out on the field. It must be preparing for one of its departures. It often does so at night, presumably to avoid being observed."

Jason and Mondrago followed his pointing hand, then looked at each other. No question about it: this was a standard shuttle, of a type normally used to service orbital stations, of which there were none here. Jason wished he had brought binoculars, but across the quarter-mile distance he could discern human figures moving purposefully around the shuttle in the floodlight.

"There's only one answer," Jason said. "They've got a ship in orbit—probably a heavily stealthed ship—and they want to keep it there, for security reasons. They use this shuttle to load it, and then it goes to . . . wherever it's going."

"So," said Mondrago slowly, "whatever they're up to, it isn't on this planet. They're just using Zirankhu as a source of supplies."

McGillicuddy tapped Jason's arm and pointed. Across the field, a moving light had appeared, and was drawing closer. At first Jason thought it was a glide car, gliding about a foot above the pavement on the wings of its fixed-altitude grav repulsion. But as it entered the floodlit area it became clear that it was a larger, open-top cargo-carrying model, loaded with bales, crates and containers to its maximum capacity. It came to a halt beside the shuttle, and native workers—reasonably efficient, Jason noted, with no low-level imperial bureaucrats looking over their shoulders—loaded the cargo aboard the shuttle.

Through all this, the recorder feature of Jason's implant was activated, and what his eyes were seeing went onto ultra-miniaturized computer media. Sounds could also be recorded, but the range was far too great for the implant's amplification capabilities—which was frustrating for Jason, for he wished he could be listening in on the conversation of the humans standing beside the shuttle. Presently the loading was completed, the cargo carrier swept away, and after a final inaudible exchange one of the humans went aboard and the others entered the hangar. After a few minutes the shuttle's running lights came on and it rose into the air, swooping away into the night. Jason didn't expect to see the glow of its minimal photon thrusters, which wouldn't need to be activated until it reached an altitude where the grav repulsion's propulsive efficiency fell off to an unacceptable level. In fact, the shuttle could reach low orbit without using it at all, if the Transhumanists were willing to take their time about it.

Jason turned away. "All right. Let's get back. I've seen enough. Mario, Lizh'Ku . . . much obliged." He couldn't repay their help with much more than this. But he had a feeling the possibility of doing the Transhumanists one in the eye would be sufficient compensation for McGillicuddy. And as for Lizh'Ku, he couldn't avoid the impression that the aged Zirankh'shi was in it for the sheer fun of it. "From here on, it's up to us to pursue this matter further. Fortunately, we have the ship to do it with."

"For which," Mondrago reminded him, "we'll have to get Major Rojas' permission."

"I know, I know," said Jason unhappily.

CHAPTER NINE

Elena Rojas glared across the small desk in the office Patel had put at the disposal of the IDRF unit. "You might have involved me, instead of striking out on your own. Remember, I am in charge of this investigation."

Jason, who had faced some truly formidable glares in his time, maintained his equanimity under this one, although he had to admit that Rojas was no slouch. "IDRF involvement would have frightened off my sources."

"And you refuse to tell me what these 'sources' are?"

"That's right. I've given my word to protect their identity—and I keep my promises. So you'll just have to take my word for the fact that the Transhumanists, operating from an out-of-the-way hangar on the fringes of the spacefield, are sending the stuff they're purchasing through go-betweens off-planet, by way of a surface-to-orbit shuttle that presumably has something to rendezvous with in orbit. That's all I can tell you definitely. But the implications ought to be obvious."

"Yes." Rojas' gaze turned inward, as though the possibilities temporarily banished her vexation with Jason. "So, we'll keep the hangar under observation. And when the shuttle has returned, if it hasn't already, we'll raid the hangar."

"I strongly advise against that, Major. Admittedly, you'd put a temporary crimp in their operations. But then they'd just fall back on something else, with tighter security, and you'd be back to square one. I might remind you that IDRF operations have already spooked them once." Jason didn't flinch under Rojas' reignited glare at this bit of calculated tactlessness. "And even if you took any Transhumanist prisoners . . . well, we all know the uselessness of trying to interrogate them."

"Well then, Commander, what do you suggest? That we do nothing?"

"Hardly. I suggest that we play them along and follow this trail wherever it leads."

"Explain." Rojas voice seemed to grow a couple of degrees less cold.

"We wait until my sources tell me the shuttle is getting ready for departure." Jason reflected that he'd give Lizh'Ku a small communicator—a matched pair of them, in fact, and let him keep them in payment for services rendered. "Then we take the *Comet* class ship that brought us here into orbit and wait—remember, it has a state-of-the-art stealth suite. The Transhumanist ship is undoubtedly also stealthed, but watching the shuttle dock with it will enable us to pinpoint its location and get a lock on it with the *Comet*'s highly sophisticated sensors. Then we wait until it departs for wherever it's going, and follow it there. That shouldn't be a problem, as the *Comet* is as fast as anything in space."

"It is also completely unarmed. What will we do once we track the Transhumanist ship to its destination? I hope," Rojas added with what might have been a heavy attempt at humor, "that you're not planning on any of the heroic deeds of derring-do for which you've been renowned in the past."

"A twentieth-century North American acquaintance once told me, 'A hero is nothing but a sandwich.'" Rojas blinked with incomprehension, and Jason decided he'd better meet her on her own literal-minded ground. "I assure you that I have no intention of trying anything reckless. We'll just have to play it by ear. Probably we'll simply observe and record, from within the *Comet*'s stealth envelope, then come back here. After which, we'll be able to return to Earth with some concrete recommendations as to what action should be taken."

"That all sounds eminently reasonable . . . except that you keep using the pronoun 'we.' It seems to me that this is a matter for the IDRF. It does not really concern the Authority."

"I must beg to differ. Have you considered that this may that the Transhumanists have a temporal displacer on one of this system's lifeless planets? It would have the gravity field it requires, and at the same time would offer great security advantages, since nobody pays any attention to any planet in this system except this one. It would at least explain what they're doing here on

Zirankhu. If they have a staff on such a planet, they'd need to bring in food for them; they couldn't exactly live off the land!"

"What conceivable purpose would such a displacer serve?"

"I admit that I have no idea as yet. But we know they have the capability. And we know that they're engaging in some kind of off-planet activity in this system. It may not be something time-travel-related—but that makes as much or as little sense as anything else!"

"Hmm . . ." Rojas cogitated a moment and then gave Jason a look of grudging acquiescence. "All right. I concede that the Authority may have a legitimate interest in this. You may accompany me."

"I, and Superintendent Mondrago. And I must insist that Dr. Frey also come along, given her unique insights into the thought processes of the Transhumanists."

"No!" Rojas reined herself in, as though in search of a reasonable objection. "I prefer to bring Captain Chang. And the *Comet*'s accommodations only allow for four passengers."

"That's right, in the two staterooms. Of course, with three men and one woman, depending on how long we have to wait in orbit, this may give rise to an awkward situation . . ."

Rojas' glare was back at full force. "Very well. You may bring Dr. Frey, if you feel you must."

The *Comet*'s crew consisted of captain-pilot Gaspar Van Horn, and navigator-electronics operator Juliana Tomori. Jason and Rojas, squeezed into the tiny control room, looked over the latter's shoulders as she tracked the shuttle's ascent from the surface of Zirankhu.

As Jason had more than half expected, the shuttle used only minimal thrust from its photon thrusters, relying on grav repulsion even as it drew further and further from the planetary surface and thus grew less and less efficient as a means of propulsion as opposed to lift. The Transhumanist underground's obsession with security was practically inbred by now.

But of course something as small as a shuttle had no stealth suite. Tomori tracked it effortlessly.

"Are you sure they won't be able to track *us*?" Rojas demanded of her, somewhat nervously.

"This ship has every stealth feature that could be built into it, including an invisibility field," the young Eurasian woman assured her. "Nothing that a basic shuttle like that could mount could possibly crack it."

"But what about the ship that, presumably, they're going to rendezvous with?"

"We know nothing about that ship, Major, so I can't answer that." Tomori spoke distractedly, absorbed in her instrument readouts. "But no matter what they've got, they have nothing to point it at. They have no idea we're here, and they can't scan the entire sky at the level of detail that would be required to . . . Ah! The shuttle is using its grav repulsion to maneuver to a rendezvous. This gives us the kind of definite target we need for . . . *Yes!* Got it!"

Jason didn't need Tomori's triumphant ejaculation to know they had acquired the Transhumanist ship through all its layers of stealth. Columns of figures awoke on the readout screen, and he studied them. This was a larger ship than the *Comet*—almost all interstellar ships were, actually—but not very large. And certainly not a warship. A small-to-medium-sized transport, probably fitted for general merchandise, including passengers.

They continued to watch as the shuttle made contact and transferred its cargo, and then applied retro-thrust to depart low orbit and return to the planet below.

"Well," said Rojas in a near-murmur, "now we wait."

"Right," said Jason, just as softly. Then he smiled at the irrationality of their low voices. It was a natural instinct, even though no conceivable—or even inconceivable— technology could enable the Transhumanists to detect sounds across the vacuum of space. He departed the control room and sought out Mondrago and Chantal. After bringing them up to date, he turned to Chantal. "Does any of this suggest anything to you?"

"No," she admitted. "I have no idea what they could be up to."

"Then we wait and keep their ship under observation. Hopefully they don't have too many more visits from the shuttle before they—"

The intercom awoke, in Van Horn's voice. "Commander Thanou! They're moving."

Jason grinned at the other two. "Sometimes you just get lucky." Then he hurried to the control room.

The mystery ship accelerated outward on photon thrusters with the *Comet* following at a safe separation, cloaked in stealth. It passed Zirankhu's Primary Limit and engaged its negative mass drive. Van Horn followed suit, and they surged outward at a pseudo-acceleration higher than they'd expected of a transport, and which seemed somewhat high for a mere interplanetary hop.

"Where are they going?" Rojas asked Tomori.

"Well, I can tell you one thing. They're not headed for any planet of this system." She brought up a system-wide display on her small nav plot, featuring the planets in their current positions. One didn't have to be a navigator to see that none of them were anywhere near the mystery's ship's projected course. It seemed to be simply heading for the Secondary Limit as expeditiously as possible.

Jason and Rojas looked at each other. They hadn't counted on an interstellar trip.

"Captain," said Rojas, "have you already laid in supplies for our return trip to Earth?"

"Yes, Major," Van Horn nodded. "It was one of my first orders of business after landing on Zirankhu."

"Well," Jason philosophized, "we won't starve."

"And I told Captain Chang not to expect us back at any particular time." Rojas drew herself up and spoke unflinchingly. "Very well. We follow that ship wherever it goes."

Their quarry reached the Secondary Limit of Zirankhu's sun, formed its space-warping field, and outpaced light. Now, following behind it, they had no fear of being detected. Nevertheless, Rojas insisted on maintaining full countermeasures.

It immediately became possible for Tomori to infer the Transhumanists' destination, for a ship under negative mass drive was impervious to outside gravitational influences, so its course could be a straight line. In this case, that line could be projected outward, deeper into the constellation Serpens, to intersect a star designated SS+28 9357.

"How long?" Rojas wanted to know.

"It's seventeen light-years from here," Van Horn replied. "At our top pseudovelocity of slightly more than 1600 c, we could make it in less than four days. But that Transhumanist ship is doing not much more than 1000 c, so we're looking at about six days."

"I see." Rojas turned to Tomori. "What can you tell us about this star?"

"Not much." Tomori brought up data. "At sixty-three light-years from Earth, it's well beyond the periphery of human expansion. It's a single K2v, which means that while it's on the main sequence it's near the lower limit of mass for stars likely to have a 'Goldilocks' world. Any planet orbiting close enough to it for liquid water to exist would probably be tidelocked, which means that—"

"Yes, yes, I'm not entirely ignorant of these matters," Rojas snapped. She turned to Jason. "Do you have any insights as to why the Transhumanists would be interested in this remote, rather marginal star?"

"Absolutely none. And I suggest that we not theorize in advance of the data."

"Still," said Rojas with a trace of waspishness, "the chances of time travel being involved in their machinations would seem to be growing less and less."

"As to that, I can only repeat what I said before: it's neither more nor less likely than any other idea we've been able to come up with. Zero equals zero."

Rojas had no answer to that, and they left the control room. Jason sought out Chantal Frey, and told her where they were going. "Can you think of any reason why the Transhumanists would be shipping food to this miserable cosmic afterthought of a star?"

"No. When I was among them, they never said anything to suggest they were engaged in any kind of off-world, much less extrasolar, activity. Of course," she added with quiet bitterness, "given their obsession with secrecy, there were undoubtedly limits to what they'd say in the presence of a Pug." She used the Transhumanists' contemptuous term for humans in their natural state, an acronym for *products of unregulated genetics*.

"One thing," said Mondrago, looking thoughtful. "If they've got people on a lifeless planet of this star, it makes logistical sense to bring in provisions for them across seventeen light-years from Ziranhku, rather than from Earth, sixty-three light-years away."

"Besides which," Chantal added, "on Earth they'd have to do all the transshipment under the eyes of law enforcement agencies that are alert for any sign of their activities."

"Very valid points," said Jason. "Which leave us with the basic question of what they're doing in this system in the first place. "He sighed resignedly. "Well, we'll find out soon enough."

Nevertheless, they were no more able to refrain from fruitless speculation than a dog can resist chewing a bone. They had little else to do as the days went by and the sun of Zirankhu fell behind, merging into the star-fields, and the tiny glow of SS+28 9357 appeared and grew in the view-forward. Six days of this left them irritable and on edge by the time that orange-tinted glow waxed from a star to something resembling a sun.

Before they approached the Secondary Limit and disengaged their drive-field, Tomori's instrumentation, though certainly not in the same class as that of a survey ship, had told them most of what they needed to know about the local planets. Aside from a few iceballs orbiting in outer darkness, there were only two: a tiny, charred cinder close to the sun, and a small rocky globe just outside this sun's narrow "Goldilocks zone." It was for the latter that the transport shaped its course.

As they followed their quarry through the maneuvering necessary for a ship under negative mass drive to approach a planet—decelerating to zero pseudovelocity and disengaging the drive before entering the Primary Limit, then killing the retained intrinsic velocity that had been built up departing from Zirankhu—they studied the planet. It was within the normal size and density parameters for terrestrial planets of its mass range, with a surface gravity of 0.55 G. It had no moons. There were polar ice-caps, partly carbon dioxide snow but holding an impressive amount of water, indicating that there was a lot more in the underground cryosphere. But there was no apparent liquid water, even though the topography, with its dry channels, made clear that the planet had possessed it in the past. In fact the atmosphere, mostly carbon dioxide with a little nitrogen and argon, was just barely dense enough for water to exist in a liquid state. These were not vacuum conditions, which would simplify the problems of constructing a base there. And it didn't take Tomori long to detect such a base.

As Van Horn put them into a high orbit, they all waited, tensely wondering if that base had anything that could crack their stealth suite. But they watched without incident as the transport settled down into the atmosphere—no need for orbital transfer here—and landed.

"Can you give us visuals of that base?" Rojas asked Tomori.

"Yes. We're on the right side of the planet. I'll increase the magnification." On a small screen, the desert surface of the planet seemed to rush toward them, and the base grew into recognizability. It was located on the desert floor at the base of a low plateau. There was a landing field on which the cargo carrier now rested, a very large powerplant, a cluster of domes, and . . .

Jason drew a sharp breath. Rojas turned and gave him a curious glance. "What is it, Commander?"

Jason couldn't keep his hand altogether steady as he pointed to a large circular expanse surrounded by machinery of, at least to his eyes, unmistakable purpose.

"That, Major, is a temporal displacer. If you don't immediately recognize it for what it is, that's understandable. It's a bigger one than I've ever imagined."

CHAPTER TEN

They all stared, speechless, as Tomori produced the figures for the size of what they were looking at.

"That would be enormous even for us," Jason finally said. "Not that we could afford to build it. Using the Transhumanists' technology, which can produce small, cheap displacers, and scaling it up to *that* . . ."

"Something else," Mondrago pointed out. "Their time travel technology is also an order of magnitude more energy-efficient than ours, which is one of the things that makes it so cheap. But look at the size of that antimatter powerplant! If they need to pump all that power into one of *their* displacers, then whatever it is they send back in time must either be massive as hell, or else go back a lot of years, or both."

"Buy why send anything at all?" demanded Rojas, clearly perplexed. "Building this installation out here, sixty-three light-years from Earth, must have been a supreme effort for them. Why should they make such an effort to go back into the past of this godforsaken, lifeless, historyless ball of sand?"

"Well," Jason deadpanned, "at least they don't have to worry about the Observer Effect." Rojas' expression told him this was not the time for levity. He turned to Tomori. "Your sensors were going throughout our approach to this planet, right? Can you go back over the readings, visual and otherwise, and see if there's anything here besides that base?"

"Certainly. I'll just tell the computer what sort of things to look for." Her manipulations didn't take long, and the computer scan was even briefer. "No," she stated unhesitatingly. "Aside from the base, this planet is exactly what you would expect it to be. There's not another artifact on it."

"So," said Chantal, "they're not doing—or, I should say, haven't done—anything on this planet in the past that has left any traces in the present."

For a moment they all reverted to silence in the face of the unfathomable.

"Can you zoom in closer?" Jason finally asked Tomori. "I want a closer look at that displacer."

"Yes. We still have a while before our orbit carries us around to the other side of the planet." The base expanded still further, and Jason studied the vast circular displacer stage, as he decided he must continue to think of it even though, unlike the Authority's Australian facility, it wasn't covered by a dome. Such a dome would have been a colossal feat of engineering for an expanse this size, and on this planet there wasn't the same need to shield it from the weather. The control stations surrounding it were, however domed . . . and as Jason watched, tiny antlike figures moved purposefully into those small domes.

"There's activity around that displacer," he said in a voice charged with tightly controlled excitement. "Is there any energy buildup from that powerplant?"

"No," Tomori told him. "The emissions are holding steady."

Jason and Mondrago met each other's eyes. Mondrago spoke. "That can only mean—"

All at once, the displacer stage was no longer empty.

There was never any warning of a temporal retrieval, which was why they were always timed according to a rigid schedule. The person or object, its temporal energy potential restored, simply appeared with a slight swirl of displaced air. Only . . . this time the swirl was not slight. Even in this thin atmosphere, a small, brief dust storm blew over the control domes, for the mass that had materialized was that of a spaceship of the same class as the one that they had followed to this system. It rose slightly on grav repulsion and moved off the stage. That was the last thing they saw before their orbit carried them around the limb of the planet.

Chantal broke the silence with a chuckle.

"What, exactly, is funny?" Rojas demanded.

Chantal continued to smile. "There's an old saying, Major: many a true word is spoken in jest. And I think Commander Thanou may have hit on the truth with his earlier crack about the Observer Effect."

"Explain."

"Clearly the Transhumanists are doing something—and of course we still don't know what—off Earth, and in the past. Suppose the Observer Effect somehow makes it impossible for them to perform temporal displacement on whatever planet is the scene of their operations? Or—which somehow seems more likely—it's impractical for them to build a displacer on that planet in the present? The solution would be obvious: find a planet like this one, that isn't and never has been inhabited—let's call it 'Planet A'—and build a displacer large enough to send back interstellar transports, which could then proceed to . . . 'Planet B.'"

Rojas frowned intently. "But why go to the colossal effort of coming all the way out here to build this displacer? Why not somewhere closer?"

"You don't fully appreciate the Underground's obsession with security, Major. They'd want a planet altogether outside the sphere of human exploration, in a worthless system."

"But," Mondrago objected, "humans will eventually explore out here. The Transhumanists' privacy won't last."

"Maybe it doesn't need to last very long," said Jason slowly. "Remember, we don't know when *The Day* is."

The temperature in the overcrowded control room seemed to drop a few degrees. It was the cloud under which they all lived. The most closely guarded secret of the Transhumanist Underground remained as secret as ever. The moment when all their elaborately laid plans came to catastrophic fruition at once could be tomorrow.

It was worse when one was in interstellar space, because for all anyone could prove to the contrary *The Day* might have *already* have occurred on Earth. Although, Jason reflected, the fact that this interstellar/transtemporal transshipment operation here on what he decided he must call Planet A was still a going concern indicated that the moment was not quite yet.

"Well," said Rojas briskly, "be that as it may, we're now in a position to abort whatever it is they're doing. We'll return to Earth with our knowledge of the location of this system, and the Deep-Space Fleet will come here and blast this installation into its component atoms! Or, rather," she hastily amended, recalling the nightmarish political delays involved whenever the Deep-Space Fleet was called upon to do anything, "it ought to be possible to do it as an independent IDRF operation—I've seen no defenses here."

"Not so fast," said Jason. "We still don't know where this, ah, Planet B is, or how far back in its past they're operating, or what they've done there—or if that operation has already become self-sustaining even if we cut off their supply line here. We can't leave yet."

"But we've obtained all the information we can."

"Not by a long sight!" Jason grinned wolfishly. "For one thing, we can deduce how far into the past they're displacing these ships."

"How?"

Instead of answering Rojas directly, Jason turned to Tomori. "Your sensors can measure the output of that antimatter reactor, right?"

"Of course."

"And when we got a sensor lock on their ship, in orbit around Zirankhu, you got a mass reading on it?"

"Yes."

Jason turned back to Rojas. "There's your answer, Major. It is a truism that the energy expenditure required for temporal displacement is a function of two factors: the mass being displaced, and how far back in time it's being sent. The Transhumanists' displacers are equally subject to this tradeoff, even though their overall energy efficiency is incomparably higher than ours. And now that we've been able to study their captured displacer on Earth, we know the energy figures to feed into the equation. Knowing that, and the mass, it's just a matter of simple substitution to get the temporal 'distance.'"

"And you know these energy figures?"

"Approximately. I'm no specialist, you understand, but I've naturally taken an interest in the subject. If we can observe the displacement of one of these ships, I can tell you roughly how far into the past it's gone."

"Very well. We will remain in orbit and watch for an impending displacement."

◆◆◆

As it turned out, they didn't have long to wait. Fortuitously, their orbit had carried them over the hemisphere where the displacer was located when the transport they had followed from Zirankhu—having offloaded some but seemingly not all of its cargo—rose on its grav repulsion and maneuvered out onto that vast outdoor stage.

The sensors involved were passive, so they were in no danger of detection as they measured the output of that antimatter reactor as it built up to the surge that would send the mass of the transport back in time at least the minimum three hundred years. They all stared as the figures mounted and mounted—especially Jason, who had some inkling of what such an output must mean when channeled into a Transhumanist displacer. It seemed as though the planet itself must shake, or at least that there ought to be some visual manifestation of these titanic energies . . .

Then, with the usual anticlimactic absence of any such visual effects, the transport was gone.

"Did you get that?" Tomori asked Jason.

"Yes." Recalling the mass of the transport (adjusted for a reasonable guess as to its cargo), he could do it in his head. He turned to Rojas. "Assuming that the energy efficiency of this displacer is the same as that of the one we captured on Earth, that ship has gone back approximately five hundred years."

"The 1880s, more or less," Chantal remarked.

"On Earth, that is," Mondrago demurred. "Out here, in this barren system, nothing in particular." He shook his head and voiced the question in all of their minds. "*Why?*"

Rojas ignored his perplexity. "All right. We've been more successful in obtaining information than we could have reasonably expected. We need to return to Earth with that information without further delay. Captain Van Horn, prepare for departure."

"No." Jason's blunt monosyllable drew a sharp look from Rojas, and he decided he'd better put a little more care into deferring to her as officer in charge of what was, after all, an IDRF investigation. "I mean, Major, that you might want to reconsider that order in light of the fact that there's one extremely crucial datum that we haven't yet obtained: where these transports are going after they've been displaced five hundred years into the past."

"And how do you propose to obtain it?"

"I want to get aboard the transport that's still here— the one we saw return—and access its nav computer."

Jason couldn't avoid a certain satisfaction at seeing Rojas, for the first time in their acquaintance, completely flabbergasted. "*What?* But . . . but how—?"

"Look, we haven't seen any sign of any weapon emplacements around that installation. You said so yourself." Jason turned to Tomori for confirmation. "Isn't that so?"

"Right."

"And it makes sense. They know they couldn't possibly build any defenses here that could stand up to a serious attack from space if they were discovered. So instead of trying, they're relying entirely on secrecy—the fact that we don't know they're here. And they have no reason to think that secrecy doesn't still hold. As far as they know, they're all by themselves on this planet and have no reason to mount guard over that ship. We can land under cloak, a short distance from their base, and approach it unnoticed."

"And what do you propose to do once we get there? Do you think they're simply going to let you stroll aboard their ship?" With an effort that obviously cost her a great deal, Rojas turned to Chantal in search of support. "Didn't you say that the Transhumanist Underground is obsessive about security?"

"I think, Major, that Commander Thanou may have a

point about this perhaps being a case where they think they can afford to relax from that. And don't forget another characteristic of theirs: arrogant overconfidence, rooted in their contempt for us Pugs."

"And," Jason added hurriedly, before Rojas could think of a rejoinder, "I recall that you brought a nice little toolkit of IDRF intelligence-collection goodies along from Earth—including items which, in less respectable hands, might be called extremely sophisticated burglar's tools. Is that stuff still aboard this ship?"

"Well, yes. We never had any use for it on Zirankhu."

"And carrying whatever we need ought to be easy, in this gravity." Jason held Rojas' eyes. "We'll never have this chance again, Major. If the IDRF attacks this place with guns blazing, anything they don't obliterate the Transhumanists will blow up themselves." Chantal nodded in confirmation.

Rojas looked grim even for her. "Very well. We'll try it. But I want two things clearly understood. First, I'm coming along, and I'm in charge."

"Of course," Jason assured her.

"Secondly, our objective is to get in and out tracelessly with the information we want, so they won't know they've been compromised. We'll approach the installation and wait for any opportunity to do that. If no such opportunity arises—in other words, if your assessment of their security proves to be overly optimistic—then we abort the mission and get out while still undetected."

"We'll have no disagreements in this regard, Major." Jason grinned. "Remember what I said before about heroes."

CHAPTER ELEVEN

✧✧✧

Invisible and—they hoped—effectively undetectable by anything the Tranhumanists had installed on what was supposed to be a secret planet, the *Comet* settled cautiously down to the surface on grav repulsion.

Van Horn landed them a couple of miles east of the Transhumanists' landing field—a compromise between security considerations and minimizing the distance they'd have to walk. The landing site was behind a low ridge which lent its own low-tech concealment. As soon as Tomori confirmed that they had not been detected, Jason, Rojas and Mondrago (whom Jason had insisted be allowed to come along) suited up.

Like all passenger-carrying spacecraft, the *Comet* carried, as a legal requirement, enough light-duty survival suits for all souls aboard. Jason (from his days with the Hesperian Colonial Rangers) and Mondrago (from his former life as a merc) were about as familiar with these as Rojas, whose training included them as a matter of course. This was not a bulky full-scale spacesuit, with its array of accessories. Instead, it appeared to be a jumpsuit made of electrically active, self-repairing nanofabric, flexible even when expanded slightly by pressurization. That "skin," powered by sunlight and the wearer's body heat, recycled waste and exhaled carbon dioxide, providing air and water practically indefinitely. Near-microscopic thermocouples woven into it maintained a comfortable temperature. A pullover clear plastic hood stiffened to form a helmet when the suit was pressurized. The gloves, with their sensory-input finger pads, allowed for dexterous manipulation of tools—including the electromagnetic needle pistols the three strapped to their belts. These suits were not military models, so their electronic camouflage systems did not automatically match the background, conferring near-invisibility; but the wearer could manually set the skin to any of several stock patterns. They chose "desert" and passed through the airlock.

The ship's artificial gravity had never been reset from Zirankhu's 0.72 G, so the transition when they left it and stepped onto the surface of "Planet A" was not as disconcerting as it might have been. They soon adjusted to a gravity little more than half Earth-normal as they mounted the ridge and proceeded across the barren landscape. Van Horn had landed shortly before sunset so they would have some light for at least the first part of their trek, but be in darkness by the time they neared their destination. (The planet's rotation was only about a third longer than Earth standard.) So they walked west toward the dim light of the small westering sun, traversing a boulder-strewn plain which was mostly sand but reddish in color due to significant amounts of iron and sulfur oxides. They made good time in the low gravity, despite the satchels they were carrying.

The sun had almost set when they arrived at the edge of the plateau overlooking the Transhumanist installation. Lying prone, they peered down. The temporal displacer was in the distance to the right, beyond a cluster of pressurized domes. But the landing area was below and to the left, and the transport lay there. Discouragingly, there was activity around it.

"They must be preparing for departure," said Rojas into the tiny communicator stuck to the base of her throat.

"Right. Another milk run to Zirankhu." Jason studied the scene through small electronic binoculars. "Maybe they'll quit work after dark."

"And leave the ship unguarded?" Mondrago sounded skeptical.

"Remember, they don't think they need to guard it."

"All right," said Rojas. "We'll wait here and observe for a reasonable length of time."

"How long is 'reasonable'?" Jason wanted to know.

"Until I say it no longer is," snapped Rojas.

There was little in the way of dusk in this thin atmosphere; almost at once, the moonless sky darkened from deep blue to black, spangled with stars that barely had the twinkling effect produced by Earth's denser air. The temperature, already low, fell rapidly. But floodlights illuminated the transport, and the figures around it, clad in suits like theirs, continued their activity. It was difficult to keep count of how many entered the ship and how many left.

"This isn't going to work," muttered Rojas.

"Just a little longer," Jason urged. "I can't believe they're going to keep at it all night."

Time went by and Rojas was growing restless again when the workers began to head back toward what must be the residence dome, which showed a flicker of lights. The lights of the nearer domes began to go off and finally the floodlights went out. The transport lay alone, in darkness.

"This is our chance!" exclaimed Jason. Without waiting for Rojas' assent he got to his feet and started off.

Inside their flexible transparent helmets they wore passive light-collecting goggles—vastly more compact descendants of an earlier era's "starlight scopes." This enabled them to scramble down a ravine that cut down through the plateau to the desert floor. Moving cautiously, they kept the bulk of the transport between themselves and the domes as much as possible. At Rojas' insistence, they stopped at the edge of the landing area and waited a couple of minutes. There was no indication that they had been discovered; evidently no security field enveloped the transport. They proceeded in a low, crouching run to the transport's side and worked their way around it to where a standard model like this would have a personnel airlock.

To their surprise, the access ramp was extended. And the airlock was as standard as everything else seemed to be, so the paratronic lockpick Rojas carried sufficed to open it from the outside. They stepped into the tiny chamber, illuminated only by the dim lights of the control panel, on which Rojas punched out a command. The outer door slid shut automatically, and then the inner inner door began to open . . .

All at once, Jason's entire universe was a blinding glare of light.

Hastily, he shut off the light-gathering goggles he had left on, expecting the ship's interior to be dark. Instead, it was fully lighted, and the goggles had enhanced that illumination into an intolerable glare, which now abruptly ceased. But his field of vision was still full of exploding suns, which he tried desperately to blink away. Just ahead, he could make out the figure of Rojas, who had stumbled into the ship, and a second figure who brought some kind of tool down on the back of the IDRF major's head.

Still frantically trying to clear his eyes of the stroboscopic aftereffects, Jason lurched forward and grappled Rojas' attacker. But he was hopelessly disoriented, and his opponent's muscles were products of genetic upgrade. He was flung aside, to smash against a bulkhead . But then his gradually returning sight made out Mondrago, grasping the Transhumanist from behind in a chokehold with his left arm and, with his right, giving a quick, vicious sideways twist to the head, breaking the neck.

Jason got unsteadily upright, smiling weakly. "You must have had your light-gatherers deactivated."

"Just being cautious," said Mondrago modestly as he helped Rojas to her knees. "Rest a minute, Major."

"No time!" Rojas got to her feet, holding her head and swaying slightly. "Let's see if there are any others."

They drew their gauss needlers and fanned out through the transport, ending in the control room, but there was no one. "So there was just the one, still in here working," said Jason.

"And now he's dead." Rojas shot Mondrago a look that Jason thought had a rather high acid content, considering that the Corsican had just saved her life. "When they find him—or if they *don't* find him—they'll know someone has been here."

"I've got an idea on that," said Jason. Rojas muttered something in Spanish about Jason's ideas, which he decided he was just as glad he couldn't understand. "But for now, let's hurry up and do what we came to do."

"All right," said Rojas stiffly, as though agreeing only grudgingly. She turned, knelt and fumbled in her satchel.

"You're welcome," Mondrago murmured inaudibly in the direction of her back.

The device Rojas pulled from her satchel was the heaviest item in it, even though it was vastly lighter and more compact than its distant ancestor, the late twentieth-century's TEMPEST (Transient Electromagnetic Pulse Emission Scanning Technology) gear. And, unlike that ancestor, it could read data already stored on a computer, not just what was currently being keyed in or displayed. Even though the transport's interior lights made clear that it was operating under minimal auxiliary power, they took no chances. They booted up the nav computer on its integral battery power before Rojas began her probing. The process took a while, during which interminable minutes Jason's nerves crawled. Finally Rojas looked up.

"All right. What we need should be in here. Now let's go. And . . . let's hear your 'idea' regarding the highly inconvenient corpse."

The dead Transhumanist was wearing a suit not unlike theirs. They pulled his helmet cowl over, pressurized the suit, and carried him out of the airlock. The inner door could, with suitable manipulations, be closed while leaving the outer one open. They then arranged the corpse at the base of the ramp in such a way as to suggest he had finished his work, departed the transport, tripped, and fallen and broken his neck.

"Do you really think this will fool them?" Rojas demanded irritably.

"I think it might. Given their belief that they're alone on this planet—and all indications point to them thinking that way—it will make better sense to them than anything else. And . . . do you have any better ideas?"

"No," Rojas admitted. "Let's go."

They scrambled back up the ravine to the plateau and retraced their steps in the darkness with the aid of their goggles and Jason's brain implant. Rojas still seemed intermittently dizzy, but she kept up.

Tomori took several minutes to download the data and interpret it, while Chantal attended to Rojas' head injury, which the latter accepted with fairly good grace. Finally the navigator looked up.

"All right. Got it. That ship's destination, after going back five hundred years, was the star HC+32 8213." She brought up a display on which a star-symbol blinked for attention. "It's fourteen point eight light-years from here, so it would only be a trip of less than five and a quarter days for them."

"And afterwards they don't have to make a return trip to this system at all," Jason observed. "All they have to do is restore the ship's temporal energy potential, and it simply reappears here in the present."

"How can you be sure it works that way, Jason?" asked Chantal. "You've always told me that, for any number of reasons involving fundamental physics, temporal displacement can only work in a planetary gravity field."

"Well, I can't be absolutely sure," Jason admitted. "We've never practiced time travel anywhere except on the surface of Earth, and you're right about the displacement itself. But as for the retrieval . . . well, everything we know and understand indicates that the object *has* to return to its own time in the linear present, at the location from which it was displaced."

"We'll have plenty of time to indulge in this kind of speculation later," said Rojas, standing up and shaking off Chantal's ministrations. "What do you know about that star?" she asked Tomori

"It's a single G3v star, only a little less massive and less hot than Sol. Beyond that, I can tell you nothing. It's almost sixty-four light-years from Sol, and therefore has never been visited."

"By us," Mondrago amended drily.

"Very well, then. Now we know where 'Planet B' is." Rojas gave Jason a hard look. "And before you can even make any suggestions regarding that star, Commander—"

"Actually, I hadn't intended to."

"—let me be quite definite on one point. It is now our

duty to get back to Earth with the information we now possess, and we will take no further risks that might jeopardize our chances of doing so." Rojas turned to Van Horn. "Captain, are our remaining provisions sufficient for us to return to the Solar system directly from here?"

"A sixty-three light-year hop—that would be a little less than fourteen and a third days for this ship." Van Horn did some mental arithmetic. "Yes, I believe so, if we go on rations."

"Good. We won't have to waste time returning to Zirankhu."

Where I left my Scotch, moaned Jason inwardly.

CHAPTER TWELVE

"As it turns out, Jason, your calculation was quite accurate" said Kyle Rutherford, gazing down the long table. "Since your return, the specialists have reviewed the sensor data you collected and applied it to the performance figures for the Transhumanist temporal displacer we captured. And, in fact, that transport was displaced almost exactly five hundred years. I say 'almost' because absolute precision is impossible in the absence of exact figures on the mass of the transport's load."

They sat in the conference room adjacent to Rutherford's office, deep in the heart of the Authority's Australian facility. Mondrago and Chantal were also present, as was Rojas. Seated beside her at the table was a big, squarely built man with short iron-gray hair and general's insignia on the shoulder straps of his dark blue uniform—Viktor Kermak, the chief of staff of the IDRF.

He had brought a retinue of staffers, but they now sat unobtrusively back from the table, along the wall. This was a preliminary conference, to determine the recommendations that would be given the higher governmental authorities.

Alastair Kung was also present. Ordinarily Rutherford, as operations director, represented the Authority in meetings such as this. But Kung had gotten wind of what was afoot here, and had muscled his massive way in. Now he sat, somewhat resembling an overweight owl, occasionally looking down his nose over his nest of chins to give Jason a look of disapproving suspicion.

"Also, Jason," Rutherford continued, "it is the opinion of the experts that you were correct in your surmise concerning temporal retrieval. It seems the mathematics of the effect predict that an object does not have to be in the same gravity field as the displacer to 'snap back' to it when its temporal energy potential is restored. This, despite all the seeming problems involving the laws of conservation of energy and momentum. And those same mathematics suggest no theoretical limit on the distance over which the effect obtains. Of course, the problem with general mathematical statements is that they contain no automatic cutoff points to tell you when they cease to apply to the real universe. And we've never tested this out. Indeed, it's never occurred to us to think in these terms before." Rutherford shook his head slowly. He still hadn't altogether recovered from the whole concept of extrasolar temporal displacement.

"If this is true," Mondrago mused, "then on their return trips the Transhumanists effectively have the kind of 'teleportation' the science fiction writers are always talking about, with interstellar range. That would be a terrific logistical advantage."

"Which, in turn, may help make this whole project cost-effective," Rojas nodded. "Even though it still must be a colossal effort for them."

"And," added Chantal, "we still don't know why they're making that effort. What can they have been doing on Planet B, five hundred years in the past, that would be worth it?"

"At least," rumbled General Kermak, "we know where this, uh, Planet B is. We also know the location of Planet A, through which it is being supplied. And they don't suspect that we possess this knowledge . . . we hope," he added with a hard look at Jason and Mondrago. "So the solution is clear: direct military action!"

"You're familiar with the arguments I advanced against an attack on Planet A when Major Rojas suggested it, General," said Jason mildly.

"Yes, Commander, I have taken cognizance of them. Which is why I'm not proposing it as an isolated operation. I say, at the same time we hit Planet A, we also go to Planet B. Whatever the Transhumanists went back in time to do there, it must presumably have consequences in the present. Otherwise, why would they have done whatever it is?"

Rutherford looked alarmed. "Surely, General, you're not advocating an all-out attack on Planet B in the current state of our ignorance of it? What you suggest may be more than the IDRF can manage on its own." This, Jason knew, was true. The IDRF's space-combat capability was limited to relatively small, lightly armed ships, for political reasons and also due to the seeming lack of a need for any heavier metal.

"No, of course not. First we need to perform a reconnaissance." Kermak pronounced it correctly. "If it turns out they've got more than we can handle there, then we'll just have to set the wheels in motion to bring in the Deep Space Fleet." He made no attempt to keep the distaste out of his voice.

Jason framed his words very carefully. "General, your duties don't normally involve time travel, so you're accustomed to thinking entirely in the 'linear present' as we call it. But I ask you to consider something. The Transhumanists are taking an enormous amount of trouble to go to Planet B five hundred years in the past. They must have a reason for doing so. If it's like all their other machinations, it can only be to plant the seed of something that's not going to come to fruition until *The Day*—which self-evidently hasn't occurred yet. Now, the Transhumanists could quite easily go across space to Planet B in the present. *Why don't they?*"

"What are you driving at, Commander?"

"General, are you familiar with what we call the Observer Effect?"

"I've heard of it. I can't claim that I entirely understand it."

"If you did, you'd be the only one," said Jason with a smile. "But it seems clear to me that for reasons related to the Effect, the Transhumanists have to leave what they've started on Planet B alone. This suggests that whatever they're doing there is vulnerable at its inception." He glanced at Rutherford, who had clearly grasped where this was headed and appeared to be experiencing some difficulty breathing. Kung still wore a look of blank incomprehension, which was just as well. Jason continued to address Kermak. "I propose that we nip their little scheme in the bud. And if we do it after they've finished setting their project up and have ceased going to Planet B, we'll have destroyed it without them knowing we have. And then won't they have a surprise on *The Day*?"

Mondrago spoke up, breaking the silence. "General, you might say time travel adds a new dimension to warfare. If I may draw an example from history, military men were used to thinking in two dimensions before the invention of airplanes allowed operations in the third dimension. In addition to going around an enemy's flanks on the ground, they could—"

"Yes, yes, I know," snapped Kermak. "They called it 'vertical envelopment.'"

"Well, General, think of what Commander Thanou is describing as 'temporal envelopment.'"

Jason held his breath, hoping Mondrago, an ex-merc, hadn't strayed over the line with Kermak. But at the same time, he reminded himself that this was no mere boneheaded warhorse; such types did not rise high in today's military. And after a moment, the general's thin lips formed a slight smile.

"I get the concept, Superintendent. Of course, its usefulness would be very much limited by the Observer Effect. Good thing, too; otherwise the consequences would be . . . unimaginable. But in this particular case, we just may be able to put it to use." Kermak turned back to Jason. "Do I understand, Commander, that you are proposing—"

"—That we ourselves perform an extrasolar temporal displacement?" blurted Rutherford, who had regained the power of speech. Kung had not; he finally understood, and his face was a frozen mask of slowly purpling blubber.

"Right. If the Transhumanists can build a displacer on that scale, then so can we, now that we have their technology. We can send a ship back almost but not quite as far as those transports of theirs are going—maybe to a point in time about a decade later—and proceed to Planet B in that time period. If possible, we can go ahead and abort their scheme, whatever it is. If that's not possible, we can return with enough ships to do it." Jason turned to Kermak with a smile. "But I would be very surprised, General, if the IDRF couldn't handle this strangle-in-the-cradle operation on its own, without the need to involve the Deep-Space Fleet."

"Hmmm . . ." Kermak stroked his craglike chin, and Jason saw he had struck a chord. "Yes. There's something to be said for avoiding all the complications *that* entails."

"Especially considering the impossibility of avoiding security leaks when something has to be taken into the political arena," Rojas added.

"And security is going to be a problem anyway," said Mondrago morosely. "Where are you going to build this displacer? The Transhumanist underground is bound to notice a project of that size."

"That's right," nodded Jason. "It can't be on Earth, for that reason—not to mention the Observer Effect, since nobody on late nineteenth-century Earth noticed any spaceships popping into existence out of thin air! We'd have to make it in modular components and ship them to some other planet for assembly." Out of the corner of his eye, he saw Rutherford and Kung seemingly go into shock.

"Mars, perhaps?" suggested Rojas. Sol's fourth planet had been the subject of extensive terraforming studies in the twenty-first century, but nothing had come of them. By the end of that century, the competition for the finite funding available had been won by the first slower-than-light interstellar probes. And then, in the early twenty-second century, had come the takeover by the Transhuman Dispensation, which hadn't been interested. And after its overthrow, no one had been interested because the negative mass drive had opened up a galaxy full of more promising planets. So Mars continued to orbit the sun in its pristine state of cold lifelessness—like Planet A, only smaller and even more inimical to life.

"It's still too close for comfort, right here in the Solar System," said Jason. "I'd prefer an extrasolar planet. I'd also prefer a planet with a breathable atmosphere. Mars is almost airless, and having to build a base there would complicate our engineering problems, besides being expensive."

Rutherford, who had managed to recover his composure, spoke with icy sarcasm. "I am reassured that you are thinking in terms of expense! Jason, do you have any conception of the magnitude of this undertaking?"

"This *unprecedented* undertaking, I might add!" blurted Kung. "Kyle, I cannot believe that your latitude as operations director can possibly be stretched so far. I would insist that it be put to the full council."

"I know it may be a hard sell to the council," Jason understated. Then he had a sudden inspiration. "But you might point this out to them. To avoid all the political headaches of achieving unity of command in a large-scale military operation, the government will almost certainly want the Authority and the IDRF to handle this, in conjunction with each other but still acting *independently*."

Rutherford's expression instantly grew more cheerful. As usual, preservation of the Authority's status as an independent agency would be uppermost in the minds of the council, and he knew it. Even Kung's face began to grow a lighter shade of purple.

"Well," Rutherford said after a moment, preening his beard thoughtfully, "if it's put to them that way . . . perhaps . . ."

Kung, however, was still not mollified. "But Kyle, the *impropriety!* I remind you that all Special Operations Section activities are at present in abeyance pending the Section's official disbandment."

"And I remind you, Alastair, that this is not an expedition of the Special Operations Section as such. Commander Thanou is, indeed, acting for the Temporal Service—"

"With which his connection is, at present, somewhat ambiguous," Kung interjected darkly.

"—but as a consultant to the IDRF, not in his capacity as head of the Section." Something seemed to firm up inside Rutherford. "And in *my* capacity as operations director, I am provisionally approving this project, and authorizing funding from my discretionary monies. You, of course, have every right to subsequently raise the question before the council of whether I have exceeded my authority." Before Kung could speak, he spoke in a more conciliatory tone. "So you see, whatever happens I will bear all responsibility."

Kung brightened visibly. In his bureaucratic world, what mattered was not success but avoidance of accountability for failure.

Well ,well, thought Jason, looking at Rutherford with more respect than he had felt in a while. *Is it possible that his conscience is bothering him for not fighting harder—or at all—for the Section? It should.*

"But Jason," Rutherford continued sternly, turning to face him, "before I can finalize my approval—and in anticipation of later council review—I must have a specific proposal as to just where we want this displacer constructed."

"Well, there are a lot of habitable extrasolar planets—"

"What about Zirankhu?" Chantal suddenly interjected. "Yes, I know it might not ordinarily occur to us. But remember, it's a dry world with extensive empty areas like . . . this." She gave a gesture that indicated Australia's Great Sandy Desert, which stretched away from the installation in all directions. "And we could purchase many of our supplies locally, rather than hauling them from Earth. And furthermore, it's not far, as interstellar distances go, from Planet A—which, if I understand the spatial relationships correctly, means it also can't be all that far from Planet B."

"Just a moment." Rojas manipulated her wrist computer, which projected a holographic display of stars in the air above the table. She made various calculations. "Yes. From HC-4 9701 to HC+31 8213—that is, from Zirankhu to Planet B—is nineteen point forty-five light-years, a figure which the proper motions of the stars won't have changed much in merely five hundred years. A considerably shorter voyage than from the Solar System or anywhere near it. Less than a third as far, in fact." She must, Jason decided, be sold on the idea. She had forgotten to glare at Chantal on general principles before supporting her.

"I think Chantal may have hit on something," he said.

"But," Rutherford objected, "we don't precisely own Zirankhu. How will we induce the Manziru Empire, which claims to rule the entire planet, to permit this?"

"The same way everything else is done on Zirankhu," said Jason with a grin. "Bribery. We can go under the table and offer the imperial officials some high-tech goodies if they'll go along. *Not* up-to-date weapons," he hastily added in Kermak's direction. "But there are other things that they'd like to have. And since those things are forbidden by their own laws and import restrictions—and also because they'll think they're swindling us by leasing us some patch of worthless, out-of-the-way desert—the individuals we deal with will agree quickly, before we come to our senses. For the same reasons, they'll be sure to keep the whole thing under tight security."

"Speaking of security," Mondrago cautioned, "what about the Transhumanists on Zirankhu. Won't they notice what's going on?"

"I don't think so—not if we handle it right, using dummy private shipping outfits to clandestinely bring in the components. Remember, they're just coming and going to buy provisions. They don't have any kind of ongoing intelligence operation in place there. Why should they? They have no interest in the planet, as such." Jason smiled reminiscently. "And remember, Alexandre, we know some people there who might be of assistance in the security department."

CHAPTER THIRTEEN

"I had a feeling I'd find you like this," said Jason with a *tsk, tsk*. "Or else dead."

"Fortunes of war," sighed Mario McGillicuddy, leaning back on the cushions. He reached for his cup of *tchova* with his left hand, awkwardly but unavoidably inasmuch as his right arm was no longer there. His features were still somewhat pale and drawn, but his characteristic cocky enthusiasm was unabated. "We had some successes at first, and I can't deny that I may have gotten a trifle overconfident."

"Just a trifle, from what I've heard of your attempt on that last Dazh'Pinkh-held town," said Jason drily.

"I tell you, if that fathead Patel had given me any support—"

"Come on, Mario. You know he can't."

"All right, all right—I overreached. But damn it, we

managed an orderly withdrawal back here to the Khankhazh area. And I'm learning from my mistakes."

"As long as they don't kill you."

"This one *was* close," the mercenary admitted. "Fortunately, I lasted long enough for Captain Chang to get me into the infirmary at the legation. Damned good of him, too; if it had been up to Patel, I would have been left outside to rot. Seems I'm an embarrassment, making it harder for him to maintain his pose of neutrality. Anyway, the infirmary is small, but they've got some basic field versions of regen devices—dermal closers and skeletal knitters and such."

"So what now?"

"Now I'm going back to Earth for a while to get the arm regrown. Naturally they don't have that kind of regen equipment here."

"Naturally," Jason nodded. The Human Integrity Act's prohibition of bionic replacement limbs and organs had been one of its most controversial provisions, for they were one of the more defensible forms of man-machine interfacing. But the framers of the Act had been adamant. And after a while the issue had been rendered moot by the development of regeneration technology. Portable versions like those at the legation infirmary could take care of most wounds in short order. But to regrow whole limbs required a short stay in a reasonably well-equipped hospital. It was less expensive than bionics would have been, but . . . "Won't the trip cost money?"

McGillicuddy flashed a grin. "Didn't I tell you I had the backing of the merchants that do business here? I still do. They've still got confidence in me, in spite of this recent mishap. They paid me one hell of a commission for rocking the Dazh'Pinkh back on their heels with those early victories. And now they want me be back here on Zirankhu, good as new, as soon as possible."

"Back here—!" Jason took a deep breath, leaned forward, and spoke earnestly. "Mario, please listen to me. You're a good sort, as raving lunatics go, and I'm going to give you some sound advice. Go back to Earth, grow a new arm . . . and stay there. Enjoy your ill-gotten gains. You were lucky this time. But if you keep on pressing your luck, you're going to end up—"

"—In Shandu, accepting the emperor's appointment as commander in chief of his armies! I tell you, Jason, the other mercenary companies are coming around to my idea of a kind of cartel, under exclusive contract to the empire. The promise of financing from the merchant houses works wonders. When I come back here I'll put together something that will sweep the Dazh'Pinkh out of existence, and then there's *nothing* I won't be able to do here!" McGillicuddy's black eyes gleamed with a light Jason had seen too often for him to entertain any further hopes of talking sense to the man. But then the mercenary abruptly took on a shrewd look, and his tone shifted.

"By the way, Jason, speaking of returns to this planet, I can tell you that Captain Chang was very relieved to see Major Rojas again. He was wondering what had become of her, since you and she had been away for so long. In fact, he was afraid he'd seen the last of you."

"Well," Jason temporized, "we were sort of drawn away, following a lead."

"But now you're back." McGillicuddy paused and gave

Jason a quizzical glance. "I can't help being curious about what you and Rojas have been doing all this time—and what you're doing here now. I've heard rumors . . ."

Jason maintained a poker face but swore inwardly. Aloud: "What kind of rumors?"

"Oh, nothing definite. Just an increase in off-world traffic—and still more buying up of food and other basics. And then you arrive. People can't help wondering."

Uh-huh! thought Jason dourly.

So far, everything had gone according to plan. An advance party of negotiators had gingerly approached the imperial bureaucracy, working up through well-known channels as high as necessary—but no higher, for the functionaries were firm believers in not bothering their superiors with things they didn't need to know. So, without disturbing the blissful oblivion of the imperial court, they had leased a stretch of land in the barren Xinkhan Desert, halfway around the planet and uninhabited even by the scruffiest of nomads, but sitting atop an underground aquifer, accessible to modern drilling equipment though unreachable and in fact unknown to the locals. They had also bought secrecy, which the officials involved had been only too willing to sell as long as it had been clearly understood that it worked in both directions. Then, working through layers of small private shipping lines following indirect routes, the initial personnel and components had been inconspicuously brought to Zirankhu and transported to the site. After the installation had acquired a certain minimum of accommodations, ships began to drop unobtrusively down from orbit directly to it, safe from detection because the only traffic control for the planet was handled by the legation in Khankhazh.

It must, Jason thought, have been in the early stages that they had, despite all precautions, begun to attract notice.

He himself had only just arrived, in the same *Comet* class as before, and once again in the company of Rojas, Mondrago and Chantal. They had landed with no attempt at dissimulation. But in orbit, the *De Ruyter*, the small *Hawke* class IDRF warship that had accompanied them remained in cloak, awaiting the signal to descend to the Xinkhan Desert and be hurled five centuries into the past.

He became aware that McGillicuddy had been giving him an inquiring look. "I don't suppose," said the mercenary with elaborate casualness, "that you'd care to—?"

"Sorry, Mario. I can't tell you anything about what we found, or what we're doing now. You haven't got a need to know."

"I figured that," sighed McGillicuddy.

"But I'll tell you what. As soon as I'm able to give you any information, you'll get it—if you'll tell me something I'm particularly interested in knowing."

"Which is . . . ?"

"These rumors you've been hearing—have the Transhumanists been taking any interest in them?"

"I wish I could help, Commander, but I won't lie to you. I don't even know if there are any Transhumanists currently in Khankhazh." McGillicuddy paused. "Of course, if there's anyone who *does* know, it would be . . ."

"Yes. I know who you mean." Jason stood up. "And I know the way, now. You just get some rest."

"Yes," said Lizh'Ku in his odd but intelligible Standard International English. "My informants have recognized certain Transhumanists among the *fahnku* currently in the city. Among the humans, I meant to say," he added smoothly.

"Of course," said Jason, with a smile at Lizh'Ku's lapse. He didn't know the literal meaning of the Zirankh'shi street term for the human species, and he wasn't sure he wanted to know. "How could they be sure? I imagine it's not always easy to tell individual humans apart."

"I assure you, only the ignorant are of the opinion that all humans look alike. My sources are familiar with Transhumanists who have already been here, and have identified several."

"But are these Transhumanists merely buying more food, or have they taken an interest in our activities?"

"Who can say?" Lizh'Ku paused and spoke briefly in the Zirankh'shi language to his assistant Luzho'Yuzho, who had been crouching in a corner of the shack. Then he turned back to Jason. "I almost forgot. One member of the Transhumanist party is new to us. Evidently he has a rather distinctive appearance."

"Hmm . . ." This was bad. If they had found it necessary to bring in someone new, he might be an intelligence specialist. "What do you mean about a 'distinctive appearance'?"

"Well . . . you must understand that to us, your skin seems quite . . . well, smooth."

"Right," said Jason. "No fur." *Naked apes*, he did not add.

"But this one was . . . shiny, over certain areas. Slick. My vocabulary fails."

"I see." Jason really did see, or was fairly sure he did. What Lizh'Ku seemed to be trying to describe reflected one of the limitations of regen technology. Really serious burn tissue was very resistant to the more cosmetic aspects. It could be regrown . . . but there was no mistaking what it was. *This individual must be important*, he thought, *or they wouldn't have risked bringing in anyone with such a readily identifiable peculiarity.*

"I'd like to get a look at him," he said.

"That can be arranged . . . as long as there is no IDRF involvement. Or at least, none that can be traced to me."

"That goes without saying." Jason paused, curiosity overcoming caution. "I'm grateful for all the help you've been willing to extend to me. Grateful . . . and a little surprised."

A moment passed before the aged Zirankh'shi replied. "All things considered, I take a favorable view of the human presence here. Before you arrived, we were getting . . . stale. That's not a fashionable view, you understand. Most of our educated class like to bemoan the way you're corrupting and mongrelizing our ordained, immemorial social order." Lizh'Ku spat a two-syllable sound in his own language. Jason suspected it was so obscene as to defy translation. "The truth is, what was once a great civilization had settled into dry rot. We needed something to jolt us out of our smug complacency."

"Aren't the Dazh'Pinkh rebels trying to do that?"

Lizh'Ku expelled a non-verbal sound of scorn. "Lunatics like that only strengthen the reactionaries by seeming to confirm their argument that social stasis is the only alternative to chaos. No, the needed stimulus could only come from the outside. You humans were a breath of fresh air. Of course, a breath of fresh air can be chilling, and blow things over. But . . ." He lapsed into silence until Jason wondered if he had dozed off. But then his huge eyes twinkled. "At any rate, I have a clear conscience in helping the Temporal Regulatory Authority. You have no interest in our past, even though I gather you will soon have the capability to journey back into it."

"That's true. However, my particular branch of the Authority does have an interest in safeguarding the future."

"Yes. From what I know of the Transhumanists, I think that may include everyone's future—including that of Zirankhu. I wish you well."

"Rojas won't like this," Mondrago predicted dourly.

"She'll get over it," Jason assured him, projecting more confidence than he felt.

They moved as inconspicuously as possible through Khankhazh's central market commodities exchange, a vast, noisy outdoor expanse cluttered with stalls and teeming with Zirankh'shi and a smattering of humans. Moving parallel to them, without emphasizing the connection, were Luzho'Yuzho and Lizh'Ku, the latter in his usual traveling position on the former's back. In response to subtle signals from Lizh'Ku, they worked their way toward one of the exchange buildings. As they neared it, three humans emerged, bending over to exit the door. This gave Jason and Mondrago the chance to duck behind a stall where they could watch unobserved.

As the trio came closer, a cluster of flashing blue dots appeared at the lower left of Jason's field of vision. He didn't even need his implant's notification of nearby bionics to know that these were Transhumanists. The two he could clearly see had the look of the middling varieties, higher than the goon-caste types and a good deal cleverer, if one knew the signs to look for. The third was behind them and could not be clearly seen.

They came abreast of the stall, and Jason and Mondrago flattened themselves to stay out of sight. Then, as they walked past, the third member of the trio paused, turned, and looked around with a sharp, suspicious expression. Then he shook his head, annoyed, and continued on after only a second or two.

But he had been in plain sight long enough.

The left side of his neck and head did indeed bear the look of regenerated burn tissue, and no hair grew on that side. His mouth was somewhat twisted, and his nose slightly crooked. But his features, at least on the right side, were still recognizable.

Jason and Mondrago stared at each other.

"Stoneman!" they breathed in unison.

"Who?" demanded Rojas.

"Of course that's not his real name," said Jason. "He naturally has one of those Transhumanist designations. But it was the name he used when I knew him, in

Virginia, North America, in the winter and spring of 1865. It was the name of a certain Union cavalry officer. Coincidentally, as I've subsequently learned, it was the name of a character in an early twentieth-century silent motion picture. For whatever reason, it tickled him." He took another gulp of much-needed Scotch.

Rojas leaned forward and stared across the desk, clearly perplexed. "I remember now. I've read a *précis* of your report on that expedition. But I thought he was killed."

"So did I. I'd shot him in the chest, and was certain he was dead—as certain as I've ever been of anything. But he must have had one of those bionic automatic-release implants that can keep a barely alive body going with massive injections and electrical jolts. Because after we left him, he followed us." Jason paused for a more cautious sip, and let his memories take him back to the pandemonium of a burning city. He spoke as much to himself as to Rojas. "We were in Richmond when the Confederates were evacuating it. We got across Mayo's Bridge just before it was due to be blown up . . . and he was staggering along right behind us like some kind of undead zombie out of nightmare, just ahead of the explosions of the tar barrels they were using as fire bombs. But they caught up to him and he was enveloped in flame. Then the bridge collapsed under him and he fell into the river. We never saw him come up."

"Then how can he be alive now? How can you be sure this was him? You admit that the man you saw had disfiguring injuries."

"Like those you'd expect Stoneman to have. Anyway,

it was him. Believe me, I'd know him anywhere. He held me and all but one of my party as prisoners for months."

"But how do you account for his survival?"

"I can only suppose that he also had some kind of Transhumanist artificial gill implant that automatically kicked in when he went underwater. And of course the water would have put out the flames. And his TRD must have been set to activate very shortly after that—come to think of it, he'd mentioned that he didn't expect to be in the nineteenth century much longer. So he was retrieved in time for them to save his life." Jason laughed humorlessly. "Knowing them, I'm surprised they didn't kill him themselves, after learning he had lost that data chip."

"It would seem they didn't, inasmuch as he's here now, disfigurement and all." Rojas scowled. "But judging from your assessment of him in your report, he's not an individual they'd employ as some kind of purchasing agent! The question is, why *is* he here?"

"I can't even guess."

"I can." Rojas' eyes grew hard. "They didn't fall for that ploy of yours with the body on Planet A. They may not definitely know we were up to anything there, but they have to consider the possibility that we were—and that therefore we know the location of Planet A, and maybe of Planet B as well. So now this Stoneman—or whatever he's called—is here to investigate, since their food-buying coupled with our presence on this planet provide the only possible link."

"Well, Major, there's an old saying: you've got to take the bad with the good. If we hadn't made the incursion that resulted in that body, we wouldn't have any idea of the location of Planet B, and our options would be very limited."

"Admitted," said Rojas with no particularly good grace. "But considering that the displacer out in the Xinkhan Desert is nearing completion, I want a look at this man before we actually perform our displacement. And yes, I know," she added, raising a forestalling hand, "you won't reveal your sources of information. So I won't ask for them. But you can lead me yourself, without compromising them."

"Yes, I suppose I can try," said Jason slowly and—for reasons he couldn't quite define—hesitantly.

CHAPTER FOURTEEN

"Are you sure he's going to be here?" Rojas asked in an irritable undertone.

"Of course I'm not sure," Jason replied as quietly as he could and still make himself heard above the hubbub of the central market. "My sources say that Transhumanists came to the commodities exchange earlier today. But they couldn't be certain Stoneman was among them."

Lizh'Ku had notified him via the communicator Jason had given him. But his own information had come indirectly, from a source he had indicated wasn't exactly the sharpest knife in his drawer of informants. Still, it had been worth a try, and Jason had alerted Rojas. The two of them and Mondrago had gotten into the scruffiest and most nondescript clothing available—including, at Jason's insistence, face-concealing slouch hats, for Rojas as well as himself and Mondrago. He didn't think she was known by sight to any of the Transhumanists, never having done any actual field work here in Khankhazh. But all his instincts were crying out for caution.

And now it was late afternoon as they mingled with the crowds, trying not to seem to be paying undue attention to the exchange buildings as they watched everyone who emerged. A few humans had, but none of those they sought.

"We'd better keep moving around," Mondrago muttered.

"Right," agreed Jason. Humans were a familiar sight here, but extended loitering might attract notice.

"Look!" said Mondrago suddenly.

Jason looked in the direction of his pointing finger. The range was too great for his implant to detect the presence of functioning bionics, but he recognized the two mid-level castes he had glimpsed before. And, as before, there was another figure with them, half crouched as though sheltering from sight behind them.

"There!" Jason hissed to Rojas. "But I can't be sure Stoneman's among them."

"Then let's follow them until we can be sure." Rojas started off without waiting to see if she was being followed. Not to Jason's surprise, she knew enough to move inconspicuously, without revealing that she was shadowing her quarry. He and Mondrago followed suit. Fortunately, humans were easy to keep in sight at a distance, over the heads of the Zirankh'shi crowd.

The Transhumanists moved steadily toward the extensive parking field adjacent to the markets, where occasional human-built glide cars nestled among the rows of ZIrankh'shi steam cars, and headed toward one of the former. With no more crowds to blend in, Jason and his two companions waited on the outskirts of the field and watched as best they could. As the Transhumanists entered their car, the third member of their group was, for an instant, in plain sight.

"I think that's Stoneman," said Jason. "It's hard to be absolutely certain at this distance, but—"

"Then let's follow them," said Rojas. Before Jason could counsel caution, she was off in the direction of their own glide car.

Tailing the Transhumanists through the disorderly and over-crowded traffic of Khankhazh was difficult, but Rojas clearly had experience at this sort of thing. And it helped that their quarry was following the most direct route toward the spacefield that was possible in this urban labyrinth.

"I know where they're headed," Jason told Rojas. "After they enter the spacefield, they're going to go to that little out-of-the-way hangar from which their orbital shuttle operates. What, exactly, do you plan to do that won't reveal our knowledge of what they're up to?"

"We'll play it by ear," said Rojas grimly. Then she turned and gave him what was, for her, a charming smile. "I seem to recall that that's a favorite expression of yours."

Jason had no answer for that, so he shut up and let Rojas concentrate on driving. Presently, the congestion thinned out into a scattering of shanties as they neared the drainage ditch between the city and the spacefield. The season had changed, and now the ditch was filled with water. There were no formalities about access to the field, and up ahead the Transhumanists' car was crossing one of the bridges over the ditch and turning left.

"Their hangar is over in that direction," Jason told Rojas as they passed the last of the shanties and approached the bridge. "Now we need to decide—"

At that moment, with a grinding scream of tortured driving machinery, the car came to an instantaneous, shuddering stop, sending Jason and Rojas forward against their safety belts while Mondrago, seated in the rear, tumbled against the back of their seats. Before their minds had fully registered what was happening, the grav repulsion expired with a wheeze and a cloud of acrid smoke, and the front end slewed into the dirt road just short of the ditch.

Grav snare, flashed through Jason's brain. Someone concealed in one of the shanties had had one of the small, portable devices that could project either a continuous tractor beam, holding a person immobilized, or a brief, high-powered one that could stop a vehicle and set up destructive harmonics in its gravitics. *And in this case, they've used the latter. So . . .* "Out! Out of the car!" he shouted as he slapped at the catch of his safety belt.

They all tumbled from the crazily canted car, and Jason drew the guass needler pistol at his side. Mondrago, he noted, was already holding his, and crouching behind the car as he exchanged fire with a couple of goon-caste types who had emerged from a shanty with similar weapons. There was the characteristic snapping sound as the steel slivers broke mach, and a metallic whining as several of them whanged off the roof of the car.

Jason immediately dropped beside Mondrago in the shelter of the car. But Rojas, who had gotten out the other side, had no such protection. Standing exposed, she brought her needler up and opened fire, getting one of the goons. But then a sleet of the vicious little flechettes swept across her body. Blood sprayed from tiny holes and, with a gurgling scream, she toppled over the edge of the drainage ditch and was lost to sight.

"Bastards!" yelled Jason as he and Mondrago fired on the remaining goon, who ducked back into the shanty. Jason spared a fraction of a second for a look across the bridge. The Transhumanist car had stopped. Stoneman—yes, it was definitely him—was standing beside it and giving directions to his underlings, who were scrambling down into the ditch from their side. Jason endeavored to keep out of his line of sight, on the chance that he hadn't already been recognized.

Yes, thought Jason with bitter self-reproach. *He always was the careful type, and he was sure he had spotted something in the market the other day. So he set up this little ambush here in case he was followed. And we fell right into it. And even if these goons had been close enough for my implant to detect them, it probably would have been too late by then.*

"Sir!" said Mondrago. "Let's get out of here while that goon's taking cover. I think we can make it to those shanties over there, across from his. And . . . it's too late to help the major, even if we could."

Jason nodded. "On my count of three." He counted, and they sent a fusillade of flechettes toward the shanty, forcing the goon to keep his head down. Then they sprang to their feet and sprinted toward the nearest alley on their side of the road.

They entered a noisome maze, where the few Zirankh'shi they saw scampered away at the sight of armed humans. Because they had no TRDs, Jason's neural map display was useless in helping them find their way. "I think," he said after a while, "if we turn here we'll—"

"Freeze," came a cold voice from behind them.

He must know a shortcut, thought Jason sickly. Beside him, Mondrago tensed almost imperceptibly and drew a breath.

"Don't be stupid even for a Pug," said the voice, sounding almost bored. Mondrago sighed and relaxed muscle by muscle. "Now drop your guns and turn around slowly."

They obeyed, to face the goon and his pointed needler. He stepped closer, coming into the range of Jason's implant. *A little late*, he thought at the mocking blue dot.

"Now come on. You're wanted for—"

Something flashed in the corner of Jason's right eye. All at once the goon's throat sprouted the handle of a knife, and his blood spurted. With a convulsive movement, he yanked the knife out, and the bloodflow immediately began to slacken as his life-preserving implants kicked in.

But by then Jason and Mondrago had dropped to the mud, scooped up their needlers, and fired as one. Jason's shot hit the goon's head. The little flechette was not one of the heavy slugs of military-grade gauss weapons, which would have blown out the top of the skull with hydrostatic pressure as it made its hypervelocity way through. But it went straight into the goon's brain. He was dead before his legs had finished buckling under him.

From the shadows between two buildings, a Zirankh'shi stepped out, retrieved the throwing knife, wiped it on the goon's shirt, and hung it beside two others dangling from his harness. Then he turned to Jason and made an unmistakable follow-me gesture.

Jason, who was getting better about individual Zirankh'shi characteristics, recognized this one as a small specimen even for his race, and wiry. But what was most noticeable was that his tapering snout terminated in a pattern of scar tissue where a nose was supposed to be. Evidently someone, at some point in his career, had decided he was in need of chastisement.

But Jason was neither in the mood to be particular nor in any position to do so. "I think I know where he wants to take us," he told Mondrago. "And it's exactly where we need to go just now."

Without another word, they followed the little Zirankh'shi into the squalid maze that was Khankhazh's criminal district.

Night had fallen by the time they reached Lizh'Ku's shack. Jason used the communicator he had given the aged Zirankh'shi to inform Captain Chang of what had happened and assure him that he and Mondrago would be back in the legation before morning. Now he sat and drank *dugugkh*. The stuff was repulsive. He didn't care. Up until now he and Mondrago had had other things to occupy their minds, but now Rojas' death was sinking home and they had nothing to shield themselves from it except alcohol.

Lizh'Ku was having a muttered colloquy with No-Nose. Over in a corner, the hulking Luzho'Yuzho was sitting and writing. He often did that, Jason had observed. Lizh'Ku must have taught him the skill, which was almost unheard of among the Manziru Empire's peasant class. Jason wondered what he was writing down. The tales of his master's cases, perhaps. *This one ought to be one hell of a novelty*, Jason thought. He took another gulp of *dugugkh* and managed to avoid gagging on it.

No-Nose departed, and Lizh'Ku walked over to Jason and snagged the bottle. "Zhagk'Urv is an old acquaintance," he explained between swigs. "He fancies to consider himself in my debt for a few favors I've done him in the past. And he has . . . contacts. After informing you of the Transhumanist activity at the market, I asked him and a couple of his associates to keep watch there and also at the approach to the spacefield that they generally use, as a precaution."

"A necessary one, as it turned out. I'm sorry I couldn't thank him." Jason took another vile-tasting swallow. He needed it, for now the mortification of having had to be nursemaided was added to everything else. "But now we have to get back to the legation."

"Luzho'Yuzho will guide you."

"At least I can *thank you* . . . for everything. I only wish I could *repay* you."

"Where will you be going now?"

"I'm not supposed to tell you, and if I did you wouldn't

believe me. Let's just say it's a matter of *when* as well as *where*."

Lizh'Ku thought a moment. "If you really wish to repay me, do me one favor. On your return, tell me the story of your travels. You may be surprised at some of the things I can believe. And Luzho'Yuzho will need it to complete his narrative."

Hey, I was right about Luzho'Yuzho's subject matter! "Very well. I can't promise that we'll ever see each other again, but if we do you'll hear the full story. Then we'll see how far your capacity for belief really goes!"

"Grave," was Narendra Patel's lugubrious assessment of the situation. "Very grave."

He and Captain Chang sat across a small table from Jason, Mondrago and a very subdued Chantal Frey. "Did Stoneman recognize you two?" Chang asked anxiously.

"I can't be sure," said Jason. "It was at a distance, and I tried to keep out of sight behind our car."

"Although," Mondrago added drily, "we had other things on our minds at the time, what with being in a firefight."

"So," said Chang, "we don't know whether or not they know that you personally—or the Authority, for that matter, is involved."

"Right," Jason agreed. "And given that the possibility exists, we have to act without further delay. The three of us will take our *Comet* class into orbit tomorrow morning and rendezvous with *De Ruyter*. As soon as preparations can be completed, we'll set her down at our displacer and proceed with the mission."

"Yes, yes," muttered a still shaken Chang.

"One other matter, you're the senior surviving IDRF officer here. But your assignment is here on Zirankhu. Even though I'm not IDRF, I've been acting as Major Rojas' *de facto* second in command for our team. As such, I'm assuming command now that she's dead." Jason looked Chang in the eye. "It would probably help if you'd so instruct the IDRF personnel aboard *De Ruyter*."

Chang hesitated momentarily at the prospect of a non-IDRF officer in command of IDRF personnel. But he knew Jason's reputation. And there really was no alternative.

"I'll cut the necessary orders," he said, after only the briefest pause.

CHAPTER FIFTEEN

✦✧✦

The *Hawke* class (one of several classes named after wet-navy admirals from Earth's history) was not a major space combatant, intended to deal out cataclysmic violence in fleet engagements. It was fast, compact, and versatile, with enough ship-to-ship firepower to overcome even the most well-armed smuggler, and also capable of surgical planetside strikes, but optimized for stealthy insertion of ground-assault teams, for whom there was a bunkroom just aft of the almost equally Spartan quarters of the ten-member crew. In shape it was a thick, blunt arrowhead just under a hundred and fifty feet long, with the bulges of twin drive nacelles on the sides near the stern. A dorsal turret held an X-ray laser, ideal for space combat but essentially useless in atmosphere, which absorbs X-rays. This deficiency was supplied by two waist turrets mounting lasers that could be adjusted up and down the electromagnetic spectrum from visible light through IR and UV, as conditions required. Under the chin was a retractable missile launcher with a nasty variety of munitions. Nestled in a ventral housing was a sleek gig.

Of course Jason and his companions could see none of this as their *Comet* class courier approached *De Ruyter*, for the latter circled Zirankhu under full stealth, including invisibility, even though its orbit was practically at right angles to the one used by the Transhumanists' cargo carriers. But Van Horn and Tomori, using *De Ruyter*'s tight-beam transponder, rendezvoused expertly and extended a passage tube between airlocks.

"Who was this De Ruyter, anyway?" asked Jason as the connection was established.

"Michel Adriaanszoon De Ruyter," said Van Horn (whose probable ethnic origin Jason belatedly remembered). Seeing Jason's blank look, he kept his expression respectfully expressionless. "Well, sir, let's put it this way. The only question about him is this: was he the greatest fighting admiral in history, or merely the greatest fighting admiral of the seventeenth century?"

Jason glanced at Mondrago, who nodded in agreement. He decided he'd better leave well enough alone.

Passing through the always-queasy sensation of transition from one artificial gravity field to another, they entered *De Ruyter* and requested permission to come aboard from Captain Jared Palanivel, the pilot/captain. In this case, at least, there was no naval nonsense about rank titles versus the sacrosanct title of a ship's skipper. The IDRF used the traditional army titles for all purposes, and Palanivel was a captain—the equivalent of an old-time wet navy lieutenant senior grade, which meant he was fairly junior for command of a *Hawke* class. But Jason had been assured of his competence, and what he saw in that young predominantly Malay face inclined his instincts in the same direction.

"Captain Chang has been in communication with you, has he not, Captain?" asked Jason.

"He has, Commander. He explained the situation. And he indicated that you wished to address the Commandos."

Commandos. That was the term—*Marines* was not permitted, lest jealousies be aroused—for the IDRF's planetary assault units. "Yes. In the flesh." Jason had decided he'd better start establishing a rapport with this commando squad, and the sooner the better. "The ship's company can listen in via intercom."

"Certainly, Commander. The commandos are already waiting in the wardroom."

The five-member commando squad rose to attention as they entered *De Ruyter*'s tiny wardroom. The squad was standard for ships of this class, consisting of two sections. The first, of three members, was armed with standard gauss battle rifles with integral underslung electromag grenade launchers. Then there was the two-member special weapons section, one with a Mark XI plasma gun and the other with a shoulder-fired missile launcher. They all wore fatigues at the moment. For EVA, they did not use the massive space marine powered combat armor, but rather the kind of combat environment suit with which Jason and Mondrago were already familiar, and which could function as a vacuum suit.

These were not people you really wanted to trifle with.

"As you were," said Palanivel. "This is Commander Jason Thanou of the Temporal Service. He has been assisting Major Rojas, due to the special nature of this mission. He wishes to address you on certain matters of which you have not yet been apprised."

Jason let them have it point blank. "Major Rojas has been killed in action. I have assumed command of this expedition." He let the stunned silence last a second or two, during which he ran his eyes over the five faces, silently asking if anyone had a problem with that. The staff sergeant in charge, who doubled as leader of the rifle section, looked vaguely familiar . . .

"Yes, sir," was all the sergeant said, and suddenly Jason remembered him: Emil Hamner, who had led a squad in the attack on the Transhumanist base under the southern Andes. Jason decided he might not have so much trouble after all.

"This," Jason resumed, "is Superintendent Alexandre Mondrago of the Temporal Service. He will function as my ADC." He didn't think Hamner would have any objection to an outside aide-de-camp. "And this is Dr. Chantal Frey, who will accompany the expedition as a consultant on Transhumanist matters." Again he scrutinized the commandos' faces, not knowing if Chantal's name meant anything to them. But all he saw was the expected grumpiness at having to be responsible for a civilian's safety.

"Due to certain security concerns," he continued, "we must proceed immediately. You already know that the mission involves time travel, having volunteered for it with that understanding. As soon as possible, we will descend to a desert area of the planet below, where a temporal displacer has been constructed that is capable of sending this ship back slightly less than five hundred years in time. Now, as some of you may know, a temporal retrieval device is required to restore the temporal energy potential of a displaced object and return it to the displacer stage from which it came, in its proper time. This ship has such a device, and everyone and everything inside it will be retrieved with it."

"Question, sir," said a member of the rifle section—a stocky female PFC. "What if the ship comes to grief in the course of the mission, while we're separated from it?"

"This is a genuine possibility, Private Armasova," said Jason, reading her name tag. "Against such a contingency, we will also have individual TRDs implanted in us. This is a very simple, painless procedure which the ship's surgeon will perform presently." The five faces showed less distaste than might have been expected in products of their culture; worse things happened to these people. "These TRDs are of the 'controllable' variety used by the Service's Special Operations Section. What this means is that they are not timed to activate at a preset moment as is usually the case. My own TRD is a special one which I can activate by direct neural interface at my discretion— and when I do so, all the others, including the ship's, are simultaneously activated, as long as they are within a rather short range." It had always been a source of potential awkwardness, with Rojas in command but Jason holding the power to terminate the mission at any time. That problem, at least, no longer existed.

"Uh . . . but what if something happens to *you*, sir?" Armasova persisted.

"That," Jason deadpanned, "is something they didn't emphasize when they called for volunteers." They all chuckled with the grim cynicism of veterans. "I assure you that I'm renowned for my caution concerning my personal safety." He stonily ignored the faint choking noises from Chantal, behind him. "But it has to be this way, because as on-scene commander I need to be able to exercise my judgment on the basis of the situation as we find it. We have no way of knowing in advance how long this mission is going to take. The displacer stage will be kept empty until such time as we return—which isn't a problem, inasmuch as we're the only traffic it has to handle."

"Speaking of the mission, Commander," said Hamner, "we've been told very little about it. Can you fill us in?"

"Not as much as you—or I—would like. After our temporal displacement, we will proceed to the star HC+31 8213, just under nineteen and a half light-years from here. That should come to about five days for this ship." Jason glanced at Palanivel, who nodded in confirmation. "We know nothing about this star except that the Transhumanist underground commenced some kind of project beginning a little over ten years before our target time period, on some planet of that system that we've been calling 'Planet B' for convenience. We don't know what this project is, or why they've gone to enormous trouble and expense to go back so far in time. So I can't tell you even approximately what kind of opposition you're going to be facing. But we have reason to believe that whatever they're doing is—or, I suppose I should say, was—vulnerable in its early stages, and that after those stages they left it alone. The magnitude of our displacement represents out best guess as to when their ships had ceased going there, for we want the Transhumanists in the present era to be unaware that their project was aborted.

"We're going to reconnoiter the system very cautiously and ascertain what the Transhumanists have there. We will then do whatever seems indicated. If we have sufficient force to destroy whatever it is, we will go ahead and do so. But if it looks like more than we can handle, we will depart without making our presence known— quite easy, inasmuch as the ship's temporal retrieval will snatch it instantaneously back to the displacer stage from which it departed, here on Zirankhu." They all goggled a bit at that. "After which, an expedition strong enough to do the job can be dispatched. If that happens, I for one would like to be on it. I'm thinking you might, also, after . . . what happened to Major Rojas."

There was no bloodthirsty bluster, no dramatics. These were professionals. But their expressions told Jason all he needed to know. *Yes*, he thought. *We'll get along just fine.*

"One final point. At the beginning, I mentioned security concerns. The Transhumanists have known for some time that the IDRF has been taking an interest in their activities on Zirankhu. But now there is a possibility that one of them has sighted me—and my face is rather well-known to them. If I've been recognized, they may have put two and two together and concluded that we know their little game involves time travel. This, in turn, could result in them being put on the alert at our destination system, even though there's no indication that our displacer here has been compromised."

"Well, then, sir," said Hamner, "it ought to be all right if we act quickly enough, when the ones at Planet B haven't been alerted yet."

"Whatever 'yet' means in this context, Sergeant," Jason pointed out. "They might go back from sometime in our future to a point prior to our arrival at Planet B."

Hamner opened his mouth to speak, then closed it again.

"But what we call the Observer Effect will prevent them from giving the warning early. Because if the Transhumanists at Planet B had already gotten the word, then they would have been able through the regular supply runs to inform the ones back here, who would then have made it their business to sabotage our displacer before it was finished—which, in fact, they haven't."

The commandos' eyes were starting to glaze over.

"But don't worry about any of this," Jason concluded reassuringly. "There are no paradoxes. We have a saying: 'Reality protects itself.'"

"Sir," said Hamner with out-of-character plaintiveness, "I'm very confused."

Jason grinned. "That means you're starting to get it."

De Ruyter was, of course, under maximum stealth for her descent from orbit. But Jason was taking no chances. It was midnight over the Xinkahn Desert when they swooped down under grav repulsion and approached the lights of the displacer facility.

Had it been daylight, Jason knew he would have viewed a scene of raw, crude newness. To call this a no-frills installation would have been an understatement. As it was, the lights were all that was visible. They made for a circle of them that defined the perimeter of the two-hundred-foot-diameter displacer stage. Off to the side, a cluster of lights marked the powerplant and massive capacitors that would provide the energy surge to send them back in time.

In what Jason was already thinking of as the old days, when the Authority's Kasugawa/Weintraub technology had required a bigger power plant than this to displace a few humans, the idea of displacing *De Ruyter*'s almost three thousand tons of loaded mass almost half a millenium would have occasioned howls of laughter. Even with reverse-engineered Transhumanist technology, it required an antimatter powerplant which had presented the biggest engineering problems in the whole clandestine construction project. In particular, the converter which processed the sand of the Xinkhan into antimatter had not lent itself to modular construction techniques.

But now all was ready. And as *De Ruyter* settled down in a cloud of dust, Jason radioed the chief technician and confirmed that the capacitors were fully charged.

Jason turned to Palanivel. "With your permission, Captain?"

Palanivel nodded, picked up his intercom mike, and spoke a command he had never dreamed he would give. "All hands, this is the Captain. Prepare for temporal displacement. You will receive a ten-second countdown."

Jason spoke again to the chief technician, then

patched him into Palanivel. The two coordinated, and the countdown commenced.

Jason had never been inside a vehicle that was being temporally displaced—the Authority had never even considered such a thing until now. He wondered if the sensation would be the same as his accustomed individual displacements—an indescribable dreamlike disconnection of reality—or if everything within the ship would remain normal to his senses. He eagerly awaited the answer to this question.

The countdown ticked down to zero . . . and afterwards *he couldn't remember*. He should, he ruefully realized, have expected it. As always, there was no sensation of time having passed, and no recollection of anything having happened.

There were only the snowfields of Zirankhu's north polar region, gleaming below in the control room's viewscreen in the early-morning light.

After such a profoundly unnatural experience, there was the inevitable moment of sickening disorientation which all personnel had been briefed to expect. As an old hand, Jason came out of it first. He waited until Palanivel had recovered his equilibrium, then spoke formally.

"The displacement has been completed, Captain. We are now in what is, by standard Earth dating, the late 1890s. Please ask your navigator to shape a course for HC+31 8213."

CHAPTER SIXTEEN
✦✦✦

Astronomical observations had long ago determined that HC+31 8213 had at least one gas giant planet, and that that planet was not a "hot Jupiter" that had migrated inward and settled into a close orbit around its sun after wiping out any potential life-bearing worlds. *De Ruyter* was no survey ship, but as she approached the system even her necessarily compact instrumentation was able to detect the small terrestrial planets, and ascertain that one of them showed the spectroscopic lines of free oxygen—a sure indication of life.

As they drew closer, details of that planet began to emerge. It orbited at an average radius of almost exactly one AU. But its primary was a G3v star, slightly less massive than Sol and only seven-tenths as luminous, so this put it near the outer limit of what was traditionally held to be the "Goldilocks Zone." However, it was somewhat more massive than Earth but not significantly larger, yielding a surface gravity of 1.12 G and suggesting both a higher allotment of heavy elements and a denser atmosphere; the range of temperature should be more or less Earthlike. Likewise, the two moons—relatively small, but close—had slowed its rotation to a diurnal period of thirty-five and a half hours. Those moons also served, like Earth's Luna, to stabilize the planet's axis in its nineteen-degree tilt, which should produce interesting but not extreme seasons.

All in all, a prime world. This, beyond doubt, was Planet B.

Palanivel disengaged the drive field sooner than strictly necessary, outside the star's Secondary Limit. He then performed the pseudovelocity-cancelling maneuvers with great caution, with all stealth measures engaged. But nothing triggered *De Ruyter*'s array of sensor-detectors. It seemed the Transhumanists were relying on the supposed secrecy of their presence here.

And of that presence there was no doubt. Their sensors picked up low-level but inarguable energy emissions from Planet B as Palanivel inserted them into a hyperbolic orbit outside the plane of the ecliptic but eventually intersecting Planet B's orbit. This would give them time for further observations, and also for deciding on a course of action.

"The great imponderable," said Chantal thoughtfully, "is whether or not they really have stopped coming here yet. The fact that we haven't detected either of their transports doesn't prove anything."

"Well," said Mondrago, leaning forward and resting his elbows on the table the three of them sat around in the wardroom, "it stands to reason that they must have, doesn't it? I mean, we caught them coming here from our era, so as far as they're going to know then . . ." His brow furrowed, as it often did when he contemplated the logic of time travel. "What I mean is, if any of them come here after we're finished, then they could go back and report that—"

"Not necessarily," Jason cautioned. "A Transhumanist ship here now could come from a time a little in advance of our own. Not much, I think, given all the indications we have that *The Day* isn't all that far in our future. In that case, they could have been—or will be—retrieved into their own time, and not have an opportunity to go back and warn their buddies in our time."

"Or," said Chantal gloomily, "it could simply mean that our mission here is going to fail."

"I prefer not to assume that," said Jason firmly. "Let's not theorize in advance of the evidence. Let's wait for some hard data."

That data was not long in coming.

"We've detected a ship entering this system and going sublight," said Palanivel as Jason, Mondrago and Chantal crowded into the control room. "It's making no attempt at stealth."

"Does its profile match the figures I gave you?" asked Jason.

"That's affirmative, Commander."

"So it's one of their transports," said Mondrago, sounding as glum as Jason felt. "Which means they're not quite finished here after all."

"Our options have suddenly become more limited," said Jason grimly.

They watched in silence as the new arrival proceeded sunward. It was no surprise that its projected course not only intersected with Planet B's orbit but was calculated to accomplish an exact rendezvous. Jason studied the system display, comparing that course and their own orbit.

"It looks," he said to Palanivel, "like it ought to be possible for us to follow that ship in. Please do so—very cautiously, and at a safe distance."

Palanivel applied the requisite vector, and *De Ruyter* eased out of its orbit into a course that would converge with the transport and Planet B—not that Jason had any intention of going that far, at least not until he had more information.

Observing from afar in their stealth cocoon, they watched as the transport, puzzlingly, took up a geostationary orbit around Planet B. Given the sophistication and power of *De Ruyter*'s sensors, they were able even at this range to make out a shuttle lifting off from the planet's surface.

"This isn't right," Mondrago stated. "Why don't they land on the planet? They've got no security worries here, like they did on Zirankhu."

"I don't know," said Jason slowly.

Palanivel eased them into a fairly distant matching orbit, and they watched as the shuttle rendezvoused with the transport. The two vessels remained linked for a surprisingly short time, after which the shuttle departed from orbit and descended toward the surface. And the transport simply remained in its orbit, seemingly dormant and lifeless.

"What's going on here?" Mondrago demanded irritably of no one in particular. "Did the transport's crew take the shuttle down and just leave their ship deserted in orbit?"

"I hope to find out." Jason turned to Palanivel. "Captain, please ready the gig. I'm going to take Superintendent Mondrago and the commandos and reconnoiter."

"Very well, Commander. Ah . . . you realize, of course, that the gig doesn't possess this ship's stealth features."

"I do. But I don't expect to need them, given its small size and the fact that the Transhumanists aren't expecting intruders here."

"But Commander, if I may ask, what do you plan to actually do?"

"That depends entirely on what we find the situation to be. Which is why I'm taking the commandos. I want as many options as possible, and the gig is unarmed."

"So why not take the ship in, under stealth?"

"Too risky. We still don't know what they've got on the planet. And we also don't know what kind of Observer Effect-related obstacles we're going to encounter. So I don't want all our eggs in one basket. You will remain out here and simply observe. And Captain . . . if anything happens that causes you to lose contact with us, you will take no action, but rather remain out here where you're safe from detection and wait for us. In fact, in such an event I want you to move into a new orbit—one that I don't know about."

For an instant, Palanivel's dark eyes held a mutinous spark, as though he wanted to ask just exactly what Jason thought *De Ruyter*'s weapons were for. But he restricted himself to a stiff nod. "Very well, Commander. I will do so . . . under protest."

"As I would have expected," said Jason with a conciliatory smile.

He and Mondrago went to the ship's locker, where they donned combat environment suits and drew gauss pistols. Mondrago also took a satchel of highly specialized tools. They were checking each other over when a small female voice was heard from the forward hatch.

"I wish I was going with you."

"Hey, the gig can only hold seven passengers—us and the commandos," said Mondrago to Chantal with a grin. Then, more seriously: "Anyway, this may not be any place for a non-combatant."

"I know," sighed Chantal. "I'd probably be useless, and certainly in the way. But . . . I'm worried. Frightened, in fact. I just hate the thought of not knowing what's happening to you."

Jason frowned. Chantal wasn't usually like this. "Don't get yourself into a state. We'll be in tight-beam communication with the ship."

"I know." She didn't really seem reassured, but she put on a brave smile. "Good luck," she said to Jason. Then she turned to Mondrago and said nothing, except with her eyes. Jason looked away as they embraced. Then she was gone.

They walked through a hatch into the gig ready room, just forward of the locker. The commandos were there, fully beweaponed. Jason had had time to get to know them all. Besides Hamner and Armasova, the rifle section included PFC Anton Bermudez. The special weapons section consisted of Corporal Askar Bakiyev, a chunky flat-faced Kirghiz, and PFC Raoul Odinga, predominantly African and giving the impression that he could have handled the missile launcher even without the combat environment suit's strength-amplification feature. There was barely room for them all in the tiny ready room.

"Stand easy," said Jason, before Hamner even had a chance to order attention on deck. He then gave them a quick run-down on the arrival of the Transhumanist transport and its enigmatic behavior. "We're going to take a closer look, without committing this ship. As I told you at the outset, I can't tell you what to expect. Just be ready for anything."

They took a grav tube down through the lower deck and into the gig's dorsal airlock. The slender diamond-shaped craft was eighty feet long, with a photon thrusters for space propulsion as well as for atmospheric maneuvering under grav repulsion. Forward of the engineering spaces and a small cargo bay was the cabin into which they now filed, with seating for seven passengers and a pilot, who was already seated at her console and was running through her checklist. Jason settled into the foremost passenger seat, to her right.

"Everything on the green, Lieutenant?" he asked.

Lieutenant Sita Hansen nodded. "Yes, Commander. We're cleared for departure whenever you give the word." Jason nodded in turn, and she activated the "detach" sequence.

The gig's maneuvering thrusters nudged it far enough from *De Ruyter*'s hull, and the photon thrusters kicked in. The artificial gravity's inertial compensation feature prevented them from feeling the G-force as the gig accelerated on its new course.

The gig was definitely not intended for long-term occupancy. This was an exceptionally extended trip for it, and they were all stiff and cramped by the time the transport grew in the viewscreen, silhouetted against the cloud-swirling blue day side of Planet B, about twenty-two thousand miles below—or "away," if one chose to so view it, for at the distance required for a geostationary orbit it could be thought of either way.

"You realize," said Hansen, "they're orbiting well outside Planet B's Primary Limit. So at any time, they could accelerate away at over a hundred Gs."

"Yes," nodded Jason. "If, that is, there's anybody aboard. It doesn't look like it."

"So you think they all went down in the shuttle?"

"I don't know." Jason peered at the planet. The gig's sensor suite was rudimentary, but they had been able to ascertain that the transport's orbit kept it over a point on the west coast of one of the continents, and that this was the point from which the fairly weak energy readings emanated. There was some kind of small base or camp or something down there.

He reached a decision. "I want to investigate more closely—see if that ship really is as deserted as it seems. And if it is, we can use a paratronic lockpick to board her. Bring us a little closer."

Hansen obeyed, and the gig drew into a range where it was surely visible to any operating sensors aboard the transport. Jason, Mondrago and the commandos attached modular EVA packs to the backs of their suits and, with a rattle of equipment, went single-file through the cabin's after hatch into the cargo bay.

EVA procedures were a matter of routine. Hanson bled the air from the sealed cargo bay and, after it was in vacuum, opened its ventral hatch. The seven-member party then drifted out, using the EVA packs. The latter were small grav repulsion units, unable to provide much in the way of propulsion this far from Planet B's surface, where they only had a gravity field of less than 0.1 G to work with. But it sufficed, given that they were in free fall and at any rate had no desire to build up a possibly uncontrollable velocity. And returning to the gig would be no problem; it mounted a small tractor beam projector in the cargo bay, so Hansen could simply pull them in one by one. Jason, wanting to keep radio communications to a minimum, gave a hand signal and they moved slowly toward the darkened transport, tightly grouped for safety.

They were about halfway there, with the gig growing tiny in the distance, when it happened.

Without warning, lights awakened up and down the transport. And a retractable ventral turret began to extrude itself. In the light of the planet, Jason instantly recognized that turret for what it was. Horrified, he watched it swivel in the direction of the gig.

In the vacuum of space there is, of course, no sound. And laser beams—even those in the visible-light wavelengths, much less the X-ray lasers of space combat—are invisible. The only manifestation of the energies that turret released was the glare as explosive energy transfer tore the gig apart.

It had all taken little more than a heartbeat. Jason hadn't even had a chance to break radio silence. Now it was broken for him, and a harsh voice crashed into his earphones.

"Attention! Your craft has been destroyed. If you do not wish to be left in orbit to die slowly, you will discard your weapons and stand by to be tractored aboard. Anyone found in possession of weapons afterwards will be killed. This is your only warning."

Jason, Mondrago and Hamner looked at each other through the transparent nanoplastic hoods of their suits. No words were necessary. It was hopeless. Odinga's missile launcher could probably damage that hull, but then the laser turret the transport wasn't supposed to have would be turned on them. Or the transport could simply accelerate away at the rates possible to negative mass drive inside the Secondary Limit, leaving them adrift.

"Do as he says," said Jason in a dull voice, still trying to deal with Hansen's death. Their weapons drifted away into infinity.

A crack of light appeared on the transport's side, and widened as a cargo port slid aside. Jason felt the rubbery grip of a tractor beam, and was drawn irresistibly inside a harshly illuminated cargo bay when he fell to the deck under the sudden force of an artificial gravity field. The others followed, and the port rumbled shut. Jason felt the pressure as the bay filled with air.

"Out of your suits!" came a command from a

loudspeaker. They obeyed, stripping to the body-stocking-like liners worn under the combat environment suits.

"They were waiting for us," Mondrago muttered as they stripped.

Jason nodded. Not knowing what kind of audio pickups might be focused on them, he said nothing about the one positive feature of their circumstances: that *De Ruyter* was safe, and would remain so if Palanivel followed his orders.

Hamner seemed to be thinking along similar lines about audio surveillance, for he muttered low in Jason's ear. "Uh, sir, as I understand it, you can get us out of this any time you want to, just by mentally commanding our TRDs to activate so we're snatched back to Zirankhu in our own time. Right?"

"Right . . . except for one little thing. *De Ruyter* is outside the range of my TRD's command function. If I activated our TRDs now, then the ship would be permanently stranded here in the past, as would everybody aboard her . . . including Dr. Frey," he added, with a glance in Mondrago's direction.

Mondrago's face was frozen into an expressionless mask.

A hatch opened, and a squad of goon-caste Transhumanists filed in, armed with laser carbines, safely usable inside a spacecraft but deadly against soft targets. "Come!" the chief goon commanded. They were herded out of the cargo bay, along a passageway, and then down to a lower deck.

As they went, Jason activated the map-display function of his brain implant. For a normal extratemporal expedition, it was programmed for the area in which Jason expected to be, and showed the locations of his team members' TRDs as red dots. In this case, with an unpredictable destination, no such programming had been done. But in its absence the implant built up a map on the basis of Jason's. The further they were marched, the more the ship's layout grew, seemingly floating in mid-air a few inches in front of his eyes.

Finally they were shoved through a hatch into a large dimly lit chamber filled to capacity with rows of narrow triple-level bunks stretching away into the darkness. The hatch slid shut behind them, leaving them alone with their despondent misery.

Jason heard gagging noises from behind him. He himself fought not to retch. The chamber was filthy, and the ventilation system fought in vain against a sour stench. The chilliness of the air probably helped.

"What the hell *is* this?" demanded Hamner.

"'Hell' is exactly the right word—it's slave quarters," came a dull, apathetic voice, and Jason saw they weren't really alone after all. The voice came from one of the bunks, where a raggedly clad female figure lay on her side, turned away from them, showing no inclination to get up or to look at the new arrivals.

Jason strode to the bunk. He grasped the woman by the shoulder, turned her over . . . and stopped dead.

"Yes, it's me," said Elena Rojas.

CHAPTER SEVENTEEN

There was only ominous silence from their captors, save for a bell that Rojas said meant feeding time. A greasy, lumpy mess flowed into a trough beside a water spigot. They tried it, and unanimously decided they weren't that hungry yet. All excretory functions had to be performed at a hole in one corner of the deck. Otherwise they had nothing to occupy their time except listen to Rojas' story, which she told in a toneless voice.

"It was a matter of luck. The flechettes that went through me missed all vital organs. They picked me up and took me to that hangar of theirs, where they have a dispensary with field regen equipment. They patched me up. They . . . ." Suddenly she seemed unable to continue.

"They must have interrogated you," Jason prompted. "Torture . . . ?"

"No," she said—a little too emphatically, Jason

thought. She shook her head, and then took a deep breath. When she resumed, her voice finally held an emotion. The emotion was self-loathing. "No, they didn't bother with that. They didn't have any mind-probe equipment available, but they pumped me full of babble juice."

And so, Jason silently added for her, *you spilled the details of our plan. Which was why they knew when to be in wait for us here.* Neither of them had to say it out loud. Her haunted eyes said all that was needed.

"It wasn't your fault," he assured her.

"Hell, no!" Mondrago chimed in, understanding without being told just exactly what wasn't her fault. "Nobody can withhold information when under truth drugs. You're only human, damn it! Don't presume to hold yourself to a higher standard than God does."

Jason shot a sharp glance at the Corsican, who he had never suspected of being even remotely religious. Then he turned back to Rojas, needing to extract all possible information. "So then they put you on this transport and went to Planet A. And there, as you must know—"

"—They performed a temporal displacement," she finished for him, and the dead hopelessness was back.

Without a TRD. Once again, Jason felt no need to verbalize what they both knew.

"So," she continued in the same monotone, "I'm stuck here in the past, permanently."

"Like hell you are! *De Ruyter* has a TRD of its own, in addition to our individual ones. All we have to do is get you, and the rest of us, aboard her."

"Oh, is that all?" The humor was wry if not bitter, but

it was the first flicker of it she had shown. It died out at once. "So the ship is all right?"

"Yes. The gig and its pilot were lost, but Captain Palanivel has orders to lay low if he loses contact with us. If we can just get away from this ship—"

"An extravagant hope," came a new voice.

Crouching in a semicircle around Rojas and intent on her story, they hadn't noticed the hatch opening. Now, at the sound of that cold, oddly distorted voice, they sprang to their feet and whirled around. Four armed goons had filed in and taken position flanking the hatch, in which stood the source of the voice.

"Stoneman!" gasped Jason.

"I suppose you may as well go on calling me that, Commander Thanou." He stepped forward under one of the dim lighting fixtures, which revealed him to be even more disfigured than Jason had thought from the glimpses he had gotten. And it was easy to see why his voice was odd, for his mouth was down-twisted to the left. But, if anything, it further enhanced his sneer. "I trust the accommodations meet with your approval."

Jason glanced around at the filthy bunkroom. "I can't say much for your standards of shipboard sanitation."

"In general they are quite high. But this compartment is good enough for Pugs and other animals." Stoneman stepped closer, and Jason saw a gleam in his eyes, which as he recalled never held anything but coldness. He recognized it for what it was: a gleam of sheer, unspeakable hate. But hate held under iron control. "Perhaps it will have more occupants after we locate your ship."

"You won't." Jason took on the irritating tone he did so well, hoping to goad Stoneman into revealing useful information. "A ship in cold orbit in deep space is practically impossible to find, unless you know where to look for it."

"As I will know after questioning you."

"Wrong again. Her captain is under orders to alter his orbit in these circumstances—but I left the details up to him. So you see, it doesn't matter what you shoot into me. Truth drugs can't extract information the subject doesn't possess."

The gleam in Stoneman's eyes seemed to intensify, but it immediately died down and almost vanished, and the Transhumanist spoke in level tones, with the closest his half-ruined face could come to a mocking smile.

"A pity. You won't be as useful as Major Rojas was. She was a cornucopia of information. For one thing, she revealed your plan to be here at a later date than our earlier supply runs to this system. In accordance with her revelations, we displaced this ship less far back in the past by about a decade . . . and, as it turned out, we arrived at precisely the right time to lay our trap. In addition, she identified you by name. I thought I had glimpsed you, across that drainage ditch in Khankhazh, but I couldn't be sure. And I had been *so* wanting to renew our acquaintance." The gleam flared up again for the barest instant, and Stoneman leered at Rojas. "And she made herself useful in other ways as well."

Jason looked into her face. And all at once he understood her dull, beaten apathy, so unlike her. He understood it even before Stoneman spoke on.

"To be sure, she was not precisely willing. Resisted quite violently in fact. In the end, we had to strip her and tie her down, spread-eagled. Which made it somewhat boring. But I had the full use of her, and then placed her at the disposal of my subordinates."

Rojas had by now gone into fetal position, and was making small, whimpering noises.

"Some of those subordinates," Stoneman continued, openly gloating, "have, ah, particular tastes. For them we had to turn her over so she was prone rather than supine, so that—"

With an inarticulate roar, Hamner lunged. One of the guards, with the almost invisible speed of his genetically upgraded reflexes, smashed him in the knee with the butt of his laser carbine, then clubbed him on the back of his head as he collapsed. He fell to the deck, unconscious. All the rest of them remained rock-still.

"In the end, though," Stoneman went on as though nothing had happened, "there was no longer any satisfaction even in hurting her. But I see you have a female among you," he added with a glance at Armasova. "An ugly one, unfortunately. But beggars can't be choosers, as the saying goes."

Jason held his hand up, horizontally, in a gesture he hoped Mondrago and the commandos would understand. They did, for no one, not even Armasova, rose to Stoneman's goading. He forced himself to speak in level tones.

"I'm surprised you didn't kill her after she had ceased to be . . . satisfying."

"That would have been wasteful, Commander. She

can still serve a purpose—as can you. A purpose that will make you wish I had killed you. Wish it every conscious moment of the rest of your life!" The gleam in Stoneman's eyes was practically incandescent now, and the snide mockery in his voice was washed away by madness. "Killing you would be too merciful, after what you did to me! Do you have any conception of what I suffered? And now look—!" With a convulsive effort he fought his voice down from the scream to which it had risen, and brought his breathing under control. "No I won't grant you death. Instead, I grant you slavery, here on Drakar."

"Uh . . . Drakar?"

"The planet we are orbiting. According to Major Rojas, you call it 'Planet B.' We named it after Armin Drakar. He was one of the founders of our movement."

"I know who he was."

"You should! His name towers in history alongside such great men as Shi Huang Di, Hitler, Stalin and Pol Pot—forerunners of his, within the limitations of their eras' technologies. His was the great insight that nanotechnology and genetic engineering and bionics had finally provided the means to fully realize magnificent dreams like theirs, but only if those means were used without limits and without regard for obsolete sentimentalities like freedom and individuality."

"Yes," Jason agreed expressionlessly, "he is certainly remembered in those men's company."

"And this world beneath us will be his eternal monument," continued Stoneman, with the imperviousness to irony of the true ideologue. Then, with a madman's abruptness, he turned practical. "But our underground movement's personnel are limited. They cannot be spared for routine, unskilled labor . . . and machines can't do everything. For such purposes, we use Pug slaves."

"You mean you've been kidnapping people of our era and bringing them back in time?"

"We did at first. But then we decided it is more cost-effective to obtain our slaves in this era and bring them across space to Drakar, thus reducing the need for expensive temporal displacements. It also frees us from the security concerns we have to deal with in the twenty-fourth century; no one on Earth in the late 1800s suspects our presence. And in this era Earth has primitive, out-of-the-way places where people can vanish without being much missed. There's one area, in particular, that we find useful. However," Stoneman continued with a return of his earlier mockery, "we'll take Pugs wherever we can conveniently pick them up. Major Rojas, for example. I had intended to drop her off here on Drakar. However, that would require another trip by the shuttle. So I believe I'll just take her along with us on this, our final slave run to Earth. Along with the rest of you, and then bring you back here with the rest of the slaves. We'll be departing directly."

"Wait a minute!" said Jason. He *had* to wring as much intel as possible out of Stoneman, on the chance that he would ever be in a position to use it. "One thing I don't understand. I gather you're starting a colony here on, uh, Drakar. Does this mean you've given up your dream of restoring the Transhuman Dispensation on Earth? And if so, what about all the various time bombs you've planted? I can't believe we've found all of them."

Stoneman smiled. "You really don't understand, do you? And why should I explain it to you?" He turned on his heel to leave . . . and then paused. He turned back to face Jason, and his smile broadened. "On second thought, I think I *will* explain it to you. I'll tell you why presently. And when I do, it will also become apparent why I'm doing *this*."

As they watched, with the goons' weapons and watchful eyes on them, Stoneman knelt beside the still-unconscious Hamner and reached into a tool-pouch on his belt. He took out a small knife, with which he cut off the sergeant's left sleeve. He then took out a sensor device and ran it over the inside of the arm until it gave a tiny *beep*.

"Secure him," Stoneman ordered one of the goons. He then used the knife to make a shallow incision. Pain brought Hamner awake with a groan, but he was immobilized in the goon's unbreakable wresting hold. The groan became a gasp when Stoneman probed inside the opening in the flesh and withdrew a tiny object. It became a scream when the Transhumanist took out miniature soldering iron and cauterized the wound, before he slipped back into unconsciousness.

"You are correct that we have planted a small settlement here," Stoneman told the horrified but helpless Jason as he stood up and wiped the blood from his hand with Hamner's sleeve. "The colonists were voluntarily displaced without TRDs, such is their dedication—they are the true heroes of our movement. And yet, haven't you wondered why we've gone to the trouble and expense of sending them back in time five hundred years? The three-hundred-year minimum would have been easier. But five hundred years—actually, a trifle more—is how long our extremely sophisticated sociological, economic and demographic projections tell us it will take the very small colony we've planted to develop into a major military power, if driven by single-minded dedication.

"And I am one of those heroes!" Stoneman's voice rose almost to a scream. "I, too, have volunteered to be temporally displaced without a TRD! I am to be the founding leader of this colony, which I conceived, and persuaded our leadership to place the underground's resources solidly behind it. Now it is the cornerstone of our grand plan to reconquer Earth. I will be remembered for all time! My name will stand beside Drakar's!"

I suppose I can stop wondering why the Transhumanist leadership trusted you after your failure in 1865, Jason thought. *You've redeemed yourself in their eyes by exiling yourself into the past.*

I can also stop wondering about your sanity.

"This slave-catching expedition will be our last visit to Drakar," Stoneman went on in a more nearly normal tone of voice after catching his breath. "There will be no further contact with it, to avoid any possible Observer Effect problems. It will then be left to increase its population and build its industrial base, all the while cherishing its tradition of fanatical devotion to our movement. On *The Day*, a whole new civilization—the concentrated and distilled essence of the Transhuman ideal, resting on the labor of a slave population that by then will have been degraded to a subhuman level—will seem to the Pugs to pop into existence out of nowhere, just beyond the frontier. It will be a civilization that is nothing more than a pure military machine, animated by a single purpose. Its space fleets will sweep past the periphery of your so-called civilization, obliterating the pathetic forces of your imbecile Confederal Republic, exterminating the colony worlds—including your own homeworld, Commander—and assuring our triumph.

"*That* is the goal toward which you will be toiling, Commander Thanou. And that is why I'm telling you all this. I want you to know that you're not just a slave, but a slave whose labor is contributing to the destruction of your own people. And there is more." Stoneman approached closer, so close Jason could smell the hate. "One of the things we learned from the good Major Rojas is that you have one of the Authority's 'control' TRDs implanted in you. So I know you can escape back to our own time whenever you wish, with the knowledge I've just imparted to you. Except that you won't, will you? You can't. In addition to Major Rojas, you would leave your ship and its crew stranded."

Including Chantal. Jason looked at Mondrago, then looked away. He had seldom seen such a stricken look on a human face.

"Now you understand why I removed this Pug's TRD while he was obligingly unconscious." Stoneman nudged Hamner with a toe. "It complicates matters still further, doesn't it? If you activate your party's TRDs, you'll be leaving him behind as well.

"Actually, I had originally considered rendering you unconscious and having the 'control' TRD cut out of you, which would be the obvious way of solving the problem.

But I think I'll leave it in you, at least for now, and let you be tantalized by the knowledge, and tormented by the dilemma."

Stoneman whirled around and departed, followed by his guards. The hatch slid shut on Jason and the others and the horror with which they now lived.

CHAPTER EIGHTEEN

At the transport's pseudovelocity, the 63.7-light-year voyage from HC+31 8213 to Sol took twenty-two and a half standard days. That was how long they had to endure the squalor and discomfort of the slave quarters, with the chill gradually biting deeper and deeper into them, periodically driven by sheer, gnawing hunger to eat the nauseating swill that flowed into the trough on a regular schedule.

An attempt to escape and take over the ship was never a real option. The hatch was very seldom opened to admit any of their captors, and on those occasions the guards were very watchful and armed with laser carbines and worse—much worse: the highly illegal nerve-lash batons that could, at a touch, reduce the victim's nervous system to nothing more than a carrier of unendurable, sickening agony.

Those batons were very much in evidence when guards came and their leering leader hooked a finger for Armasova to accompany them. Slowly and with great dignity, she stood up and gave the six men in the compartment a look that said *Don't try anything foolish* more clearly than words could have—for which Jason was thankful, for he hadn't been certain he would have been able to restrain Mondrago if Stoneman carried through on his threat to use her to service the Transhumanists sexually in the brutish way Rojas had been forced to undergo. Then she turned and allowed herself to be marched through the hatch. For a time that seemed longer than it was, they were left with their seething frustration at their helplessness. Finally, the hatch opened again and a guard shoved Armasova through it with an expression of disgusted disappointment. Without a word, she went to a corner and sat crosslegged, her face turned toward the bulkhead. For a time, no one disturbed her. Then Rojas settled down beside her and put an arm around her shoulders. She went into convulsive shudders and gasping, sobbing sounds. None of the men could think of anything to say, and they all kept their distance.

At least Armasova was never removed from the compartment again. Nor was Rojas summoned for more of the same. Jason suspected that it was a matter of the usual iron Transhumanist discipline while the ship was actually underway. At any rate, he was glad of it—and not just for the obvious reason. He wasn't certain he would have been able maintain discipline—including self-discipline—if it had happened again.

Jason, however, was taken away after a time, and interrogated. Stoneman had brought along a supply of truth drugs, so torture wasn't necessary. Nor was it used . . . during the interrogation itself. It was only after Jason had been wrung dry that Stoneman indulged himself with the nerve-lash. Over and over again.

"I don't want to use physical methods that would damage you and depreciate your value as a slave," he explained in a soft voice during one of his pauses. Jason heard him as though from a vast distance away as he lay shuddering with aftershocks of agony, the ocean of pain receding a little for the time being. "I also don't want to use this for very long at a stretch. There's always the danger that it might drive you into outright insanity. That too would make you useless as a slave. Even worse, it would be a form of escape for you. And we can't have that." By now Stoneman's voice was rising, his breath was becoming uneven, and his eyes were glowing with hate. "No. I want you to feel some fraction of what I endured!" He thrust the baton home again, and once again Jason was nothing more than a mindless vessel of torment.

Finally it was over. Jason, unable to walk or otherwise use his convulsively twitching limbs—but still observing everything he saw and letting his implant process that input—was dragged back to the slave quarters and flung through the hatch. His companions did their best to make him comfortable. As they did so, he saw that Mondrago was having difficulty meeting his eyes.

He was fairly sure he knew why.

For the entire voyage so far they had, like people avoiding talking about the elephant in the room, skirted the one subject on all their minds: the fact that Jason could get them all out of this at any time but at the same time could not. And not just because of Rojas and Hamner, both of whom would have insisted that Jason not let it influence his decision. And Mondrago had seemed even more awkward than the others, feeling that he, in particular, was to blame for Jason's intolerable dilemma simply because Chantal was aboard the ship that would be left stranded half a millennium in the past.

Now, knowing what Jason had endured and declined to escape from, his misery was complete.

And it suddenly came to Jason that this was one of the very reasons Stoneman had tortured him.

"Alexandre," he said as soon as he could talk in an unshaken voice, "it's just a part of the sick little psychological game Stoneman is playing."

"I know," said Mondrago. The Corsican's expression told Jason that no elaboration was necessary. He finally looked Jason straight in the eye, and spoke with uncharacteristic formality. "Sir, the decision has to be yours. None of us can make it for you. But in making your decision, don't let any . . . considerations involving me influence you. And I think Chantal would tell you the same thing, if she could."

"I think she just might," said Jason. *But would everybody aboard* De Ruyter? he didn't add. "But I'm not ready yet to give up on the possibility of getting *all* of us back." He saw the commandos' expressions—they obviously wondered if torture had affected his mind—and he managed a grin. "Hey, people, in the Temporal Service I used to have a reputation for never losing any member of an expedition of which I was mission leader. Now that we've discovered the existence of the Teloi and the Transhumanist Underground, I've had to adjust to losses." *Sidney Nagel. Bryan Landry. Henri Boyer. Pauline Da Cunha.* The never-forgotten litany ran through his mind as always. *And, of course, Deirdre Sadaka-Ramiriz, who wasn't killed, just stranded in the Bronze Age—admittedly by her own choice.* "But I've never learned to like it. If it happens, it happens—but I refuse to accept it until it actually does." He tried to wring from his torture-ravaged brain something to say other than *Where there's life there's hope* or some such cliché. "Remember, Stoneman plans to bring us back to Drakar, as I suppose we have to call Planet B. So maybe a chance will present itself for us to be back within control range of *De Ruyter*." He didn't add what they all knew: that Rojas and Hamner would have to actually get aboard *De Ruyter*, adding a further complication that they didn't need.

"But how can you be sure *De Ruyter* will still be there after we've been to Earth and back in this tub?" asked Bakiyev.

"I can't be. But remember, I'm the only one who can activate the ship's TRD. Besides, I told Captain Palanivel to wait for us. Unless I'm very mistaken in my assessment of his character, he'll do just that, for as long as his supplies hold out. And they should hold out for quite a while." He smiled wryly and gestured toward the trough. "After all, the Transhumanists are feeding us."

"If you can call it that," quipped Bermudez, who Jason had spotted early as the unit smartass.

The grim snorts of non-laughter that ran around the

squad were exactly what Jason had hoped to hear. Any military outfit that could still gripe about the food was still in business.

In one respect, there was light at the end of the tunnel. Jason and Rojas knew the transport's capabilities from their previous experience of following it, and also knew the distance to Sol. So they had no difficulty calculating their ETA. It therefore came as no surprise when their nervous systems registered the very slight subliminal sensation that always accompanied the activation or deactivation of a drive field. Shortly thereafter the hatch slid open to admit Stoneman, preceded by a double file of guards.

As he met Stoneman's eyes, Jason decided his earlier impression had been correct. The Transhumanist, who on their previous acquaintance had been merely an ideologue and a sadist, was now insane. A sane man— even, perhaps especially, a sane sadistic ideologue—would never have spilled the Transhumanists' master plan for the Drakar colony without afterwards killing Jason or at least cutting his control TRD out of his flesh, thereby slamming the door on any possibility that the information could ever be transmitted uptime. Instead, he had sacrificed absolute security for the sheer joy of watching Jason squirm on the horns of a moral dilemma.

It made Jason wonder why the Transhumanist Underground's hierarchy would tolerate him. But then, the answer was obvious: they wouldn't have to worry about his stability, given his self-exile into the past. They had adopted his plan for Drakar, put their resources behind it, and based their strategy on it . . . and then let him indulge his martyr complex by going back in time so they wouldn't have to risk the consequences of his insanity anymore. The best of both worlds.

And at any rate, Stoneman's probable long-term future was of no help to them at the moment.

"We have passed Sol's Secondary Limit," Stoneman announced. "Naturally we have no need for caution in approaching Earth, in this era. After our landing, we will round up as many Pugs as possible. So," he added with a twisted smirk on his half-ruined face, "the luxurious spaciousness to which you have become accustomed is about to come to an end. We intend to fill this compartment to capacity for our final slaving run."

"But where are you landing?" As always, Jason knew he could keep Stoneman talking by asking the questions his flunkies never would. "You said something about an out-of-the-way area."

"Yes. The region has other advantages as well. The dominant group speaks English, as it is spoken in this era. It is ancestral to our own language, so its speakers can learn to understand us promptly, given . . . proper stimulus." Stoneman smiled and twirled the baton in his hand. "And they can pass on our commands to their non-English-speaking subordinates."

"And of course it helps that you had nineteenth-century English neurally imprinted on your brain's speech centers when you were sent back to the American Civil War, just a little over three decades earlier than this," said Jason. He didn't remind Stoneman that the same applied to Mondrago and himself. "Come to think of it, I vaguely recall that in the United States there was a rash of reported sightings of mysterious 'airships' in the late 1890s, rather like a lower-tech precursor of the 'flying saucer' craze of the 1950s. Is that where we're going—North America?"

"No. We've previously conducted operations there, among other places. But we never like to arouse suspicions—or risk running up against the Observer Effect—by operating too intensively in any one milieu. We've found a better harvesting ground: the North-West Frontier of the British Indian Empire. It's sparsely populated, so we can easily come and go unnoticed. And it's a fairly wild, lawless area. In fact, many of our activities get blamed on Pathan tribesmen from across the border in Afghanistan. We once tried gathering slaves from those tribesmen, in Afghanistan, but they're simply too wild to be tamed. So we carefully take our pickings among the British and their Indian troops, and from villages in the region, where we usually kill most of the males but take the females. The Indians have a long history of subjugation to foreign masters in any case; once we break the British and the Indian noncommissioned officers—the linguistic go-betweens—the rest generally give us no trouble." All at once, Stoneman looked annoyed at himself for his verbosity. He turned businesslike. "At any rate, I may use you and your subordinate here as assistants, since like me you speak nineteenth-century English, if only the American variety."

"Why should we want to assist you?"

"You know perfectly well." Stoneman juggled his baton again. "And you will, of course, be very carefully watched at all times." Abruptly, he turned and departed, followed by his guards.

They all looked at each other. Mondrago was the first to speak. "Do you think maybe . . .?"

"We'll just have to be alert to any possibilities that may come our way," said Jason. "But there's one problem."

"What's that?"

"Whenever we've gone into the past before, we've always received an orientation on the target milieu, and taken along a specialized academic historian who could tell us more or less what was going to happen next. This time we're being thrown in off the deep end without either. And it's for damned sure I don't know anything about late-Victorian British India." Jason ran his eyes over the IDRF people. *Naturally there's nobody here whose ethno-cultural background is Indian or British*, he thought grumpily. *That would be too convenient.* But then he recalled Mondrago's interest in military history. "I don't suppose you—?"

"Uh . . . I recall a little about the British Indian Army. It was an unusual organization. Unique, in fact."

Jason smiled. "Well, then, Professor Mondrago, you're now our resident historian."

"Just don't assign us any term papers," Bermudez cautioned.

Mondrago made a rude noise with his mouth.

CHAPTER NINETEEN

There was never any sense of motion when the negative mass drive was operating, even in its slower-than-light mode within the Secondary Limit. But subtle fluctuation of the artificial gravity let them know, even in the dim depths of the slave compartment, when the Primary Limit had been entered and the transport was maneuvering under reaction drive.

By then, they had decided on their basic strategy, although they had no idea how to execute it.

"After we land, we've got to take any chance we get to escape," Jason stated.

"But sir," said Hamner, "that doesn't get us any closer to the Drakar system, and *De Ruyter*. What can we accomplish here on nineteenth-century Earth, in what I gather was a pretty godforsaken area?"

"We can search for allies. We're going to be among

some very warlike people." Jason looked at Mondrago, who nodded. "If we can get enough of them on our side, we can start thinking about seizing this ship and taking it back to Drakar."

"Even assuming that we can take this ship," said Rojas, in a tone that said she didn't consider it a very high-probability assumption, "how do we operate it? Even if we capture some of the crew alive and force them to work for us, I wouldn't trust them not to do something suicidal. We know how fanatical they can be."

"Still, it may come to that. And even if we can't go that route, Superintendent Mondrago, in his former life as a mercenary, checked out on combat craft. And I've had some familiarization with the same kind of vessels in the Hesperian Colonial Rangers. Alexandre, remember that Kestrel when we were being pirates in the seventeenth-century Caribbean?"

"Yeah," said Mondrago dourly. "But that was a very small craft—as small as interstellar-capable vessels get. This tub is something else again. And besides, all I ever actually did with a Kestrel was atmospheric and orbital work—never an interstellar hop."

"Something else, Commander," said PFC Odinga, his dark face very serious. He seldom spoke, but when he did he invariably made sense. "About these local allies you hope to find . . ."

"Yes?" Jason prompted.

"Well, sir, from what little I understand about this 'Observer Effect' you people talk about, aren't we asking for trouble? There's no record of people in northwestern India seizing a spaceship in the late 1890s. And what if they were to go home afterwards and start talking about what they've seen?"

"They'd be laughed at as liars," Bermudez scoffed. "Or else everybody would think they'd been on drugs."

"But what if they collect some souvenirs to corroborate their story?" countered Odinga.

"You've raised a very real concern, Private Odinga," Jason admitted. "The lack of any recorded mention of any such incident does seem to suggest no local people transmit any such story. Which in turn may mean that we may have to take measures to see that they don't." He recalled what he had done to Henry Morgan because reality had required it. *Only this time I don't have any fancy memory-erasure device*, he reminded himself.

"You mean, sir . . .?"

"Yes, Private Odinga. It might mean that we end up having to take locals back to the Drakar system with us. In a lawless, primitive area like the one we're headed for, missing persons won't raise any eyebrows or suggest any abnormal causes."

He didn't mention what else it might mean. He didn't know whether any of these people had already thought that through on their own. If so, they kept quiet about it. And he himself didn't want to think about the possibly necessary nature of those "measures."

I've killed a number of people, he thought. *But I've never killed anyone in cold blood without what I considered a sufficient reason. This may put that to the test.*

Rojas interrupted his thoughts. "It could also simply mean that we're going to fail."

That could just as happily have been left unsaid, Major. But, Jason reflected, it at least had the virtue of taking everyone's minds off whatever choices they might have to make.

Then their weight seemed to momentarily waver and there was a very brief surge of acceleration before the inertial compensators took over. The transport was approaching an Earth that could never have imagined such a visitor.

"So, Alexandre," said Jason, "tell us all you can about the area where we're going to be landing. Stoneman said something about the 'North-West Frontier.' What does that mean?"

"It was the area on both sides of the border between the British Indian Empire and Afghanistan. The border was pretty vague, but I think that sometime shortly before this it was marked out in accordance with an agreement the British made with the Russians."

"With the Russians?" queried Hamner. "What about the Afghans themselves?"

"They weren't consulted. Abdur Rahman, the amir, just had to sign on the dotted line. Afghanistan was pretty anarchic, and part of the reason it kept its independence was because neither the British nor the Russians wanted the other to have it. They were always intriguing over it— 'The Great Game,' they called it."

"What was the other part of the reason?"

"The fact that the tribes that inhabited it were simply too wild to be permanently conquered—the British have tried, a couple of times in this century and failed, as other people, including the Russians, will at different times."

"Stoneman called them 'Pathans,' I think."

"Right. They live on both sides of the border. They have no sense of nationalism—their loyalties are only to their tribes, or more likely to their clans, septs and extended families. These people are barbarians—savages, really. They're nominally Muslims, but with them that just means going on a *jihad* whenever some mullah gets them pumped up. The rest of the time they're fighting blood-feuds among themselves, or raiding the Indian plains and valleys to the south. But those on the Indian side of the Frontier are perfectly willing to fight for the British against their fellow Pathans—no nationalism, remember. In fact, they make up some of the best recruits for the British Indian Army, as opposed to the British Army in India."

"Uh . . . what's the difference?" asked Hamner.

"The British Army in India is simply the British units stationed in India, and it consists entirely of Brits. The Indian Army is a separate organization, recruited locally. All its enlisted men—or 'other ranks' as the British call them—are Indians, called *sepoys*, or *sowars* if they're in the cavalry. But British Army warrant officers and NCOs are sometimes seconded to the Indian Army for limited terms. All of the Indian Army's officers are Brits . . . except for a special category of 'Viceroy's Commissioned Officers' or 'VCOs' who command units but all of whom, even the most senior, rank below the most junior British officer."

"Why?" Bermudez sounded puzzled.

Jason answered that one, on the basis of his knowledge of the attitudes of European and European-descended people in this era. "Because it's unthinkable that British troops could ever find themselves commanded by someone with a skin darker than theirs."

The commandos' faces looked blank. "What has the color of their skin got to do with it?" Armasova wanted to know.

"Trust me—it's just the way they think."

"But apart from that," said Hamner, looking more perplexed than ever, "how does this army function when the enlisted troops speak a different language from the officers?"

"Languages," Mondrago corrected. "The Indian troops speak dozens of languages and dialects. But the Mughal Empire that preceded the British had come up for a solution to that: a common language called Urdu, a mixture of Hindi and Persian and various northern Indian languages. All recruits have to learn it—not too difficult for most of them. And so do all the British officers."

"Still, language must be a problem."

"Not to mention religion," said Mondrago—who, Jason had begun to suspect, knew more about this area of military history than he had indicated. "These other ranks are Muslims or Hindus or Sikhs. The Muslims look on the Hindus as pagan idolaters—even worse than Christians and Jews, the 'People of the Book.' The Hindus are divided into various castes that can't stand the thought of physical contact with each other. The Sikhs are the result of an unsuccessful attempt to merge the other two—and since Muslims killed a particular martyr of theirs, they have a reputation for killing any Muslim they can catch, in ways he almost certainly won't enjoy. And they all have different dietary restrictions—the Muslims think the pig is unclean, and the Hindus think the cow is sacred—so they have to be in separate companies. The failure of the British to remember that helped bring about a nasty mutiny forty years ago. But then, the Brits think the lot of them are a bunch of benighted heathens."

Hamner shook his head slowly. "How can an army like this possibly work?"

"But it did . . . or I should say it *does*. Ever since the mutiny I mentioned, the Indian Army has been practically a byword for loyalty. And it will stay loyal right up to the time, about sixty years from now, when India will become independent. Somehow, a bond formed between these troops and their British officers." Mondrago looked thoughtful. "It may have had something to do with the fact that the Brits do their recruiting among what they call the 'Martial Races' of India: castes and ethnic groups that have a warrior tradition and consider soldiering an honorable profession. There's never any problem getting recruits, and they never resort to conscription. During World War II this will be the largest all-volunteer army in history."

"So," Jason reflected, "the British are able to put a medieval ethos to work for them in the First Industrial Revolution era."

"And it's a tremendous military asset to the British Empire—a pool of military manpower. Indian troops serve in places as far apart as China and Africa, and in the World Wars they'll fight for the British on all fronts. And when the Indian Army is fighting the kind of wars it's intended to fight and not playing out of its league—as when they try to put Indian troops into the trenches in World War I—it doesn't lose very often."

"So what, exactly, is going on here on the North-West Frontier right now?" asked Rojas.

"I'm sorry, Major, but I don't have that kind of detailed knowledge. Punitive operations are frequent, but I can't say what's happening on a particular date. The British permanently hold the key passes through the Hindu Kush mountains from Afghanistan—especially the Khyber Pass—with the Frontier Scouts, recruited among the Pathans. Well back from the frontier, they have camps where British battalions are brigaded with Indian Army units. In between, the wild Pathans are pretty much left alone."

"In short, good slave-hunting ground," said Jason morosely.

At that moment there was a seeming hiccup in their weight as the artificial gravity cut off and the brute pull of Earth's mass took over. Simultaneously, they felt a slight bump as the transport landed under grav repulsion and settled onto its landing legs. There was no change in their weight, for the ship had been using the standard one G of the world on which they now rested.

After a tense interval, the hatch opened and Stoneman entered with his guards and addressed them. "As you are aware, we have landed. It is late August, 1897, as you are also aware, Commander Thanou, from your computer implant—oh, yes, we know about that. Bit of hypocrisy, isn't it, for one who claims to abide by the Human Integrity Act? At any rate, the British are conducting one of their innumerable punitive expeditions in this area—

it's known as the Swat River Valley—and we've located some isolated detachments of theirs nearby, off the main line of march. I and most of my men are about to depart, to do some collecting. As soon as we're on our way back, I'll be sending for you, to perform the function I mentioned before. Hold yourselves in readiness." He turned on his heel and departed.

They all looked at each other. Mondrago was the first to speak. "So most of them will be gone . . ."

"And I can find the way to the cargo port we were brought in through," said Jason. "My implant has had a chance to build up a partial deck plan of this ship."

"But," said Rojas, "what happens if we get there and it's closed?"

"I have a hunch they'll simply leave it open while Stoneman and his slaving party are gone. Why not?"

"What about that laser turret they used to destroy our gig?" asked Hamner. "It could fry us once we're out in the open."

"It's a ventral turret," Mondrago reminded him. "I doubt if it can protrude when the ship is on the ground. And even if it can . . . from what I recall of its location, I don't think it can cover the area astern."

"Besides which," added Jason, "I'd be surprised if they even have it activated. From their standpoint, these people around here aren't just Pugs, they're also primitives—totally beneath contempt."

"It's still a long chance," said Rojas.

"It's the only chance we've got," Jason reminded her. He gave her a close but surreptitious look. In the course of the voyage she had gradually come out of the shell of despondency in which they had found her, but her personality still hadn't altogether reasserted itself. While Jason couldn't pretend that he missed her abrasive assertion of authority, its absence wasn't entirely reassuring. He could only hope she was up to what they were contemplating.

Time passed, its pace slowed by tension. They used it to make plans and try to foresee contingencies. Finally, with the usual nerve-wracking lack of warning, the hatch opened. Two guards entered—fewer than usual, which suggested that Mondrago was right and that most of the Transhumanists were absent. Both were goon-caste. After so much time with no trouble from the prisoners, they had grown lax . . . even more so now that Stoneman was absent, Jason suspected, for only one had a laser carbine, and it was slung over his shoulder. Both held neural-stimulator batons in a contemptuously nonchalant way.

"You two," said the one with the laser carbine, gesturing at Jason and Mondrago. "Come!"

Jason rose slowly to his feet, followed by Mondrago. As he did so, he gave Rojas an almost imperceptible nod.

As Jason and Mondrago passed between the two guards, Rojas suddenly screamed and went into what appeared to be an epileptic seizure.

"What—?" exclaimed the guard with the laser carbine, who stood to Jason's left. By sheer reflex, he swung toward the source of the commotion.

As he did so, Jason grabbed the laser carbine and heaved, swinging the guard to whose shoulder it was strapped around to collide with the other guard, knocking him off-balance. Simultaneously, Mondrago dropped to the deck, avoiding the batons, and grappled the two guards' ankles.

All the IDRF people sprang to their feet. Jason grasped the wrists of the guard he had unbalanced and pinned him to the floor, desperately straining against genetically upgraded strength as the guard tried to bring his baton into contact. He only had to do so for a second before Bakiyev kicked the guard in the temple, hard. At the same time, Jason heard a scream from Mondrago, for the other guard had fallen on top of him and applied his baton. But then Hamner gripped the guard's baton-arm, rolled him over and finished him with a quick, economical chop to the throat with the edge of his stiffened hand.

"Are you all right?" demanded Jason as he hauled the trembling Mondrago to his feet.

"Never better," the Corsican managed to gasp.

"Not a bad performance," Jason told Rojas. He scooped up the laser carbine. "And now, let's go!"

Guided by Jason's map display, they rushed through the transport's passageways, encountering no one. The hatch giving access to the cargo bay was closed, but its controls were standard. Jason slapped a button, and it slid open.

The cargo port was open, as Jason had hoped, with its ramp expended to the ground, and the outside world was visible in blurred gray tones it always showed when viewed from inside an invisibility field. "Come on!" Jason ordered.

They were halfway across the cargo bay when a guard, who had been standing outside, stepped in with laser carbine at the ready. As he brought it into line with one hand, he punched a control box beside the opening. The cargo port began to rumble shut.

Odinga, who was closest to him, launched himself at the guard with a roar. There was the *crack!* of a weapon-grade laser drilling a hole through air, and Odinga's chest expelled the steam of heat-exchange. He crumpled without a sound.

But he had given Jason the split second he needed. His own laser beam speared the guard.

"Run!" he shouted.

They all crowded through the port before it had finished closing. Jason was the last, and as the port slammed shut it caught his laser carbine, crushing it.

There was no time to mourn Odinga. They ran toward the stern of the transport, not wishing to test their theories about the laser turret. Then they were out of the field, the transport was no longer visible, and the landscape around them abruptly came into focus and assumed the clarity of mountain sunlight.

CHAPTER TWENTY

There was no immediate pursuit, and Mondrago's optimism about the laser turret appeared to have been justified. Still, Jason wanted to put as much distance as possible between them and the now-invisible transport. So he kept them running for a spell, until they all needed to stop, gasping for breath—this clearly was high-altitude terrain, and they were used to standard sea-level atmospheric pressure. Only then did he permit himself to look around at their surroundings.

It seemed mid-afternoon, judging from the position of the sun. They were on an upland plateau, stony and barren like the slopes of the mountains that loomed above, although the upper reaches were covered with dense forests. Spurs projected from the sides of the ridge, forming narrow gorges, in which what looked like villages could be glimpsed. To the west, below and barely visible between two peaks, the westering sun glinted on a river—Stoneman had mentioned the Swat. He had also mentioned isolated British detachments off to the flanks, which was undoubtedly why he had landed up here in the surrounding mountains.

It was a dramatic landscape, but Jason was in no mood to appreciate it. He swallowed to wet his throat—the air was dry as well as thin, and he was growing thirsty in the August heat—and turned to face the others.

"All right, let's get moving. They'll be after us soon, and they must have sensors that can detect my implant—maybe fair-sized, long-ranged ones."

"Where shall we go?" asked Hamner.

"Toward that valley over there. We'll find the nearest village."

"How will we communicate with them?" Rojas inquired. "None of us speak whatever it is they speak around here—"

"Pushtu," Mondrago supplied.

"—and I doubt if any of the villagers speak English."

"Well, Stoneman said the Brits are operating in this area. Maybe there'll be some around . . . or maybe the headman will have picked up a few English words."

"Anyway," said Bakiyev with his usual stolid calm, "we'd better get going." He pointed back to the location where the transport rested inside the field that bent light-frequencies around it. Figures were popping into view around it.

"Move!" Jason snapped. The distant figures weren't many—Stoneman hadn't returned yet—but they had twenty-fourth-century weapons, which made numbers irrelevant. And they would undoubtedly be driven by a desire to not have to explain to Stoneman how they had lost the prisoners.

None of them needed any urging. They all got to their feet and scrambled uphill, up the rugged slopes, over tumbled heaps of boulders. They soon lost sight of the remote figures of their pursuers, but Jason wasn't about to let up, knowing what a beacon his implant provided to anyone with the right sensors.

As they gained altitude, the heat grew somewhat less oppressive. But the air also grew thinner, so that exertion was exhausting to their unacclimated bodies. It also grew drier, and Jason's thirst became ever more tormenting.

After a time, his sense of direction began to tell him that his efforts to put as much distance as possible between themselves and the Transhumanists might not be working. The topography was tricky, and they might simply be circling around in such a way as to cross the path of their pursuers. He licked his dry lips, croaked "Halt!" and tried to get his bearings.

"Freeze!"

Jason froze, and slowly turned his head to the left, from which had come the command. A figure in standard shipboard coverall stood at the edge of a cliff up which he had presumably clambered, pointing a laser carbine at them. Keeping the weapon on target with his right hand, he raised his left arm to speak into a wrist communicator. *Summoning the others*, Jason thought bleakly. *After which—*

"Hit the dirt!" Mondrago's dry-throated rasp held a tone that caused Jason and the others to instantly fall prone to the ground. As Jason did so, getting a mouthful of dust, he looked to his right. Three figures wearing khaki uniforms and pith helmets topped a ridge, and one of them opened fire with some kind of shoulder arm. He heard a cry to his left and, turning his head, saw the Transhumanist clutch his midriff and fall over backwards off the cliff.

For a moment, Jason could only lie there and cough dust out of his desiccated mouth. Then he heard a scrape of sandaled feet and looked up.

It was a small, scrawny man of indeterminate age, clad only in a dirty-white breechclout and a kind of turban. His leathery skin was a darker-than-average brown compared to most predominantly Indian-descended people of Jason's acquaintance. Over his shoulder was slung a goatskin sack which looked to be partially full of liquid and seemed much too heavy for him. He squatted beside Jason, propped up his head, and put the sack's unstopped opening to his mouth.

The water was lukewarm and none too fresh. Jason had never tasted anything so exquisitely delightful.

The man smiled, his teeth white against his dark face, and spoke in an odd singsong version of nineteenth-century English.

"I hope you liked your drink, *sahib*."

The entire party had been watered by the time the three men in khaki had scrambled down the slope and joined them. At closer range, Jason saw that all three had what he recognized as early bolt-action repeating rifles slung over their shoulders, and wore sergeant's chevrons.

The one who had shot the Transhumanist also had a tiny crown in the chevrons' angle. He had the build of a heavyweight boxer—a good one—and a ruddy face that could have been cited as evidence for the still-contentious theory of Neanderthaloid ancestry in modern *Homo sapiens*. He took off his pith helmet and wiped the sweat from his dark reddish-brown hair.

"Thanks," Jason told him, and gestured at the nearly naked Indian. "You and that man, between you, saved our lives."

The massive sergeant gave a dismissive gesture in the direction of the Indian and spoke in a kind of deep, clipped rasp in which *th* shaded slightly toward *d*. "Ah, he's just the regimental *bhisti*." Jason assumed that meant "water carrier." Then the sergeant gave him a surprisingly shrewd look, and stroked his narrow mustache. "Yank, eh?"

"Actually, my friend and I are Canadians." Jason had already decided on this dodge to account for his and Mondrago's North American accents while at the same time establishing them as loyal subjects of Her Majesty the Queen. He introduced the two of them, using their own names, which he hoped would sound French to this bruiser. "We're with a company exploring for minerals in these mountains. Our employees, here, are Americans." He pointed to Rojas and Bermudez. "Those two are Mexican-Americans, and the others are recent immigrants. So their English is limited . . . sounds pretty strange, in fact."

"Ah," nodded the sergeant. If he found anything odd about the presence of two women in the party, he kept it to himself. "I'd say you picked a bloody awful place for prospecting, especially these days with the niggers running wild up here." He gazed at the men's three-week beards and general filthiness. "And I can tell you've been out here a while. But what . . .?" He gestured in the direction of the cliff over which the Transhumanist had toppled.

"Uh . . . he worked for another company that's in competition with ours, you see. They attacked—took all our equipment. We've been running from them."

"Ah." The sergeant gave another sage nod. "That explains those buggers. We've had trouble with them ourselves. And we didn't know what to make of them. They're not local tribesmen, that's for certain. And they're dressed peculiarly . . . rather like . . ." He gave Jason's own garb a narrow regard.

"Well, as you say, that explains it," said Jason hurriedly, anxious to change the subject. "But to whom do we owe our lives?"

"McCready, Royal West Kent Regiment." He gestured at the other two sergeants, both younger than he. "This is Carver, and this is Hazeltine."

"Top o' the afternoon, mate," said Carver in an accent that was pure cockney. He was a roguishly handsome, black-haired man whose clean-shaven face featured a deeply cleft chin and an infectiously raffish grin. Jason instantly summed him up: *engaging rascal.*

"Good day," said Hazeltine in educated tones. His unconsciously languid posture didn't disguise the athleticism of his slim body. His hair and neat mustache were blond, his features clean-cut, his eyes blue and alert.

From somewhere, Jason recalled the old British army term *gentleman ranker*.

"All right, let's move our bloody arses," McCready rumbled. "There are a few of the 24th Sikhs over the ridge," he explained to Jason. "Our battalion is brigaded with them, and with the 24th and 31st Punjab Infantry, and the three of us got seconded to their regiment." Jason recalled Mondrago mentioning something about such arrangements. "We were up here on the flank of our main column, and got separated. Then we got into a bit of a dust-up with these business competitors of yours. Lost a couple of the Sikhs before we got away. By the way . . . what kind of rifles are those they're using? They don't seem to *do* anything, but—"

"New American models," Jason cut in. "Don't know much about them. But that reminds me, Sergeant. It seems you and we both want to get back at these people, and I wonder if your unit would help us to—"

"Sorry. Our duty is to rejoin our brigade." McCready turned to his fellow sergeants. "Right. Let's go." Then he noticed the *bhisti*, still doling out sips of water. "Get moving, you lazarushian bugger, before I help you along with the toe of me boot!"

"Come on, Mac," Carver remonstrated as they started trudging up the ridge. "Go easy on him. He means well. And he has a hard enough time in life, what with bein' an untouchable and all."

"Not an insuperable hindrance with the Sikhs of the 24th," Hazeltine reminded him. "They don't believe in caste. They'll drink water from him even though he's touched the bag. But you're right about him meaning well. He's so proud of the little bit of English he's learned."

"And he's given me a new tip!" Carver's dark eyes lit up. "Yes, all right, I own that the last one didn't exactly work out so well—"

"Not exactly," Hazeltine interjected drily. "It landed the three of us in close tack, as I recall. We're lucky we still have our stripes."

"But this time he swears by Rama and Vishnu and all them heathen idols that he knows the location of a buried treasure of the old Mughal emperors, in these very hills! Enough to make us all richer than bloomin' dukes! If only we could've just taken a slight diversion . . . You know, a bit of tactical flexibility, like."

McCready drew a deep breath of long-suffering exasperation into his barrel of a chest. "So help me, Carver," he growled slowly, "if I hear you mention treasure one more time . . .!"

"Ignore them," said Hazeltine to Jason with a wink. "I do so habitually."

Jason decided to risk exposing their ignorance, for he badly needed information. "I was wondering if you could bring me up to date on the state of affairs here in the Swat Valley. We haven't been in this country long, you see, and we don't know anything about the background of this campaign."

"Well," Hazeltine began, "you must understand that this entire area—the Bajaur-Dir-Swat-Buner region—is an explosively hostile Pathan stronghold, British in name only. After all, it's outside the Administrative Boundary." Realizing that a colonial like Jason wouldn't understand what that meant, he elucidated. "You see, the official boundary between India and Afghanistan—the Durand Line, it's called, after the chap who marked it out—has a belt on this side of it where we don't even try to keep the Pathan tribes from robbing and murdering each other to their black little hearts' content as long as they don't molest our forts at points where we have to keep control, like the Khyber Pass. The Administrative Boundary is the inner border of that belt. "

"Ain't he something?" declared Carver, beaming with pride at Hazeltine's education. "Would you believe, he's even learned Urdu, like a proper officer?"

"I say, let the heathen sods learn English," muttered McCready.

"But the present problem," continued Hazeltine, demonstrating his expertise at ignoring the other two members of this comedy team, "began last month, when our fort at Malakand Pass, at the southern end of the Swat Valley—one of those crucial posts I mentioned—was attacked by the followers of Sadullah the Mad Mullah."

Jason made surreptitious eye contact with Mondrago. The Corsican gave a nod that said, *Yes. Seriously.*

"In addition to all the usual tosh about Allah," Hazeltine continued, "Sadullah has been carrying around a thirteen-year-old boy he claims is the legitimate heir to the Mughal dynasty. So the local Pathan tribes—Yusafazis, Swatis, Bunerwals and the like; treacherous brutes—were ready to carry fire and sword to Delhi and restore Muslim rule so they could get back to the enthralling fun of massacring Hindus, from which we British have been cruelly restraining them. But even though the entire

Frontier has been simmering, the *sirkar*—that's our bloody government—didn't take it seriously until July 26th. Then ten thousand *ghazis*—fanatics—attacked the Malakand fort and the even smaller one at Chakdara. The garrisons—24th Punjab Infantry and 45th Sikhs, mostly—only amounted to a thousand men, but they managed to hold out until reinforced. At this point, even the politicians realized this wasn't just a few tribesmen out for an evening's amusement, and early this month the Malakand Field Force was formed under Brigadier General Blood."

Jason gave Mondrago the same look, and got the same nod.

"We've been advancing into the Swat Valley ever since, in three brigades. Ours is the first, under Brigadier General Meiklejohn. The tribesmen fought us their usual way, with ambush after ambush, but our mountain artillery cleared the way for us repeatedly, and our brigade flanked them out of position when they tried to stand. Yesterday, the 18th, we reached Barikot. Unfortunately, rumor has it that Sadullah has gotten away and is now spreading his poison among the Afridis—they're the most powerful of the Pathan tribes on the Frontier—to the south, around the Khyber Pass. But nothing's expected to come of it." (Mondrago shot Jason a *famous last words* look.) "And now we're on the way to Mingaora, where we're to halt a few days for the Swat Valley tribes to come in and tender their submission."

"They'll be lying in their teeth as usual," McCready grimly foretold. "But, as I said, our flanking party got cut off, and . . . Ah, here we are. And here comes the *naik*."

They had topped a rise and entered a hollow, where a

number of bearded, khaki-clad, turban-wearing Indian infantrymen (Sikhs, Jason assumed) were starting a fire—it was now early evening, and the mountain air's temperature was dropping even at this season. One of them, wearing two chevrons—Jason deduced that *naik* meant corporal—approached and spoke to Hazeltine in what Jason assumed was Urdu. Off to the side was a tethered horse.

"Oh, I forgot to tell you," said McCready to Jason. "We've picked up another straggler—a newspaper reporter, in fact. Young subaltern of the 4th Hussars who went on leave and got himself a job covering this campaign. He's been attached to Brigadier General Jeffreys' Second Brigade, but he went off looking for adventure, I suppose, and got separated. Cocky young feller, but likeable. Ah, here he is now."

A young man in dusty khaki tunic and jodhpurs approached. He was about five feet eight—average height in this era—and looked to be in his early twenties. Despite his youthful slenderness, a certain quality of roundness in his face suggested that he was the type to grow stout in later life if he wasn't careful. And the face itself could easily grow to be decidedly bulldoglike. But it was a not unattractive face, with a fair number of freckles, topped by reddish sandy hair and dominated by bright blue eyes and a charming smile.

"Ah, North Americans," he said when Jason and Mondrago had been introduced. He had a pleasing voice and a decidedly upper-class accent. "I'm half-American, you know, on my mother's side. Name's Churchill. Winston Churchill."

He gave the half-circle of newcomers a puzzled look, as though wondering why they were staring at him openmouthed.

CHAPTER TWENTY-ONE

faded text

✧✧✧

"My regiment, the 4th Hussars, is stationed here in India but wasn't ordered to Malakand for this little jaunt," Churchill explained as they sat around a fire that night after appeasing their hunger with the Sikhs' chapattis and chilis. "So I took leave and got myself an assignment to cover this campaign for the London *Daily Telegraph*. Well, all right," he admitted a little sheepishly, "I admit my mother's influence helped a bit—she's Lady Randolph Churchill, you know. But I *do* have some experience as a correspondent—in Cuba, year before last, with the Spanish troops operating against the Cuban guerillas. Lovely island, and wonderful cigars. That was the first time I was ever under fire," he added casually. Then he grew thoughtful. "It happened again just the other day, you know. We were passing a native village we thought to be deserted, and an ambush burst on us. Bullets were

223

flying past me. The officer in charge caught one. The men tried to bear him away, but they were driven off. A Pathan swordsman slashed the wounded officer to death with his tulwar before our eyes. At that point, I formed a resolve to kill the brute."

"And so you shot him?" Jason prompted.

"Actually, I thought that under the circumstances my saber would be more appropriate. Well," he added a little defensively, seeing the looks on his listeners' faces, "I *did* win the Public School fencing medal. However, a half-dozen of his fellow sword-swingers came running up, and upon reflection I decided my revolver would be more practical after all. I'm not sure I actually hit any of them," he admitted, "but we were able to get away to a knoll held by the Sikhs, where we were relieved by the Buffs. D'you know," he added cheerfully, "nothing in life is so exhilarating as to be shot at without result."

He would never know that his listeners were asking themselves if the world they came from could have come into being if one of those Cuban insurgents or Pathan tribesmen—or, in a few years, Sudanese and Boers—had shot *with* result.

Jason had more than that on his mind. Indeed, he could barely keep up the façade of polite, composed interest concealing his mental turmoil.

This tears it. It was easy, back aboard the ship, to talk glibly about what we might have to do if any of the locals helped us and, in the process, saw things they weren't supposed to. After all, what difference would a few lowlifes in a remote war zone matter?

But this is different. As long as this cocky youngster

on whom so much rides is with us, we can't *take any action with regard to that ship. The Observer Effect won't let us. Something will prevent us. It's a current that you cannot swim against . . . and which might just drown you.*

"You certainly seem eager to see action," said Rojas. Jason was impressed by her linguistic subterfuge. Having heard Churchill mention his Cuban experiences, she was carefully pronouncing the current version of English as she had heard it, and as a speaker of her own native Spanish would have accented it.

Churchill suddenly looked bleak. "Well, my father Lord Randolph Churchill died two years ago, when he was only forty-five. I'm haunted by the fear that I may also die very young—that I don't have much time to make my mark in the world. I suppose that's why I so often seem to people to be in a frightful hurry." Then, as an afterthought: "I have a fancy I might go into politics eventually."

"Well," said Mondrago, "you certainly ought to have opportunities to bring yourself into notice, serving against Sadullah the Mad Mullah."

Churchill's mood changed again in its mercurial way. "Yes, I suppose we British *do* have a way of characterizing those who oppose our empire as deranged rather than simply patriotic, don't we? But having said that, it must also be remarked that some of Sadullah's pronouncements are a bit . . . well, peculiar. He's assured his disciples that our bullets will turn to water, and that they can stopper up the muzzles of our guns by a wave of the hand."

"Probably hasn't worked out too well for them," Mondrago surmised drily.

"Hardly—especially with Sir Bindon Blood in command. A most impressive man—and somewhat unconventional. He claims direct descent from Captain Blood, the noted Restoration thief who came within an ace of making off with the crown jewels from the Tower of London." Churchill chuckled. "I've sometimes thought that if the Pathans knew he takes pride in having a distinguished bandit for an ancestor, they'd regard him as a kindred spirit and we could work all this out without so much bother. But," he added, turning serious, "probably not. We're dealing with Muslim fanatics engaged in a *jihad*, or holy war."

"We Westerners have had our holy wars," Jason ventured. "Do we really have any room to talk?"

Churchill gave a sad smile. "You're overlooking one thing. Holy war is a perversion of Christianity; it is *not* a perversion of Islam. The Islamic ideal is the *ghazi*—the fanatical holy warrior from the desert, sweeping away the corruptions of civilization with fire and sword."

"But your average Muslim isn't a *ghazi*."

"No, but deep in his heart of hearts he thinks he *ought* to be one. Any Muslim who believes in peace and religious tolerance isn't a very good Muslim . . . and he knows it. His religion provides him with no basis for a refutation—no philosophical defenses, as it were—when some holy man preaches *jihad*."

Jason fell silent, for he had seen enough history to know Churchill was right. The Moors of Spain had been the most civilized people in Medieval Europe . . . and not once but twice they had offered no real resistance when ignorant Berber fanatics from North Africa has swept over them, because their religion told them they had no *right* to resist having their multicultural society thus cleansed and purified. And Muslim states of the late twentieth and early twenty-first centuries had exhibited the same lack of will in the face of the terrorists who had been the high-tech descendants of the blood-mad fundamentalist desert tribesmen of old.

And besides, he thought he now had a glimpse of a way out of his predicament.

"Well," he said with careful casualness, "I imagine you'll want to be getting back to General Jeffreys' brigade." He recalled what Hazeltine had told him. "And you'll want to be in time to enter Mingaora with them. After all, the *Daily Telegraph* will surely be interested in a story about the submission of the Swat Valley tribes."

Churchill's eyes lit up. "I say, they will, won't they? The sergeants over there—rough diamonds, you may say, but splendid chaps, really—have been trying to persuade me to stay with them. They fear for my life if I set out on my own again. But you're absolutely right. And at any rate, I do need to get back before General Jeffreys thinks I've deserted. I'll set out first thing in the morning."

"We'll be sorry to see you go," said Jason. *Relieved, actually,* he mentally corrected. But he knew he wasn't entirely lying, Observer Effect or no.

"You're sure you want to try it, sir?" Sergeant McCready's face was furrowed with concern, making it even uglier than usual. "I don't think there are any hostile tribesmen left nearby, but these business competitors of Mr. Thanou's might give you trouble."

In fact, the Observer Effect won't let them, thought Jason. But of course he couldn't say so out loud.

"Thank you for your solicitude, Sergeant, but I'm certain I'll be all right. And it is my duty to rejoin General Jeffreys as expeditiously as possible." As Churchill looked down from his horse, his mouth settled into a determined look, and Jason felt a small gooseflesh-raising shock of recognition, for he had seen that exact expression. He had seen it on Churchill's four-decades-older face, in photographs taken while Nazi bombs were falling on London and Britain stood alone against a new Dark Age, armed with little more than a badly outnumbered air force and one clear-sighted man's unconquerable will.

"Well, best of luck, sir. We've got to get back to Third Brigade."

"Of course you do, Sergeant. Best of luck to you as well." As Churchill turned his horse around, his eyes met Jason's. "Cheerio," he said with a jaunty wave. "Perhaps we'll see each other at Mingaora." Then he rode off, carrying the future with him.

"All right, you lot," growled McCready after a moment. "Fall in, before it gets any hotter."

The little pick-up unit sorted itself into marching order. The three sergeants slung their rifles—Lee-Metfords, Mondrago had called them. They also had .455 Webley revolvers in holsters. The Indian sepoys carried rifles of a different kind. Jason asked Mondrago about them.

"Martini-Henrys," the Corsican explained in an undertone. "It's a single-shot breechloader, rather than a repeater like the Lee-Metford. Obsolete in the British

Army. But ever since the Mutiny the Brits have been careful to arm their 'native' troops with stuff one generation behind what the white troops get. They also keep direct control of all artillery."

They set out, the time travelers behind the sepoys and, bringing up the rear, the *bhisti*, who had filled his water sack from a nearby stream. Despite its weight and awkwardness, he wore his usual cheerful and accommodating expression. McCready detailed two of the sepoys to scout ahead.

Jason studied the position of the sun and tried to recall the direction he and the others had taken the preceding day. As far as he could determine, they weren't headed in the direction of the transport. But he had no idea which direction Stoneman and his slave-gathering party had taken.

As they began to enter a defile between two rocky slopes, he joined the three sergeants at the head of the little column. "You know," he said to McCready, despising himself for his dishonesty but having no other choice, "I'd still like to try and interest you in a little side jaunt. We could be of help to each other. If you rid us of those disagreeable competitors of ours, we could put you in the way of considerable profit."

"The answer's still no. We've got to get back to the main body of First Brigade without delay. Besides," McCready added with a sour side-glance at Carver, "this sounds altogether too much like one of Carver's schemes to suit me."

"Now see 'ere, Mac—"

A rifle shot, amplified and echoing in this confined

space, interrupted Carver's indignation, and one of the sepoys sank to the dust, clutching his thigh. At McCready's roared command, they all took whatever cover was available behind boulders, as the first shot from above was followed by a fusillade of others, with a distinctly differed sound. To Jason's ear, they sounded like the muskets he had encountered in the seventeenth century.

"Mostly *jezzails*," McCready observed.

"But that first one was a bleedin' Lee-Metford," said Carver aggrievedly, unlimbering his own and firing at a half-seen target.

"Gun-runners have been getting a few of them to the tribesmen, who'll pay all they own for one," said Hazeltine. The repeater somewhere on the crags above continued to fire away. The Sikhs, crouching or prone, returned fire at a slower rate with their Martini-Henrys.

Serve you people right if your native troops are outgunned, thought Jason as a near-miss spattered his face with dust and slivers of rock. *Bad luck for them, of course.* He surmised that the scouts were lying in their own blood up ahead, their throats cut.

McCready handed Jason his Webley. "D'you know how to use one of these?"

"I think I can manage." The revolver was a large-caliber that would doubtless kick like a mule, but at least it was a cartridge breech-loader, not one of the clumsy front-loading Colts he had used in the American Civil War. He squinted into the sun and searched for targets.

"We're fish in a barrel," muttered Carver as another sepoy screamed in pain. The *bhisti* scrambled to the wounded man's side, dodging bullets.

Then, for no apparent reason, the ambushers' fire began to slacken off, and then ceased.

They all looked at each other blankly in the sudden silence.

A voice from behind them shattered the silence, speaking in more or less contemporary North American English.

"You are surrounded. Do not attempt to resist."

Jason stood up and turned around. Stoneman stood on the trail they had followed, flanked by four of his goons. Each held a laser carbine in one hand, with which the totally recoilless weapon could easily be used. The other hand held another weapon that Jason recognized.

Other goons now appeared on the ridges above, where Jason was certain he knew what they had done to the Pathans.

One of the Sikhs turned with an oath and brought up his Martini-Henry. With a bored look, Stoneman fired the neural paralyzer in his left hand. There was the ruby flash of a laser guide beam. The Sikh toppled to the dirt, unable to move a single voluntary muscle.

With an inarticulate growl, McCready began to raise his rifle.

"Don't try it," Jason told him in a low voice. "You don't stand a chance."

"Wise advice, Commander Thanou," said Stoneman in twenty-fourth-century Standard International English. "We'd rather not kill potential slaves, even though we have something of a score to settle with this unit—we had a run-in with them yesterday. But we will if we have to."

"Here, wot's this?" demanded Carver.

"Just to demonstrate . . ." Stoneman glanced at the two wounded sepoys. "More trouble than they're worth," he said casually. This time he used his laser carbine.

The three sergeants stared, inarticulate with helpless fury. McCready was clearly exerting all his massive strength to hold himself in check. The sepoys were marbled in uncomprehending shock. The *bhisti* tried to make himself as small as possible.

"You murdering bastard," hissed Jason.

"Now what kind of attitude is that? We just saved your lives. Waste not, want not, as an old saying goes. Unfortunately, we had to paralyze those few of your attackers we didn't kill, so given their inability to move under their own power I've summoned the ship. It should arrive at any moment."

"I've had enough of this!" roared McCready, infuriated beyond caution. He glared at Jason and Stoneman alike. "Stop talking in that silly way, damn your eyes! 'Business competitors' my arse! Who are you? What's this codswallop about a 'ship' in the middle of these bloody mountains? What—?"

"*Sahib! Sahib!*" cried the *bhisti*, who was staring skyward with huge round eyes. "Look!" Something in his tone made McCready stop and look up. Then, one by one, they all looked up. No one spoke, as shadow engulfed them.

The transport was sliding overhead on grav repulsion, filling the sky over the defile, blocking the sun.

CHAPTER TWENTY-TWO

The sepoys moaned, and the sergeants muttered curses, as the paralyzed man was lifted up through the cargo port by tractor beam, followed by the equally paralyzed surviving Pathans. Then the transport settled onto its landing jacks on a flat expanse above the defile, and they were marched up to the still-open port, through the cargo bay and along the passageways, flanked by guards bearing nerve-lash batons. All the locals—British no less than Indian—stared with round eyes and open mouths at their surroundings. The sergeants, at least, would have heard of electric lighting, which had been invented almost two decades earlier although it still was far from widespread. But the materials—plastics and composites—were utterly unnatural to them, as were the humming, beeping, clicking background sounds.

All at once, it became too much for one of the sepoys.

With a scream, he turned and sought to fight his way back out of the belly of this flying monster. One of the goons, looking barely interested, jabbed him with his nerve-lash baton. The Sikh's scream turned to one of agony, and he collapsed to the deck.

"Here, you!" roared McCready indignantly, rounding on the guard. Evidently, no one *else* was allowed to mistreat his native troops. Before Jason could warn him to back off, the goon brushed the baton against his elbow. He went rigid but, astonishingly, didn't scream. With a gasp, followed by a low moan through tightly clenched teeth, he sank shuddering to his knees.

The other two sergeants went to their knees beside him. "Buck up, Mac old boy!" Carver urged, grasping the big man by the shoulders.

"Don't try anything," Jason pleaded with them. "All you can do is get hurt." Carver and Hazeltine both glared at him, but they restrained themselves from doing anything more than helping McCready to his feet. The sepoys did the same for their whimpering comrade, and the dismal procession continued.

When the hatch opened on the slave quarters, a cacophony of female screams arose. The compartment was half-full, mostly with women and children. *Taken from some nearby village*, Jason thought, *where the men were wiped out. Important to maintain the sex ratio among the breeding stock.* But four paralyzed tribesmen had already been brought in—presumably all that had survived. The women were helping them restore their muscle control. Now, with these new arrivals—especially the white ones—the women panicked and tried to veil their faces with whatever rags they had available. One hawk-faced, black-bearded Pathan, more recovered than the others and seeming to be their leader, struggled to his feet and glared at the intended victims of his ambush. The Sikhs glared back.

"Any brawling among the slaves will be punished with neural stimulation," came Stoneman's voice like a whipcrack from the hatch behind them. "Or, if that proves unavailing, with a few exemplary executions. You'd better make that clear to all, Commander Thanou. And by the way, we'll be departing directly." Then he was gone, and the hatch clanged shut.

It took only an instant to make it pretty clear to the sergeants, and through the *naik* they made it equally clear in Urdu to the sepoys. And enough of the latter spoke a little Pushtu to get it across to their erstwhile attackers. The tension in the overcrowded compartment subsided, leaving nothing but uncomprehending despair.

Rojas briskly examined the women, who only momentarily flinched away from her. Then she tried the water spigot. "It's not on," she told Jason, "and these women are nearing dehydration." She turned to the *bhisti*, who had kept his water sack through it all, and spoke in her version of the current form of English. "Give the women water."

"Yes, *memsahib*."

The women, as Muslims, objected to his Untouchable status no more than did the Sikhs. Their acceptance of his water seemed a kind of signal, and everyone settled into a formless mass of common misery and apathy. The three sergeants sat on the deck with their backs to a bulkhead.

Presently, there was a slight sensation of movement as the transport went aloft on grav repulsion and the photon thrusters kicked in, then it ceased. "What's happening?" Hazeltine demanded. "We started to move, but then stopped."

"No. we haven't stopped. In fact, we're moving very fast." Jason didn't bother trying to explain inertial compensators. Instead, he sat crosslegged on the deck facing the sergeants and meeting their eyes. *Might as well get this over with.*

"All right," said McCready wearily. "Talk. You've been lying to us."

"Too bloody right!" exclaimed Carver. "If you're a Canadian prospector, I'm a Bengali *babu*!"

"Bad form, old man," added Hazeltine with acid irony.

"I'm sorry I had to lie. But if I'd told you the truth, you wouldn't have believed it."

"Well, I'd say we're ready to believe just about anything now," said Hazeltine. He gave a wave that indicated the ship around them. "This is all like something out of one of Mr. Wells' stories."

"So talk," McCready repeated. "Who *are* you? Who are these blighters who've captured us? Where are you from? Where are we going on this great bloody airship?"

"What's *happening*, for God's sake?" blurted Carver beseechingly.

Jason turned to Hazeltine. "You mentioned H. G. Wells. Has he already written *The Time Machine*?"

"Why, yes. Year before last, I believe." Hazeltine frowned, as though he found Jason's phraseology a trifle odd.

"Good. Then you've heard of the idea of time travel."
Jason took a deep breath. "My companions and I are from
the future. Nearly five centuries in the future, in fact. So
are our captors—the Transhumanists, they're called.
Don't ask me how it's done; I couldn't begin to explain
that to you. But ask yourselves this: could this ship, or the
weapons you've seen, have come from anywhere in *your*
time?"

Hazeltine's expression was one of fascination warring
with incredulity. Carver's was simply blank. McCready's
reflected a struggle to assimilate the outrageous statement
he had just heard. He was the first to find his voice.

"See here, Mr. Thanou—or whatever your real name
is—"

"That's one of the two things I didn't lie about. The
other is that the Transhumanists are my enemies, as well
as yours. The fact that I and my party are locked up here
with you should prove that."

"I suppose it might. But . . . if what you're saying is
true, what the devil are you doing here?"

"Mondrago and I—that's also his real name, by the
way—are, well, police. The others with me are soldiers.
We came back to this time to do our duty, which is to
combat the Transhumanists. They captured us. We
escaped. That was when we met you. I was hoping to
come up with a scheme to take this ship, and persuade
you to help us."

McCready seemed able to take all this in—he didn't
even remark on the fact that the soldiers included two
women. But Hazeltine frowned with thought.

"I say, if you people are mucking about in your own

past, won't you . . . well, rather mess things up for the world you came from? Including, I should think, yourselves."

Jason's estimation of his intelligence went up another notch. "The possibility of doing that is strictly limited by something we call the 'Observer Effect.' But there are ways around it—nooks and cracks in recorded history. That's why, for example, the Transhumanists can snatch a small, isolated unit like yours in a remote war zone like the North-West Frontier. For all anyone knows, that Pathan ambush today wiped you out. And taking advantage of this to 'mess things up' for the future is exactly what the Transhumanists are trying to do. My job is to stop them."

The three sergeants spent a moment absorbing this. Then McCready shook his head as though to clear it of everything but immediate practicalities. "All right. Let's say you're telling the truth. Where are they taking us? Have they got some sort of hideout over the mountains, someplace like Kafiristan?"

Jason had to smile. "I'm afraid we're going a lot further than that. We're going to another planet—another world."

After a moment, Hazeltine broke the silence. "Another planet . . . like Mars, you mean?"

This, Jason reminded himself, was the era of Schiaparelli and Percival Lowell. "Not Mars. A planet you've never heard of, called Drakar. A planet of another sun—a star so distant that its light takes almost sixty-four years to travel here."

Carver's face was a study in rejection. "Light *traveling*? Garn! What does that even *mean*?"

"No, he's right," Hazeltine assured him. "Over thirty years ago, a scientist named Foucault measured the speed at which light travels. And recently, I've heard of some experiments by a pair of Americans named Michelson and Morley." Then he seemed to realize the implications, and turned to Jason. "But if it's *that* far away, how can we possibly get there? How long are we going to be aboard this ship?"

"A little over three weeks." All three sergeants gaped, although not, Jason suspected, for identical reasons. "Remember, I said we're moving very fast. We're going to be moving a *lot* faster."

"But *why*?" McCready's face wore a look of pained incomprehension. "We and our men and these Pathan women have got nothing to do with the games you and these, uh, Transhumanists are playing with each other. Why are they taking us to this Drakar planet?"

"As slaves," said Jason bluntly.

It seemed to stun the trio even more than everything else he had said.

"Did you say, 'slaves'?" asked McCready in a dangerous voice.

The *bhisti*, squatting nearby, overheard it and got to his feet, drawing himself up indignantly. "Who is slave? I am soldier!" Then, wilting under McCready's glare, he amended in a small voice, "Well, regimental *bhisti*."

"They're starting a colony on Drakar, so that over the next five hundred years it can grow in secret into a powerful ally for them," Jason explained. "But their numbers are very limited. They need a labor force. So they've kidnapped people—some from our own era, and taken them back in time. But you're not the first from late-nineteenth-century India."

He wasn't sure they were even listening. McCready just continued to glare. "Slaves?" blurted Carver. "*Slaves?* See 'ere, I'm an *Englishman!* What do they think I am? A nigger?"

"To them," said Jason, "we're all 'niggers.' Except that the word they use is 'Pugs.'"

"Slaves," was all Hazeltine said, in a dull dead voice.

"Not if I can help it," said Jason firmly. "I have a ship waiting for us in the planetary system of Drakar. Once we arrive, we have a chance if we can make contact with it."

"How are we going to do that?" asked Hazeltine, sounding more alive.

"I have no idea. We'll just have to improvise. But . . . well, I'm not one to give up."

"Neither are we," growled McCready.

"And as for our men," said Carver, "well, just let me tell you about Sikhs . . ."

Stoneman had gotten greedy. The compartment was hideously overcrowded, and there were more prisoners than there were bunks. They organized a system of shifts, and segregated the sexes, with Rojas and Armasova taking charge of the women.

At first, the Pathans refused to eat the mess in the trough, lest it contain any unclean items. But then, one by one, they began to consume it with no more distaste than that occasioned by its repulsiveness. And after a while, the women's improvised veils began to come off. It was as though verities dissolved in the face of incomprehensibly alien horror.

They tried to occupy their minds, simply to hold the stultifying boredom and discomfort and hunger at bay. The IDRF Commandos learned to communicate in nineteenth-century English, and all the time travelers picked up some Urdu. The Sikhs and Pathans, after they had gotten past ancestral antipathy, began to evolve a patois synthesized from Urdu and Pushtu, with a lot of English words. One way or another, they all came to be able to communicate after a fashion.

Occasionally, at odd intervals, guards with the dread batons entered on surprise inspections. Otherwise, the only times they saw their captors were the two occasions of which the guards came to bear away one of the women. It took McCready's best parade-ground roar to keep the Sikhs from trying to intervene, Muslims though the women were. Afterwards, when the desolately sobbing women were flung back in, all the men gave them as much space as possible while Rojas administered what comfort she could.

One "day," Jason was sitting with his back to a bulkhead. Carver settled down beside him. "Listen, mate, can I ask you something?"

"Sure."

"These Transhumanists . . ." The sergeant paused to organize his thoughts. "You've never really told us much about them, except that they're your enemies. But *why* are you fighting them? I mean, besides their bein' a lot of bloody slavers."

"Well . . . for about a hundred years, in the twenty-second and twenty-third centuries, they ruled the world. A revolution overthrew them, and they went into hiding. Now, in my time, they want to rule the world again."

"Oh." Carver nodded sagely. "Like Bonaparte."

"Worse. Much worse." Jason paused. *How do you explain genetic engineering and bionics and nanotechnology and all the rest?* "They don't just want rule the human race—they want to *change* it into something that's no longer even human. A ruling caste of supermen would dominate specialized castes that were more machine than man—in fact, that would blend machine and man in ways you can't imagine. They would be slaves that couldn't even *object* to their slavery, for they would be bred to it by the means of perverted science."

Carver's dark eyes were round as he stared nightmare in the face—a nightmare beyond the imagination of his time. When he spoke, it was in a tone Jason had never heard from him. "Tell me something else. Tell me about your . . . well, your country. I mean, your people. Your time. You haven't said much about that."

"Where to begin?" sighed Jason. "How can I tell you about a whole world? Could you tell me all about England—what it *means*? But I can tell you this much. We learned something from the time when the Transhumanists ruled. And what we learned was: *never again!* We've learned that Man must be kept Man."

"Well, I was with you anyway, but now I think I really see why I *should* be with you."

"As am I," said Hazeltine, who had overheard them.

"I don't want you men to be under any illusions," said Jason, prompted by his conscience. "I have nothing to offer you but a forlorn hope. The chances are excellent that we'll be killed."

Hazeltine smiled and stroked his fair mustache. "I still remember a few Latin tags from my school days. Here's one of them, from Seneca: *Qui mori didicit servire dedidicit.* 'He who has learned how to die has learned how not to be a slave.'"

CHAPTER TWENTY-THREE

By the time Jason's digital clock display showed that they must be nearing the Drakar system, a kind of standing committee had formed—a council of war.

It included Jason, Rojas, Mondrago, Hamner, the three British sergeants, and two others. One was the *naik*, whose name was Gurdev Singh. The other, to Singh's obvious lack of delight, was the Pathan leader, a certain Ayub Khan. McCready, Carver and Hazeltine had at first also had reservations about the mountain brigand's presence in their counsels. But Jason and Rojas had wanted every element of their ill-assorted band represented. And after a while the Pathan had earned the Sikh's grudging respect by holding his own in the exchanges of insults that Hazeltine assured Jason were the way their peoples expressed themselves. And he understood just enough of what Jason told him, through translation, of the Transhumanists to recognize them as servants of Shaitan.

"Before long, we will be nearing the sun of the planet Drakar," Jason told them, as they sat in a tight circle on the deck. He didn't mention how he knew the time so precisely, seeing no need to burden them with unnecessary shocks to their already-overburdened sense of reality. "When we approach it to within a certain distance, the . . . force which has been driving the ship very swiftly between the stars must shift into a different mode, moving much more slowly, so it can maneuver among that sun's worlds." He wasn't sure how much of this was getting through the murmured translations and translations of translations, but all the nineteenth-century people at least seemed to be accepting it at face value. "We'll know when that shift occurs, because there's a very slight sensation of . . . wrongness. People usually don't even feel it, when they're aboard a ship and have other ways of knowing what's happening. But down here in this hole—"

"Yes," Hazeltine nodded. "I seem to recall feeling something that couldn't quite be described, not long after we left Earth. It must work in both directions."

"Precisely. Anyway, after that it will be possible to communicate with the ship of ours that I told you about." *Assuming it's still there*, Jason did not add. He told himself that Palanivel *must* have stuck it out for over six weeks, because without him, Jason, to activate its TRD the ship would be stranded in the nineteenth century. But the deeply buried worry refused to stop gnawing away at the back of his mind.

For the first time, they all looked blank. "'Communicate'? How?" McCready wanted to know.

"Signal flags?" Carver speculated.

"No. Electronically."

"What?" McCready wore an uncomprehending look. "You mean telegraph? Or telephone? But how—?"

"Where are the bloody *wires*?" Carver blurted.

"No, wait a minute," said Hazeltine, waving him to silence. "I've heard that people have been experimenting with a wireless telegraph. Chap named Tesla, and another named Marconi . . ."

"That's the idea," said Jason with a nod. "Only this is voice, not Morse code—like a wireless telephone. It's called *radio*." He saw no point in trying to explain about different wavelengths.

"Blimey!" Carver shook his head. "What'll these boffins think of next?" Jason had a feeling that radio was close enough to things of whose capabilities these people *thought* they knew that it was somehow more impressive than time travel and space flight. Those things were so incomprehensibly far advanced that there was not even a horizon for them to be beyond.

Ayub Khan continued to simply look blank. But Gurdev Singh spoke. Over the weeks, in the linguistic pressure cooker of the slave quarters, he had picked up enough English and Jason had picked up enough Urdu that the latter was able to process the mixture he was speaking without too much difficulty.

"Forgive me, *sahib* from the future, I am only an ignorant soldier. But how does this help us? We do not have this wondrous *radio* of which you tell us."

"Good point," McCready admitted, giving the *naik* a surprised look.

"This ship has one—a long-ranged one."

"I don't fancy the blighters will lend us the use of it," said Carver dubiously.

Rojas answered that one. "If any opportunity presents itself—any chance at all, however small—we must try to get control of the ship's communications station, if only for a short time, and send out a . . ." She paused, even her impressive linguistic adaptability defeated by *nondirectional signal*. "A cry to our ship for help, in code. Our man Corporal Bakiyev is, among his other talents, the squad's qualified radio operator—the radio *wallah*, as you'd say."

"Major Rojas and Superintendent Mondrago and I have been aboard a ship of this class before," Jason added, recalling their incursion on Planet A. "In fact we've been all through it. So we'll be able to find the control room, where the radio is located." Again, he refrained from trying to explain his brain implant with its map display.

"Well and good—if we can get out of this compartment." Hazeltine gave Jason a hopeful look. "You mentioned that you and your people escaped once, just before you met us."

"So we did." Jason told them about Rojas' performance. "But they're not going to fall for that again."

Gurdev Singh looked him in the eyes. "Then, *sahib*, if the guards cannot be tricked then they must be overpowered, when they come on one of their inspections. And my men and I are the ones who should do it."

"But . . . you know those batons the guards have. One

of them was used on one of your men. He can tell you what it's like."

"So can I," McCready rumbled, barely suppressing a shudder.

The Sikh's expression did not change. "I know. But we would be useless in this *control room*. It is you from the future who must get there, to do what you alone can do. We will do that which we can do."

Jason said nothing. He lacked the words.

"By Allah!" Ayub Khan burst out. "Shall it be said in the mountains that the faithful held back when dogs of misbelievers dared this thing? Shall the others of the Maxdan sept of the Yusufzai tribe hear that Ayub Khan had less courage than a Sikh? No, by Allah! There are only four of us, but we will be in the forefront!" All at once, his villainous face wore a cautious scowl. "Just remember, Sikh, this does not make me thy brother!"

"Just as well," grunted Gurdev Singh, "since you undoubtedly bugger all thy brothers, after you tire of sheep."

"Nay, you Sikhs have left no sheep available, oh father of lambs."

"Nay, we are kept too busy by thy sisters, in the whorehouses of Peshawar—and picking off their lice afterwards."

As the exchange continued, Jason turned to Hazeltine and spoke in an undertone. "Are you *sure* these two are going to be able to work together?"

"Oh, yes," replied Hazeltine with a stroke of his by now scraggly mustache. "It's just the way they are, old man. Natives, don't y'know?"

✧✧✧

The Secondary Limit was passed, and they waited tensely, but no guards came to inspect the slave quarters. As the time crawled by, Jason began to worry that the Transhumanists were too busy for any further inspections before they reached Drakar.

The problem was that the surprise inspections *were* by surprise, so they had to stay in a constant state of readiness to spring into action without warning. The strain began to tell, most of all on the twenty-fourth-century people, least on the nineteenth-century Indians. Nor was Jason's state of mind improved by the fact that the sensation of the drive field's shutdown had occurred during the ship's "day." He had been hoping that they could make their desperate attempt during the nighttime shift, when there might be only one watch-stander in the control room and, with even more luck, Stoneman might be asleep.

But time continued to pass at the same agonizing pace. The lights dimmed, and Jason began to breathe a little easier about the last consideration, at least.

He was thinking about it when, with no more than the usual second or so of noise, the hatch slid open to admit two baton-carrying goons.

This time there was no attempt at subterfuge, and no tactical finesse of any kind. They had long since decided that their only hope lay in instant, furious action in accordance with a prearranged plan. Thus it was that as soon as the goons entered the compartment, no orders needed to be given. The three British sergeants led the Sikhs and Pathans in a sudden, silent, pantherlike rush, a wave of bodies that came as a total surprise to guards accustomed to seeing slaves cringe from their batons.

The silence lasted less than a second before being shattered by screams. The goons' enhanced reflexes took over, compensating for their astonishment, and they began to jab and slash with the batons. But the furious press of attackers swept over them and, by sheer weight, pushed them back—in opposite directions, away from the hatch, leaving the opening momentarily clear.

Knowing the agony he was leaving his allies to, and despising himself for it, Jason led Mondrago and the IDRF people between the two piles of thrashing struggling, bodies and through the hatch. As he went, he noticed the *bhisti* throwing himself into the scimmage.

"This way!" he yelled, glancing at his map display. They ran through passageways as empty as Jason had hoped, frantic to reach the control room before the alarm could be sounded.

That hope was immediately dashed. A wailing, nerve-shattering siren ululated through the bones of the ship.

Those guards must have implant communicators, thought Jason over the din. *We knew they probably would, but there was no help for it. And besides, the alarm they've raised will draw the others to the slave compartment, not the control room.* He led the way faster. It was all he could do.

They turned an angle in a passageway, and the control room hatch lay ahead. It was sliding shut, as a Transhumanist just inside manipulated controls beside its frame.

Without pausing for thought, Jason lunged ahead of the others, through the closing hatch. With the momentum of his body behind the force of his arm, he drove a fist into the Transhumanist's solar plexus. This one was of a technician caste, not maximized for combat like the goons. With a shrieking grunt, he doubled over. Jason kicked him in the temple, hard. Then he looked around. As he had hoped, the Transhumanist had been alone. He turned to the control box and slapped a switch. The hatch reopened, and his companions piled through. When they were all inside, he closed the hatch.

Mondrago looked around. There were no loose objects in sight. He took off the belt that was part of the Transhumanist's uniform, wrapped it around his fist as a kind of knuckle-duster, and used it to do the control box as much damage as he could without cutting himself too badly. "Maybe that will make it harder for them to open it from the outside," he explained.

Jason turned to the comm station, where Bakiyev had already seated himself. "Can you figure it out?" he demanded.

"Seems fairly standard," the stocky Kirghiz muttered. "Just give me a minute or two."

"I'm not sure we have that much time," Jason told him. "Make it snappy." He went back to the hatch, where Mondrago and the others had arranged themselves flanking the hatch. It was all they could do in the way of a defensive strategy, lacking any weapons. Jason had hoped the watch-stander would have a sidearm, but realism insisted there had been no reason for him to wear one.

"While we're waiting," said Rojas calmly, "should we

be smashing things in here? Maybe we could make the ship harder for them to control."

Mondrago looked around dubiously at the solid-state-based instrumentation. "I don't think these things would smash very easily, when all we've got is bare hands." He rubbed his raw and bleeding fingers.

"Besides," Jason added, "we don't know how much of it is integral to the ship's life support. And I'm not ready just yet to give up on living."

Before the discussion could proceed further, an ominous noise came from beyond the door. And a red spot appeared on the door's surface, then turned orange, and yellow, and white, and then began to spew sparks into the control room, followed by a blinding, narrow jet of flame.

Plasma torch, Jason knew.

"Bakiyev!" he called out in a strained voice.

"Just about there, sir."

Then the plasma jet vanished, leaving a cooling hole in the door. An obscenely serpentlike probe entered, with an exhaust vent at its forward point. There was a hissing sound, and a scent reached Jason's nose. He recognized it.

Knockout gas! It was, he reflected in a calm corner of his mind, the obvious tactic.

"Got it, sir!" Bakiyev called out, his voice beginning to slur toward the end. It was the last thing Jason heard before he slumped into unconsciousness among the equally inert bodies of the others.

CHAPTER TWENTY-FOUR

✧✧✧

Jason awoke in misery. His stomach churned and his head throbbed with the nausea and headache that were the invariable aftereffects of knockout gas. The rancid stench of the slave quarters didn't help. Neither did the moans from men still recovering from the neural stimulation of nerve-lash.

He felt blessed coolness on his forehead as a Pathan woman held a damp cloth to it. Mumbling his thanks, he sat up and slowly opened his eyes—agony even in the dim lighting. He lay alongside a bulkhead with the other twenty-fourth-century people, who were at varying stages of returning consciousness. Having verified that they were all present, he looked around the compartment.

The deck was littered with men, Hazeltine and Gurdev Singh among them, who lay twitching feebly and emitting the moans Jason had first heard. Others, including McCready and Carver and the *bhisti*, moved among them, helping the women dispense whatever comfort they could.

Jason was puzzled. If enough time had passed for him and the others who had inhaled knockout gas to regain consciousness, then everyone here should have more or less recovered from the experience of neural stimulation.

Carver came to his side. "I see you're awake, mate."

Jason nodded, which sent stabs of pain through his skull. "But what about these men . . .?"

"Ah. Well, the buggers somehow sent an alarm, because others arrived in a jiffy. Since you chaps had already gotten away clean, we stopped fighting and backed off."

"Yes. That was the plan," said Jason. There had been no need to prolong their exposure to unendurable pain.

"But you see, we had given a pretty good account of ourselves—"

"Yes, by Allah!" enthused Ayub Khan, who had appeared at Jason's other side. "We killed one of Shaitan's bum-boys, after McCready *sahib* broke his jaw!"

"—so they turned ugly. The leader—Stoneman, didn't you say his name is?—said they wouldn't kill us because they can't afford to waste slaves. But they picked some of us at random to make an example of. Held them down and kept those bloody batons on them for what seemed forever. The screaming went on and on, while the rest of us watched, helpless, with those carbines that you say kill with light held on us." Carver's expression turned even more grim. "One of the Sikhs died under it."

"Aye, cursing his tormentors with his last breath." Ayub Khan paused, then spoke as though the effort cost him a great deal. "That unbeliever was a brave man."

Jason nodded slowly. No one with any kind of latent cardiac malfunction could hope to survive prolonged neural stimulation. He was surprised they had only lost one man.

McCready joined them and addressed Jason without preamble. "Well? Did you—?"

"I'm pretty sure we did." Jason turned to Bakiyev, who was holding his head in his hands as though to keep it from flying apart. "Right, Corporal?"

"Right, sir. I sent the message. Of course, I couldn't receive any acknowledgment."

"Of course," Jason echoed.

"Why not?" McCready demanded. Then understanding seemed to dawn, and he nodded. "Oh. You were put to sleep with gas as soon as the message went out."

"That's right." It was true as far as it went, and Jason decided to leave it at that, without trying to explain a time lag that might be as much as several minutes, depending on *De Ruyter*'s location relative to this ship. In fact, he confidently hoped that Captain Palanivel had had the good sense not to put Stoneman on alert by replying.

"So," said Carver, "you don't know for sure whether your ship got the message."

"Or even," McCready added heavily, "if your ship is still here after all this time."

"I'm reasonably sure the ship has waited. You see, I'm the only one who can return it to its own time. But I won't lie to you: there's no absolute certainty."

"Well, then," said Carver with an attempt at his usual jauntiness, "we'll just have to wait and see what happens, won't we?"

"*Kismet*," said Ayub Khan serenely. "All things lie in the lap of Allah."

The women wailed, and the Sikhs and Pathans tried to outdo each other in stoic silence, through all of the sensations of atmospheric maneuvering and finally of landing. These sensations were their only warning that they had arrived at Drakar.

The wails continued, and the male expressions grew alarmed, when the artificial gravity cut off. Even the British sergeants looked nonplussed.

"Don't be alarmed," Jason told them. "This planet has a twelve-percent stronger gravity than Earth. In other words, you weigh a little more here."

"Gained it back, you mean," remarked Carver with a sour glance at the trough from which they had all eaten the minimum necessary amount.

With the usual lack of notice, the hatch slid open. A double file of goons armed with laser carbines entered, followed by others with batons, who herded the prisoners out and marched them to the cargo bay. There, Stoneman awaited them, twirling a baton lazily.

"Welcome to your new home, Commander Thanou. I regret to have to tell you that your quixotic stunt went for naught. Whatever coded message you sent has elicited no response of any kind, and nothing untoward has occurred." Stoneman's affectation of languid facetiousness wavered momentarily, and his eyes glowed with madness.

"I considered punishing you for that—rather severely. Then on reflection I realized that what awaits you here is punishment enough, even for you." He started to turn away, then paused. "But on second thought . . ." With a motion of almost invisible swiftness, he swiped the baton across Jason's left elbow. In a blaze of sickening pain, he collapsed. Rojas and McCready caught him. Stoneman smirked, and departed the cargo bay.

"I wish I'd been there to see it when that bastard got those burns," McCready ground out.

"I was there," Jason gasped, getting shudderingly to his feet. "I was sure he was dead. Unfortunately, Transhumanists aren't easy to kill."

The cargo port rumbled open, and the late afternoon sunlight of HC+31 8213 flooded in. The guards prodded them forward and down the ramp.

A G3v star's light was not perceptibly different from that of Sol—or of Psi 5 Aurigae under which Jason had grown up. And the sky was the familiar blue, with a few fleecy clouds. It might almost have been Earth . . . until one looked up at that blue sky.

Drakar's two moons, while small, were just massive enough to have been molded into spheres by their own gravity. And they orbited close enough to show discs far larger than that of Luna as viewed from Earth. And at the moment, both were in the sky, pale in the daylight but clearly visible. Their orbital motion of the inner one was quite perceptible, and even the outer one could be seen to move if one looked a few seconds. From somewhere a quote surfaced in Jason's mind: *The hurtling moons of Barsoom.*

There was not a sound from any of the nineteenth-century people. No wailing from the women, no curses from the men. Not even anything from Ayub Khan about Allah. Just silence. It was, Jason thought, as though the sight of those two huge swift moons in the sky, though arguably not the strangest thing they had experienced, had brought home to them as nothing else could the reality that they were on a different world, cast adrift on the cosmic ocean, severed by an unthinkable gulf from all the unquestioned assumptions that had formed the bedrock of their prior lives.

After a moment, Jason looked around at their surroundings. In one direction, below and over the top of a forest whose foliage was a bluish-green different from any native to Earth, spread an ocean, with the foreland sloping up from the shore to the forest. It must, he thought, be a west coast, for the afternoon sun hung above the ocean, laying a glistening golden trail on the waves. To the east of the rolling upland on which they had landed, the land rose into a range of mountains, the lower slopes clothed in dense forests, the peaks above gleaming with snow. Beyond loomed ever higher ranges.

Jason drew a deep breath of the moderately cool air. Accustomed to a variety of different worlds, he could tell that this air was, as expected, somewhat denser than that of Earth. But the difference wasn't a particularly noticeable one, and a higher oxygen content made it invigorating. It held the clarity only to be found on worlds that had never felt the touch of industrialization.

But that, he immediately saw, wouldn't last.

Perhaps a mile to the north of the level field on which

they stood was the beginning of a small city. Even at this distance, its architecture could be seen to be brutally functional. Around and beyond it spread tilled fields. On the outskirts were what Jason could see even at this distance were weapon emplacements, causing him to mentally curse. He had cherished a hope that the Transhumanists would rely entirely on secrecy as a defense here. But that would have been asking too much.

To the southeast the land fell away somewhat before rising again toward the mountains, and in this lower level was a large fenced-in compound, filled with rows of low buildings and surrounded by a high fence with guard towers at intervals.

There was no doubt in Jason's mind as to what that compound was.

"Get moving!" a guard snapped, and with frequent prods of laser carbines they were herded toward a row of grav carriers and packed inside. The carriers then glided along a rough dirt road, dust puffing up behind them, down the slope between fields of blue-green grass and occasional clumps of unfamiliar trees with feathery fronds. Jason guessed that the local ecology was almost but not quite as highly evolved as Earth's.

They passed through a heavily barred gate in the compound's fence—obviously an electrified fence, judging from the powerhouse near the gate. They came to a stop in an open area around whose fringes were shacks among which largely naked children played in the dirt—quite a lot of children, Jason thought. Adults were also in evidence—raggedly dressed, the men heavily bearded—and more were on the way, evidently curious in a listless sort of way to see the new arrivals. They included people of both Indian and European extraction, as well as various other stocks and mixtures of stocks. A number of the women were conspicuously pregnant. Beyond the shacks, rows of long, low, ramshackle buildings stretched away into the distance.

As soon as they were empty, the grav carriers glided around and departed, without a word from the guards.

"What? No orientation lecture?" said Mondrago in a half-ironic tone.

"No," said a new voice. "You'll be summoned whenever they want you. Otherwise, they don't give a damn."

The speaker was a strongly built man of medium height, more heavily bearded than most. He spoke in nineteenth-century English, but with an intonation that identified him as a native speaker of the twenty-fourth-century language. He stepped forward like the leader, or at least the official greeter, followed by another man, and introduced himself.

"I'm Ari Kamen. We weren't expecting any more arrivals—it's been so long. I gather you people are from India like the last few loads," he added, gesturing at the uniforms of the Sikhs and the British sergeants. But then he looked at what was left of the attire of Jason and his group, and looked puzzled.

"True, as far as it goes," said Jason. "But I and my companions are time travelers from your era." Kamen's eyes went wide. "I'm Commander Jason Thanou of the Temporal Service." He introduced the others. "We knew in general that the Transhumanists were up to something on this planet, and went back to 1897 to abort it. That was when we were captured on the North-West Frontier along with these other people."

"1897!" exclaimed the man with Kamen—an early-middle-aged man wearing what Jason recognized as the last tatters of a British uniform. "By Jove, I *told* you it's been nine years. Not easy to keep track, y'know," he added in an aside to Jason and offered his hand. "Captain Nigel Southwick, 4th Punjab Infantry."

McCready immediately drew himself up and barked, "Fall in!" As the Sikhs did just that, he went front-and-center before Southwick, saluted, and reported crisply. "Flanking party, 24th Sikhs, sir. Four dead, otherwise all present and correct." He hesitated, and added, "We were with the Malakand Field Force, sir . . . although I don't suppose that would mean anything."

"No, Sergeant. My men and I were with General McQueen's Black Mountain expedition in 1888 when we were captured. No one else has been brought in since."

"My group was the first," said Kamen. "We were working on a power plant in a remote area of Transoxania when they swooped down on us. Afterwards, they blew up the power plant to account for our disappearance. There are also others, all from out-of-the-way places. But after a while they stopped bringing in twenty-fourth-century people. Nineteenth-century ones like Nigel began to arrive." He wore a haunted look. "That was when we realized we had been sent back in time. We hadn't known what that unnatural sensation had meant."

No, you wouldn't have, thought Jason. "Yes, they explained it to us. Abducting people on twenty-fourth-century Earth was too difficult and dangerous, and besides, they were having to do too many temporal displacements. So they started doing their kidnappings on contemporary Earth, on the North-West Frontier and North America and other places. They sent their final slaving expedition not quite as far back in time as the others, because they had found out my group was going to appear in 1897." Jason could almost feel Rojas stiffen with the unjustifiable but nonetheless real self-reproach that she had never entirely overcome. "Their leader, you see, fancies he has a score to settle with me. Then, having captured us, they proceeded on to Earth to complete their quota. That's why we're a mixed bag."

"Well, we'll have to get you settled in." Kamen looked around at the shacks and the barrackslike buildings beyond. "Like everything else inside the fence, they leave that up to us. And they don't provide enough accommodations. We've cannibalized enough wood and other things from the buildings to put together the shacks. They're for people with children."

"Yes," said Rojas. "I was wondering about that. There seem to be a lot of children around . . ."

Kaemen answered her unspoken question. "Early on, we decided it would be wrong to bring children into this world. But the Transhumanists want to expand the slave population. So periodically, they come in here, stun some men and women and take them away—we've learned better than to resist. They impregnate the women by artificial insemination and throw them back in here. We have a few people with some sort of medical training. But a lot of the children die in childbirth. They don't care. They can always make more." He said all this in a toneless voice, as though outrage had worn away under the erosion of the years. "After live children are born, their mothers almost always keep them. Otherwise, some other woman takes them. Usually they pair off with some man. We've occasionally talked about killing the infants. But we can't bring ourselves to do it, even though we probably should."

Kamen stopped abruptly, his last word falling into a well of silence. After a moment, Jason spoke. "What's going to happen to us next?"

"Soon they'll come for the third shift, and you'll be in the same position as everyone else."

"What do you mean?"

"They divide the day into three shifts." (*Nearly twelve-hour shifts*, thought Jason, recalling this planet's rotation period.) "At any given time, a third of us are working—in the city, or in the fields around it, or in the mines up there in the mountains. They don't even try to regularize it; at the end of a shift they just bring back the workers and then take away another third of the adult population, they don't give damn who. So sometimes you'll end up working two shifts out of three. That's bad. But nobody resists them. They use those nerve-lash batons a lot. They like to use them. If you give them enough trouble, they keep on using it until you die."

Jason looked around. There was no one in earshot except Kamen and Southwick. "Tell me, what kind of defenses have they got here?"

"Well," said Kamen, "the guard towers around this compound have laser weapons—they've killed a few of our people who've cracked and tried to rush the fence.

Don't know why they bothered; the fence would have electrocuted them."

Those lasers will be merely antipersonnel models, Jason thought. "But what about the town over there? I could identify fixed weapon positions of some kind. Have they got any combat aircraft, or armed spacefcaft?"

Kamen look vague. "Well, I'm no military man. But they've got what look like some sort of weapon emplacements. And there are some small craft that that have a military look to them. I'm sorry, I can't be any more specific than that."

"And of course I know nothing about these confounded devices," added Southwick.

"Listen," Jason said in a low voice, "keep this to yourselves, because I don't want to raise possibly false hopes in these people. But there's a ship of ours in this system." (*I think,* he mentally hedged.) "And we think we've succeeded in signaling it. If so, it may be able to take some kind of action." He decided against sharing with these people the agonizing dilemma that prevented him from returning himself and his immediate companions to the twenty-fourth century.

The two men's eyes held a flicker of something that hadn't been there before. "What kind of action?" Kamen asked.

"And what can we do to help?" Southwick added.

"The answer to both is, I don't know. The ship's captain will have to use his judgment. But I have confidence in him."

The flicker guttered, but did not entirely go out.

❖❖❖

Night had fallen when, with a blaze of headlights, the entire fleet of grav carriers came gliding in and offloaded their passengers, staggering and reeling with exhaustion. Then loudspeakers commanded the slaves to come out of the barracks into the open, and baton-wielding guards, covered from behind by others with laser carbines, began to shove their way into the compound.

Jason looked around anxiously, trying to locate all his people. Rojas and Armasova were away, helping the Pathan women, who were encountering a good many of their fellows. (Not a great help, as those others were more likely than not to belong to tribes that were hereditary enemies of the Yusufzai.) Bermudez had gone with them to lend any aid he could. Otherwise, the commandos were not too far away, as were the three British sergeants. "Let's try to stay together!" he called out.

But that proved impossible in the shoving, terrified crowd, roiled by the guards whose batons everyone feared to touch. One of the Sikhs, along with Ayub Khan, were caught up in the mob being herded toward the carriers. And in the middle distance, Jason glimpsed Rojas, Armasova and Bermudez moving away, trapped in the press, until they too vanished into one of the carriers.

As soon as all the carriers were fully loaded, they swung about and departed, leaving Jason staring after them.

"They'll be back in about twelve hours, sir," Hamner tried to reassure him.

"Right," Jason nodded. "We'd better hope nothing else happens before then."

CHAPTER TWENTY-FIVE

The vicious crack of a weapon-grade laser in atmosphere and the roar of a collapsing guard tower shattered the night.

Jason came bolt upright from the stinking mat on which he had been fitfully asleep. Flashes of light through the slave barracks' windows illuminated the packed interior, and the crowd of sleepers awoke in shrieking panic.

"Come on!" he yelled over the uproar. Mondrago, Hamner and Bakiyev, who had bunked down as close to him as possible, responded at once. The three British sergeants, not far away, followed, their men scrambling after them with the *bhisti* in the lead. They struggled through the milling mob jamming the building's one door, and emerged into pandemonium.

De Ruyter hung overhead on gravs, its waist turrets

spitting crackling laser bolts at the guards around the compound's periphery while trying to avoid the frenzied crowds pouring from the barracks buildings. The collapsed tower lay on its side, shattered and burning. The other towers were firing at the attacker, but the same electromagnetic shielding that protected the crew from cosmic radiation in deep space could handle such relatively low-energy antipersonnel laser fire. As they watched, one of *De Ruyter*'s lasers lashed out at the powerhouse. With a buzzing roar and a spectacular shower of sparks, the electrified fence short-circuited and died.

Yelling madly, the crowd started to surge toward the area where part of the no-longer-lethal fence had been pulled down by the falling guard tower. It was a mad rush for freedom, heedless of whatever laser fire the guards could bring to bear.

As though sensing an opportunity, *De Ruyter* dropped lower and her ventral hatch began to swing down, forming a ramp that neared the ground. Palanivel must, Jason thought, must be glued to a viewscreen turned to full magnification and light enhancement, searching the crowd for familiar faces, because all at once a lateral thrust of her grav repulsion sent the ship gliding in their direction.

"Let's go!" he called to his group. They broke free of the press, and all that separated them from the descending ship was an open area . . . .

Then a file of goons appeared, deploying across the space between them and the ship, laser carbines levelled.

They must be under orders to take us—or, at least,

me—alive, if possible, thought Jason. *Or else we'd be dead. Which we will be if we try to rush that line.* And there was nothing Palanivel could do about it. *De Ruyter*'s starboard waist turret could be brought to bear, and its high-energy laser would vaporize the goons . . . and also consume Jason and the others, just beyond them.

For a moment that seemed longer than it was, the tableau held.

Jason became aware that the *bhisti* was standing beside him. In the flickering light of the fires, the sweaty brown face looked up and their eyes met.

"*Sahib*, I do not understand any of this. But this much I know: you must get away, for only you can defeat the evil ones. And I am nothing."

"No—" began Jason, who had never felt so unworthy in his life.

"Here, what's this, you?" demanded McCready, who had overheard.

The *bhisti* didn't answer him. Instead he hurled his water sack at the goons and, with an eerie scream, plunged toward them.

Startled by the sheerly unexpected, three of the goons obliterated the goatskin sack in mid-air with laser pulses. But the instant it took them to do it allowed the *bhisti* to reach them. Arms spread wide, he practically dove into their line, dragging the three lasers down. The other goons, to right and left, turned on him and fired. Steam exploded from his body as laser pulse burned their way through him.

But then a furious wave of bodies crashed into them. Jason had given no command; this was no carefully planned operation, as when they had rushed the guards aboard the transport. It was spontaneous. A couple of the goons got off shots, and Hamner and one of the Pathans died. Then the others were on top of them, punching and strangling and tearing. Jason grabbed a dropped laser carbine and used it as a bludgeon for beating the face on the goon he was straddling into bloody, broken pulp.

Abruptly, it was over. Carver and Hazeltine were standing over the corpse of the *bhisti*, and McCready was kneeling beside it. He spoke in a softer voice than Jason had ever heard him use, or ever thought he was capable of—almost too softly to be heard. "You're a better man than I am."

Jason tried to imagine what that admission, spoken of a man of darker skin, had cost someone of McCready's background. He failed. He put a hand on the big sergeant's shoulder. "Come on. We've got to get aboard."

McCready nodded and stood up. As he did, Jason looked down at the *bhisti*. It occurred to him that he had never learned the man's name. He was about to ask when Mondrago said, "Sir—look!" in a tone that made him look in the direction of the Corsican's pointing finger, through the darkness and the smoke.

In the distance, over the spacefield beside the Transhuman city, a firefly swarm of lights were rising into the night sky. Kamen had spoken of some sort of military craft based there . . .

"*Run!*" Jason shouted. And without waiting to see if he was being obeyed, he sprinted for the ramp and pounded up to the main deck, and forward toward the bridge.

There was no time to contemplate the loss of Hamner's steady competence, nor even any time to come up with an acceptable way to give the ship's captain an order on his own bridge. "Raise ship!" he snapped. "Now!"

"But . . ." Palanivel gestured at the scene in the viewscreen. A fresh wave of panicked slaves, desperately trying to reach the fence, had surged into his party, sweeping them apart, forcing them to struggle to reach the ship. "Some of your men are still out there!"

"We'll have to leave them," Jason forced himself to say. It was one more thing he might have time to try to come to terms with later. "There are fighters of some kind on the way. I don't know whether they're purely atmospheric or have space capability. But either way, if you don't move fast *none* of us are going to get away."

Palanivel needed no further urging. He rapped out a series of orders and slapped controls. Even as the ramp was retracting, the ship rose, rotated, and swept up and away. As soon as it had risen high enough to do so safely, Palanivel activated the photon thrusters, and under the combined thrust of that and grav repulsion *De Ruyter* soared aloft. In the view-aft the chaotic slave compound below, still illuminated by flames, shrank rapidly.

In that same viewscreen the fighters had also engaged their reaction drives. Behind them a larger shape was visible: Stoneman's transport. Jason wasn't worried about that; *De Ruyter* was faster and better armed. As for the fighters . . . Jason knew he could do no good here. He departed the bridge, leaving Palanivel to seek the Primary Limit, and went below to see to his men.

Mondrago had made it, as had the three British

sergeants and two Sikhs. Neither Gurdev Singh nor Bakiyev had; they, along with the rest of the Sikhs, were either dead or recaptured.

"Did you see what happened to the others?" Jason asked Mondrago. The nineteenth-century men, British and Indian alike, were sprawled on the deck in the throes of reaction and strangeness.

"No . . . I was a little busy. In fact I barely got away—jumped for it and grabbed the end of the ramp just as it was swinging shut, and rolled inside just before it closed. In fact . . ." Mondrago's voice trailed off, and he stared past Jason's shoulder. Jason turned, and saw a small slender figure silhouetted in the hatch.

For an instant, Chantal Frey gazed wide-eyed at the ragged, wildly bearded men. "I had almost given up hope," she whispered. Then she and Mondrago were in each other's arms. For a time, no one disturbed them.

After a while Mondrago, still holding her, turned to Jason, for her presence had reminded him of something. "Sir . . . I know you had other things on your mind at the time. But when this ship was down there in the compound, wasn't there a brief period when you could have activated our TRDs, and the ship's—" (a glance at Chantal) "—and sent us all back to Zirankhu in the linear present?" He paused thoughtfully. "Of course, I don't know the range of the 'control' function of your TRD, so I don't know if . . ." Then his expression went blank as the implications hit him.

"You've grasped it," said Jason with a bitter smile. "Depending on how far it is to these mines and agricultural plantations where they've been taken, I might or might not have been able to retrieve Armasova and Bermudez. But what about Rojas?"

"Rojas?" exclaimed Chantal.

"Yes. She's alive. It's a long story. But the point is, she has no TRD. The only way to retrieve her is to get her inside this ship." Jason decided not to burden Chantal with the knowledge that the fact that a similar consideration, applied to her, had been a major factor in keeping them in this time for this long.

"Well, sir . . ." Mondrago let the thought go unspoken.

"No," said Jason firmly. "I won't leave her stranded as a slave in this time unless I'm convinced there's no hope whatsoever of getting her back. Not to mention the fact that we're *really* out of range for Armasova and Bermudez by now." He reflected that Hamner's death had slightly simplified his problems, only to reject the thought with a spasm of self-disgust for having thought it. He dropped his voice and spoke to Mondrago and Chantal alone. "And besides, there's the little matter of . . ." He gestured at the British sergeants and the Sikhs.

"I was meaning to ask about these people," said Chantal with a puzzled look.

"Again, it's a long story. But the point is, there are some very real ethical issues involved in taking them into the twenty-fourth century with us. They'd be stuck there unless we returned them to their own time—which we could hardly do, with all they now know." Jason let them chew on that for a moment, while reflecting that this barely scratched the surface of the ethical issues. "And at any rate, I'm not yet prepared to give up on the possibility of doing some good here and now. Speaking of which, I need to get back to the bridge and find out if that possibility still exists. Alexandre, you handle the introductions." And he hurried out.

"We left the fighters behind just after going into stealth," Palanivel told him. "Maybe they couldn't reacquire us. Or maybe they don't have long-range deep-space capability. Either way, they're returning to the surface."

"Good," sighed Jason, gazing at the receding globe of Drakar in the view-aft. "But let's not rely exclusively on those possibilities. After we pass the Primary Limit, take us further out and put us into an orbit in the outer system where we can plan our next move."

"Right."

They had their first decent meal in what seemed like forever, and badly needed showers, shaves and haircuts. The British and Sikhs, who had been flabbergasted by the showers, had been assigned to the commando squad's now-vacant quarters, and were adjusting to the unfamiliar amenities, when Jason received an urgent call to come to the bridge.

Palanivel wore a grim look. "Our sensors are picking up something entering this system—something big."

"Another of those Transhumanist transports?" Jason was perplexed, for Stoneman had said his was the final delivery here.

"No, it's much too big for that. We're not close enough to get any detailed sensor readings, much less a visual, but we can infer how massive it must be."

Jason looked at the figure, and emitted a low whistle. Then he and Palanivel studied the newcomer's course.

"It's not headed for Planet B," said Palanivel.

"Or Drakar, as the Transhumanists call it," said Jason absently. "No, it seems to be following a search pattern. Let's get into an intercept course, so we can get more data."

De Ruyter eased out of its orbit under full stealth. As the gap between her and the mystery ship narrowed, it became clear that the latter's inferred mass was, if anything, on the conservative side. More details were hard to come by, for the target had some heavy-duty ECM . . . but not, it seemed, an invisibility field. Jason was puzzling over that lack, which seemed to remind him of something . . .

He was still trying to put his finger on it when *De Ruyter* shuddered and ominous sounds came from the engineering spaces.

"Tractor beam!" Palanivel gasped.

It was a truism that the long-range focused application of artificial gravity known as a tractor beam had the same effect on the negative mass drive as a planetary gravity field. In other words, if a ship was tractored it was the equivalent of coming within a planet's Primary Limit with the drive engaged—a sure-fire career ender for a space captain. It resulted in the drive's immediate shutdown, usually involving damage in varying degrees.

This, clearly, was what had happened to *De Ruyter*. While Palanivel took a report from his engineering officer, Jason marveled at the range at which it had been done. In addition to being big, the stranger was clearly a purpose-built warship, mounting a massive tractor beam generator and, doubtless, weapons to the same scale.

Palanivel finished his colloquy with the engineer and turned to Jason. "It could be worse. The damage to the drive is repairable. But it will take time."

"That's exactly what we haven't got. Try using photon thrusters to break loose."

But, as Jason more than half-expected, this proved futile. Inexorably, *De Ruyter* was drawn toward her captor, which soon became visible in the viewscreen under maximum magnification.

Mondrago and Chantal joined them. Mondrago didn't even need to ask what had happened. "The Transhumanists?" he queried.

"No," said Jason. "It can't be them. I don't know . . ." His voice trailed to a halt as he stared at the slowly expanding image of the strange ship. It could now be seen to be roughly an oblate spheroid, but with twin drive nacelles on the underside. No details could be made out, but . . .

All at once, Jason *did* know.

So, evidently, did Mondrago. "Am I losing my mind," he breathed, "or Is that—?"

"Yes," Jason nodded, not wanting to believe it, unable to take his eyes off the totally unanticipated horror in the viewscreen.

"What are you two talking about?" Palanivel demanded.

"Superintendent Mondrago and I have seen a ship like that. We saw it in the seventeenth century. It was much bigger than this one—a battlestation rather than a ship, really—but the same design philosophy. That, Captain, is a warship of the *Tuova'Zhonglu* Teloi."

CHAPTER TWENTY-SIX

✧✧✧

Palanivel stared uncomprehendingly. "But I thought the Teloi all died centuries ago, long before this era!"

"So does everyone else, except a select few," Jason sighed. This was no time for quibbling about security clearances or for wondering what Rutherford would say, and it looked as though Palanivel was going to have a definite need to know. "Since my expedition to Bronze Age Greece, it's been public knowledge that the Teloi were the reality behind the Olympian gods and all the other versions of the Indo-European pantheon, and that they had created *Homo sapiens*. But we've tried to be as low-keyed as possible about it, and I think most people are still in denial about the second part . . . or maybe it's just that it still hasn't registered on the popular consciousness. And we've emphasized the fact—and it is a fact—that the last of those 'gods' were long dead at least as far back as the seventeenth century.

"What we *haven't* made public is something else I learned on that seventeenth-century expedition to the Caribbean. The Teloi who, for their own crazy reasons, marooned themselves on Earth a hundred thousand years ago were the members of the *Oratioi'Zhonglu*, a . . . well, apparently 'zhonglu' is untranslatable. A subculture, or kinship group, or association, or . . . hell, club, for all I know. At any rate, while they were on Earth in their self-imposed exile, playing at being gods, their race entered into its ultimately suicidal war with the Nagommo. The military formed its own 'zhonglu,' the *Tuova'Zhonglu*, lements of which escaped the final cataclysm.

"That was sometime between the fourth and second millennia B.C.—probably a little more than forty-five hundred years before our time, hence four thousand years ago as of now, although we can't narrow it down any more precisely than that. Ever since, the *Tuova'Zhonglu* have been prowling the spaceways, stewing in their own hate, telling themselves that they didn't *really* lose the war—they were betrayed by the other Teloi, who'd proved themselves unworthy by failing to give the military their unstinting support and unquestioning obedience. As far as they're concerned, the near-extermination of the Teloi was a good thing, purging decadent, effete types like the *Oratioi'Zhonglu* and leaving only themselves—the purified and distilled essence of the race."

Palanivel stared at Jason. "And this is all they've done for *four thousand years?*"

"Remember, the Teloi gengineered themselves into near-immortality ages ago. The first generation of the *Oratioi'Zhonglu* were at least a hundred thousand years old when I made their acquaintance in the Bronze Age, although for some reason the lifespans of the younger, Earth-born generation were drastically reduced. They simply have a different time scale from ours. And the need to find something to fill their interminable, empty lives drove the Teloi insane, at least by our standards. I believe living beings simply aren't *intended* for immortality— evolution hasn't fitted them for it. But the *Tuova'Zhonglu* take the madness to another level. They are to the Teloi what people like the Nazis and the Transhumanists are to humanity."

"How do you know all this?"

"While in the seventeenth-century Caribbean, we were captured by Transhumanists who had made contact with a wandering *Tuova'Zhonglu* battlestation and, by making false promises involving time travel, tricked the Teloi into helping them found a cult by posing as gods. The battlestation was also going to share Teloi military technology with them." Jason saw the effect that had on Palanivel. "Now you're beginning to see why we've kept this from the public. No need to create panic and hysteria. Especially inasmuch as we managed to destroy the battlestation and scotch the Transhumanist scheme." *With the help of that brilliant bastard Henry Morgan*, he mentally added.

"But now here they are again, and they've got us," observed Palanivel glumly. "What are they doing here, in this system?"

"Who knows why they're ever in any particular place at any particular time?" Jason shook his head. "They wander the spaceways on the kind of incredibly extended schedules you'd expect, especially since they use suspended animation to prolong their lives even further I gather they're only occasionally in contact with each other or with their hidden base, wherever it is."

"I think you may have come up with the answer to your own question, Jason," said Chantal.

"What do you mean?" asked Jason, giving her a sharp look. It belatedly occurred to him to wonder why Palanivel didn't object to a civilian on his bridge.

"Well, the battlestation you and Alexandre destroyed came through the Solar system in the 1660s, almost exactly two hundred and thirty years ago. Given the long independent cruises you've described, many years probably went by before the others became aware it was missing. But then they naturally wanted to find out what happened to it, and where—"

"Of course!" Mondrago snapped his fingers. "Right. Remember, their movement schedules are *very* long-term—and, for something as big as the battlestation, probably pretty inflexible. So they knew what course it was supposed to follow."

"And so they sent ships to scour the systems along that course," Jason continued the thought.

"In the direction of Earth," said Chantal very quietly.

"And now," Palanivel added, gesturing at the magnified image in the viewscreen, "one of them has got us." He sagged in his seat, and for the first time Jason noticed how exhausted he looked. "I need a short break. Chantal, will you take the con?"

"Sure," she affirmed, then turned to meet Jason's and Mondrago's astonished stares. "Well, I had to find something to occupy my mind while waiting out here in the outer system all that time. So I got interested, and asked if I could have the controls explained to me, and—"

"She's turned into a pretty useful second relief pilot," said Palanivel. Then the realization seemed to penetrate his weariness-dulled brain that he had just admitted to a flagrant breach of any number of regulations. "Er . . . you won't . . .?"

"Relax," Jason assured him. "Extraordinary circumstances, and all that. We won't turn you in."

"Somehow," said Mondrago dourly, eyeing the viewscreen, "I have a feeling that getting in trouble when you get back to Earth is the least of your worries."

The Teloi reeled them in very slowly and carefully, lest undue haste cause the tractor beam's hold to waver and enable them to break loose. It gave them time to stare at the gradually waxing magnified image in the viewscreen and contemplate its implications.

Presently, details could yet be made out. The alien ship was bumpy with a variety of weapon blisters, external sensor components and superstructures of less readily obvious function. And it had the apertures that denoted a reaction drive. The battlestation had not possessed one. It had been purely a creature of deep space, and Henry Morgan, visualizing it as a hulk drifting at the mercy of the currents, had insightfully grasped its vulnerability as it approached Earth in free fall. This ship, on the other hand, would be able to maneuver within a planet's Primary Limit, although it wouldn't be exactly nimble, and it obviously wasn't designed to land on the surface and therefore wouldn't incorporate grav repulsion. Instead, it carried what looked like a fair-sized surface-to-orbit shuttle partly recessed into a ventral housing.

They made no attempt to communicate with their captors. Jason was certain any such attempt would be met with dead silence, knowing the supreme arrogance of the *Tuova'Zhonglu* Teloi. And besides, he wasn't ready to reveal the fact that he could understand and haltingly speak their language, having had it rammed into his brain by unsubtle direct neural induction during his captivity in 1628 B.C. So they could only stew.

Jason took advantage of their enforced idleness to go aft and give their nineteenth-century passengers an explanation of what was happening. It was extremely abbreviated but true as far as it went: their ship had been grappled by a ship crewed by beings from another planet. After all they had already been through, they took it surprisingly well. "I *knew* it had to come to that!" said Hazeltine with a weary smile. McCready merely grunted. The Sikhs' fatalism was unruffled. Carver gave Jason a hopeful look.

"See 'ere, mate, if there's going to be a fight, you know you can count on us. What do you want us to do?"

"We're working on that," Jason assured him, wincing inwardly at his own dishonesty. "Just wait here." He hurried back to the bridge, where Mondrago, Palanivel and Chantal were indeed hashing over plans. It didn't take long, given their extremely limited options.

"We can't fight them," said Palanivel, summing up the consensus. "Our weapons might be able to do them some damage, but this ship simply isn't intended to fight a major space combatant like that. They'd reduce us to our component atoms."

"They could have done that already," said Mondrago glumly. "The reason they haven't must be because they want information from us."

Palanivel turned to Jason and spoke like a man who didn't want to be the one to bring something up and didn't want his motivations to be misunderstood. "Sir . . . I know it's not my place to remind you of this, but you *do* have the capability to get us out of this and leave the Teloi wondering where we went."

"I'll well aware of that," said Jason, feeling all three pairs of eyes on him. *Yes, get us out of this and back to twenty-fourth-century Zirankhu. Us . . . and five nineteenth-century people. While leaving Rojas, Armasova and Bermudez permanently stranded on nineteenth-century Drakar as slaves.*

Once again, I'm face to face with my ethical dilemma.

And this time I may not be able to afford the luxury of ethics.

He was still thinking about it when Chantal spoke hesitantly. "Jason . . . there may be another way. In fact, we could even turn this situation to our advantage."

"What do you mean?"

"Well . . . are we agreed that they're probably here to find out what happened to the battlestation?"

"Yes, I think so."

"And didn't you tell me once that, for all their mutual contempt, the *Oratioi'Zhonglu* and the *Tuova'Zhonglu* did very occasionally communicate with each other?"

"Right. That's how the Transhumanists—through their *Oratioi'Zhonglu* contacts in the fifth century B.C.—learned that the battlestation was due to pass through the Solar System in 1669. Remember those extremely long-term movement schedules."

"Very well, then. Perhaps we could . . . ." She spoke on for a few moments, improvising as she went. Jason listened with gradually decreasing skepticism. By the time she was done, he was nodding slowly.

"It might work," said Mondrago.

"At least it's worth a try," said Jason with a final, emphatic nod.

They spent the few minutes remaining to them brainstorming the plan.

By the time the tractor beam brought them to a halt relative to the Teloi ship, that ship was close enough that magnification was no longer required. It filled the viewscreen in all its ugly, massive functionality, so different from the mannered, almost overdecorated look the *Oratioi'Zhonglu* had imparted to Teloi engineering.

For all its hideousness, the *Tuova'Zhonglu* aesthetic (if it could be called that) at least had the virtue of making it easier to recognize certain things for what they were. Like the point-defense blisters that stood ready to obliterate any missiles *De Ruyter* might launch in desperation. And like the heavy weapons turrets trained on them, ready to unleash gigawatts of ravening coherent energies.

As they watched, a gig detached itself from a docking cradle and crossed the space between the two ships. They made no move to resist as it extended a passage tube to *De Ruyter's* ventral airlock, in the engineering spaces near the stern. Jason left Palanivel on watch on the bridge and, accompanied by Mondrago and Chantal, both of whom knew Teloi, went aft and opened the inner hatch to admit two boarders.

This was only Chantal's second glimpse of Teloi. But by now Jason and Mondrago were almost used to the sight of the seven-to-eight-foot humanoids, with hair shimmering in tones of silver and gold, deathly pale skin, and long narrow faces whose sharp features included upward-slanted cheekbones and brow ridges. Beneath the latter were their most disturbing feature: enormous tilted eyes whose opaque blue irises seemed to have leaked some of their color into the "whites," which were scarcely less blue.

These were the characteristics shared by all Teloi, as was arrogance. But in place of the affectedly languid, supercilious arrogance of the *Oratioi'Zhonglu* of Jason's Bronze Age acquaintance, the arrogance of these two was of a harsh, stiff, intense kind, their almost nonexistently thin lips set in a permanent sneer. They seemed to belong to a different subspecies, despite the lack of physical divergence. Their clothing accentuated the difference: a kind of jumpsuit that Jason imagined could serve as an emergency light-duty vacuum suit, basically plain in shades of gray and bluish-gray but bedizened with insignia that gave it the unmistakable look of a military uniform.

They were armed with heavy handguns which seemed to combine a gauss needler and a laser in an over-and-under configuration. The one who seemed to be the leader used his to give a peremptory "through there" gesture in the direction of the airlock.

Jason didn't move. "I speak your language," he said in his best Teloi, and had the satisfaction of seeing the boarders' sneers collapse into open-mouthed astonishment.

"How—?" began the leader. Jason cut him off, in the tone of one who has better uses for his time than talking to underlings.

"That is not your concern. I wish to speak to your commanding officer—and I believe he will wish to speak to me. You see, I know what happened to your battlestation."

CHAPTER TWENTY-SEVEN

After a brief radio colloquy with their superiors, the two Teloi had ushered Jason into their gig, leaving Mondrago and Chantal to instruct the British sergeants to sit tight. The gig had crossed over to its mothership amid tight-lipped silence. Now Jason walked, under the guns of his captors, along passageways through a realm of austere functionality, feeling small in surroundings scaled to the Teloi.

Let's see, he thought as he walked, adjusting to the somewhat lower gravity to which the Teloi were native. *What was it that Henry Morgan once told me? Oh, yes: "Always behave as though you have the upper hand . . . especially when you don't."*

A hatch slid aside, and they entered what Jason decided he must call the bridge. Concentric semicircles of control consoles faced a large viewscreen in which *De*

Ruyter hung against the backdrop of stars. Overlooking it all was an almost thronelike chair behind a crescent-shaped control desk. The chair swiveled, and Jason found himself face to face with its occupant.

It never occurred to Jason to doubt that this was the captain—and not just because the insignia on his jumpsuit was more than usually elaborate. He had what Jason knew were the indicia of relatively advanced age, which was saying a great deal among a race whose lifespans were measured in tens of thousands of years. He also had the thin beard that characterized some but not all Teloi males, worked into a kind of scanty Vandyke. Most noticeably of all, he wore a patch over his right eye. Jason didn't know if the Teloi had regeneration technology, but their overall technological level suggested that they should. He wondered if, in the brutally militaristic *Tuova'Zhonglu* subculture, physical evidences of past violence carried the kind of prestige dueling scars had once carried among Prussian Junkers.

"How did you learn our language?" the captain demanded without any sort of preamble. His deep voice held a quality common to all Teloi voices, disturbing in a way that could not be defined.

So you're not going to deign to introduce yourself, thought Jason, still looking at the eyepatch. *Well, all the Teloi I've ever met have gone by names of mythological gods when dealing with humans. So I think I'll dub you "Odin."*

And I'm certainly not going to tell you anything that would reveal the existence of time travel, which you probably don't know about, since the battlestation never got to pass on the information it had acquired from the Transhumanists. In fact, I'm relying on your not knowing about a great many things, because I'm going to be telling you a great many lies.

"That," he answered, "is bound up with the question of how I know what happened to your battlestation. And I think that's what you really want to hear about."

For a moment the single alien eye flickered with fury, and Jason thought he might have gone too far. But Odin's curiosity won a visible battle with his arrogance, and he spoke in a tightly controlled voice. "Very well. Speak on . . . for now."

"First of all, I assume you know the origin of us humans."

"Of course." Odin's sneer intensified. "We were occasionally in communication with the effete exquisites of the *Oratioi'Zhonglu*. So we are aware of the subject race they produced on Earth, the planet to which they had exiled themselves, by genetic engineering of a local species." (*Homo erectus*, Jason mentally interpolated.) "Indeed, that was one of the reasons they chose Earth: the presence of a species which, due to a coincidental resemblance to our own evolutionary ancestors, lent itself to being molded into a kind of sub-Teloi. Thus they could have worshipers to lend a certain spurious substance to their dilettantish pantomime of godhood." Odin's contempt was unmistakable even across the gulf of species differences. His entire aspect fairly oozed it. "They evidently are all dead by now. Small loss."

"But we humans, as you can see, remained. And if you turn your sensors toward the inner system of this star, you will detect the energy emissions of a colony that a human faction called the *Transhumanists* founded here some time ago—more than two hundred and thirty revolutions of Earth around its sun, in fact."

Odin gave Jason a sharp look, obviously surprised that humans would have been engaged in interstellar colonization as far back as the seventeenth century. And when he got a closer look at Drakar, he might think it odd that a colony so long-established would be so small. But that, thought Jason, was a bridge they would have to cross when they came to it. For now, he hurried on, prevaricating freely.

"Shortly after the colony's foundation, your battlestation entered this system. The Transhumanists, by a pretense of friendship, tricked its commander into landing many of his personnel on the colony planet— Drakar, they call it. Then, with their usual underhanded treachery, they destroyed the unsuspecting battlestation. Those Teloi who had landed were captured. They are still there now, as slaves."

For several human or Teloi heartbeats, Odin sat rock-still. He would, Jason thought, find nothing implausible about the continued survival of the imaginary Teloi captives; two hundred and thirty years—or even ten times that—was nothing much in terms of Teloi lifespans.

"I get the impression," Odin said drily, "that you are no friend of these Transhumanists."

"Far from it. I belong to another human faction— *zhonglu*, if you will—that is their bitter enemy. They constantly raid us for slaves to ship to their colony planets. That was my fate. Along with many others, I was sent to

Drakar, where I met the enslaved Teloi and learned their language. They told me the story of how they came to be there.

"Finally, I and some friends managed to steal a small Transhumanist warship and get away. When we found ourselves tractored before we could escape from this system, I knew at once who it must be. My Teloi fellow-slaves on Drakar had told me that the *Tuova'Zhonglu* would undoubtedly send a ship in search of the missing battlestation. And now you know what happened to it. And," said Jason in conclusion, "now we are in a position to help each other."

Odin's sneer was back in full force. "For what conceivable reason would I want to help an inferior being like you? And you are hardly in a position to help anyone."

"I beg to differ. You need us, if you want to get revenge on the Transhumanists for their destruction of your battlestation."

"Need *you*?" Odin seemed to find the notion insulting. "Unlike the commander of the battlestation, who must have been an egregious fool, I will not be deceived by the Transhumanists' lies. And if your ship is a fair sample, the defenses of Drakar should give us little trouble. We will simply reduce the colony to radioactive ashes. Why do we need you for this?"

"Because," said Jason, slowly and distinctly, "we know where the Teloi prisoners are being held. If you go in without that knowledge, you will kill them along with everyone else."

This was a crucial moment, and a gamble on Jason's part. It was possible that the *Tuova'Zhonglu* ethos included a samurailike indifference to the lives of its own personnel; in fact, something of the sort would have seemed in character. But Jason was inclined to doubt it. The same species modification that had, ages ago, given the Teloi near-immortality had also—almost of necessity, if one thought about it—reduced their fertility to the point where they hardly ever reproduced. It was, Jason had often thought, one of the sources of their racial insanity. And it meant that they surely couldn't view losses with complete equanimity. He paused as though giving Odin an opportunity for a response. But none was forthcoming, and with an inward sigh of relief he resumed.

"Here's my proposal. Let our ship go. It has very sophisticated stealth, and unlike you we can infiltrate on Drakar. We'll get the Teloi aboard and out of danger. Then you can come in and destroy the Transhumanist installations at your leisure."

"Why do you want to do us any favors?"

Jason restrained himself from declaring he had seen the light and come to properly revere humanity's creators, or anything along those lines. It probably would have worked with Zeus in his decline; Odin, on the other hand, might be crazy but he wasn't stupid. "Isn't it obvious? You have us. This is all we can offer you in exchange for letting us go."

Odin seemed to reflect a moment. "Very well. Agreed—with one exception. You will take this ship's shuttle. Your ship will remain in orbit, covered by our weapons, as a . . . surety for your good behavior."

"But I told you, our ship can—"

"Our shuttle has a full stealth suite." Jason recalled

that the Teloi did not possess the invisibility field, but he had no reason to doubt that otherwise their ECM capabilities were commensurate with the rest of their technology. "It can insert you and a landing party a safe distance from your objective, then retrieve you and the freed Teloi prisoners." Jason opened his mouth to speak, but Odin cut him off with an imperious gesture. "Enough! I demean myself by offering explanations to a lesser life-form. It is for us, the universe's natural masters, to give commands, and for all others to obey. Obey this command, or die."

"Very well," sighed Jason, out of options. "We'll do it your way."

It was a subdued conference that met aboard *De Ruyter* after Jason's return.

"This changes things," said Palanivel glumly after Jason had finished his account.

"That's one way to put it," agreed Mondrago.

"What are we going to do, Jason?" asked Chantal.

Good question, he thought. Their plan had been very straightforward. They would land *De Ruyter*, break into the slave compound, and find Rojas. As soon as she—along with any of the other twenty-fourth century people they could manage to snatch—was aboard the ship, and the three IDRF commandos in the compound at least within range of Jason's control TRD, he would immediately activate it and they would all snap back to their own time and another world, leaving the duped Teloi to vent their rage on the Transhumanists.

All very neat . . . except for the problem of the five

Indian Army men. They had been forced to consider the option of simply leaving them on Drakar with the rest of the slaves, to hopefully survive the destruction of the Transhumanist colony and make do in its absence. The alternative was to keep them aboard *De Ruyter* and whisk them to the incomprehensible world of the twenty-fourth century, from whence they could never return. They had concluded that the latter was the lesser evil—they owed a debt to these men, and Jason's entire being rebelled at the thought of simply abandoning them. He had decided he would get them back aboard *De Ruyter* in time if at all possible—that is, if the press of events permitted it. That "if at all possible" was, he admitted to himself, something of an evasion—a way of putting off the final decision until circumstances took the matter out of his hands. But it was the best he could do.

Now, it seemed, some rethinking was called for.

"I can see only one viable alternative plan," he said slowly. "We get Rojas, Bakiyev, Armasova and Bermudez aboard the Teloi shuttle, and then, while its pilot is wondering where the 'Teloi prisoners' are, we overpower him—hopefully he's the only Teloi aboard—and force him to take off and go into orbit. There, while we rendezvous, I put Odin off with some story about how the Teloi slaves had already been killed. While I'm still sweet-talking him, we hastily get Rojas aboard *De Ruyter*—and at that moment I activate the TRDs."

"You realize, Jason," said Chantal, "that this means we can't even try to rescue any of the other people from our own time, because we can't possibly have time to get them inside *De Ruyter*."

"No," said Mondrago. "And if we pop out of existence with them still in that shuttle, I don't even want to think about what this Odin would do to them afterwards. They'll be better off trying to survive on the surface."

"It also means," said Jason grimly, "that we can forget about all our soul-searching where our five nineteenth-century guests are concerned. For exactly the same reason—over and above all ethical questions about taking them into the twenty-fourth century—they have to stay behind."

"We and they have been through a lot together," Mondrago reminded him. "And they've stood by us. I don't like the thought of just . . . ditching them."

"Do you think I do?" Jason reined in his temper. "Look, I'm not any happier with this than any of you. But this is a situation where there are no good alternatives. Does anybody have another plan to offer?"

None of them did.

"No," said Mondragon. "And if we pop out of existence with them still in that shuttle, I don't even want to think about what this Othu would do to them afterwards. They'll be better off trying to survive the life surface."

"It also means," said Jason grimly, "that we can forget about all our soul-searching when our five-nineteenth-century guests are concerned. Boy, exactly the sanity reason—over and above all—head questions about taking them into the twenty-fourth century—they have to stay behind."

"We, and they have been through a lot together," Mondragon reminded him. "And there we stood by us. I don't like the thought of just abandoning them."

"Do you think I do?" Jason replied in his temper. "Look, I'm not any happier with this than any of you, but this is a situation where there are no good alternatives. Does anybody have another place to offer?"

None of them did.

CHAPTER TWENTY-EIGHT

✧✧✧

To Jason's relief, at least one of his working assumptions proved accurate. The Teloi shuttle's crew consisted only of the pilot, who looked on with the expression of an Easter Island statue as they filed aboard from *De Ruyter*.

Chantal stood beside the airlock as Jason, Mondrago, and the five Indian Army men departed. She and Mondrago had had a little time together earlier, and now they parted with only a silent touch of hands. She wore the same expression she had when she had seen him off on their ill-fated reconnaissance of the Transhumanist transport . . . but, it seemed to Jason, not exactly the same. This time it seemed to hold an element of fatalism that bothered him in a way he could not define. But he didn't have time to let himself worry about it, as he led the way into the shuttle.

Jason had done his best to prepare the nineteenth-

century men for the sight of a Teloi. The Sikhs muttered
to each other and made certain signs, and the British
sergeants maintained stiff upper lips with an effort. But
that was all, and they settled silently into the outsize Teloi-
designed couches, arranging their weapons.

Their choice of the latter had, of course, been limited
to what was left in *De Ruyter*'s small armory after the
losses when they and the commandos had been captured
seemingly so long ago. For one thing, they had lost all of
their strength-enhancing combat environment suits,
without which not even McCready could have handled
the spare Mark XI plasma gun. But they had three spare
gauss battle rifles, and the sergeants carried these. There
had, of course, been no opportunity for live practice;
Mondrago had barely had time to put them through dry
runs. Jason hoped their overall familiarity with projectile
weapons would stand them in good stead, even though
they had been astonished to learn that electromagnetic
impulse, not gunpowder, propelled the slugs. Jason and
Mondrago carried the laser carbines intended for in-ship
action, as did the sepoys, whose instruction hadn't
included any attempt to explain how they worked. Jason
and Mondrago also had gauss needle pistols as sidearms,
and Mondrago had been delighted to find a vicious-
looking combat knife that must have been a private
possession of one of the commandos. He and Jason also
had, hanging from their utility belts, hand grenades
somewhat larger than the thimble-sized ones fired by the
battle rifles' integral launchers. Jason's belt also supported
a fairly bulky communicator with orbital range.

Jason looked everyone over. Carver gave him a cocky

wink. He looked away. He wasn't finding it easy to meet the eyes of these men to whom he was lying. He had assured them that the plan was to get everyone back aboard *De Ruyter*, which would then fly away in accordance with a foolproof plan he had to escape the Teloi. Their unquestioning acceptance of his assurances made it even worse.

He turned to the pilot and spoke curtly in Teloi. "Take us down."

Under cover of darkness and the shuttle's ECM, they descended from orbit and settled down just beyond a low range of hills to the east of the slave compound. It was a fairly long walk to the compound, but Drakar had a long night. And it was mostly downhill.

Jason wore light-amplifying goggles, and under the stars and the great swiftly moving moons he led the way in a half-circle around the darkened compound to the location of the powerhouse that *De Ruyter*'s lasers had fried, near the gate. Taking as much advantage as possible of a thinly wooded area, they slipped through the odd alien trees and Jason switched his goggles to magnification. As he had expected, the powerhouse was under repairs—the work suspended for the night—but the Transhumanists had rigged a portable emergency generator to keep the fence electrified.

He consulted his brain implant for the time. From the one opportunity he had had to observe a change in shifts, he had been able to extrapolate the three-shift schedule. When the night shift returned, for a short while all the slaves would be present in the compound, and the gate would be open. It had been the basis for his timing of their insertion, and he saw with relief that his calculations had worked out. The shift wasn't due to return for a little while yet. He gave a hand-signal, and they settled in to wait at the edge of the grove, grateful that this hemisphere of Drakar was in a mild season. And, in accordance with their premission briefing, Carver handed his battle rifle to Mondrago.

Dawn was near when the headlights of the grav carriers appeared, gliding along the dirt road. This time, the caravan was led by a large glide car. The gate swung open and the first of them began to glide through into the compound's open area.

Mondrago, who wore a pair of goggles like Jason's, used the slide action of the battle rifle's underslung electromag grenade launcher to ready a grenade for firing. Taking careful aim, he sent the grenade toward the generator and, with a rapid pumping action, followed it with two more while it was still in flight.

The series of explosions shattered the predawn darkness, followed almost instantaneously by a harsh rasping sound as the generator burst into glaring flame. A ripple of sparks ran along the fence as it died.

"Go!" shouted Jason, and they sprinted across the short distance. Transhumanist guards tried to close the gate, but the grav carriers had it blocked. The slaves inside one of the carriers forced its hatch open and came boiling out. The driver jumped to the ground and whipped out a sidearm. McCready cut him in two with a burst from his battle rifle, stopped for a fractional second to stare at his weapon in awe, and then ran on.

Guards were converging from both sides, and the antipersonnel laser atop the nearest guard tower began to spit pulses of energy. Hazeltine pumped grenades at it, missing with the first two from sheer inexperience, but then scoring a hit which caused the weapon mount to explode into flames and a burning guard to fall screaming to the ground like a falling torch.

Jason dashed ahead, through the milling mob of slaves around the grav carriers. He tossed a hand grenade at a file of guards, then dropped to his stomach and speared one of them with a bolt from his laser carbine just before the grenade exploded among the others. Then he sprang to his feet and ran on, the others close behind firing blasts of suppressive fire to right and left whenever they could do so without collateral slaughter. All at once they were through the gate and into the compound, where slaves were pouring from the barracks buildings.

"Elena! Bermudez! Bakiyev! Armasova!" Jason yelled the names at the top of his lungs. He was hoping that the IDRF people were all keeping together in a group. This was no time to be searching them out individually.

"I know where they are!" cried a new voice. It was Captain Southwick. "They're this way, where Kamen is organizing an attempt to breach the fence."

"Let's go!" said Jason. Southwick led them between two buildings to the fence beyond, where a crowd of slaves led by Kamen were using boards ripped from their quarters to press the wires out and down. The ground around a nearby guard tower was littered with laser-burned corpses . . . but now its laser was being used against the nearest tower.

Jason turned to Southwick. "What happened here?"

"Well, these people scaled the tower—"

"In the teeth of laser fire?"

"—and overwhelmed the guard. Good show, actually. That's your Corporal Bakiyev up there now—handy chap with that weapon."

But Jason was no longer listening, for he had spotted Rojas. "Elena!"

She waved to him and broke away from the crowd, followed by Armasova and Bermudez. In their wake came Gurdev Singh and a couple of sepoys.

"One of our men was killed scaling the tower, *sahib*," Gurdev Singh reported to McCready. "So was Ayub Khan. He led the way up, calling on his Allah even as he was burned by that devil-weapon." His voice held an admiration Jason would never have expected to hear.

"Jason," said Rojas urgently, "is *De Ruyter* here?"

"No, it's in orbit. It's a long story, which we don't have time for. Just take my word that I've got transportation out of here. Let's get you armed." He and Mondrago drew their pistols. "Unfortunately, we've only got two sidearms."

"Give them to Bermudez and Armasova," said Rojas. "I'll take that combat knife." Mondrago handed it over with no very good grace.

"The fence is down," Carver called out, pointing to the rush of slaves who were pouring through the breach into the open fields.

"Right," said McCready. "Let's step lively."

And all at once, Jason's dilemma, temporarily forgotten in the heat of battle, was back in full force, as he faced these men he could not take with him. And it could no longer be evaded.

What am I going to say . . . ?

Jason was still trying to decide when he was blinded by headlights and a glide car, the hum of its overdriven grav risen to a harsh buzz, came screaming around the corner of the nearest barracks building in a tight turn that caused it to angle crazily. Their group scattered, save for Southwick, who was caught head-on, the life crushed out of him.

It was, Jason had time to think, the car they had seen leading the procession of grav carriers—and about which they had forgotten. Now they could see that it was a heavily armored military model with a remote-control laser turret mounted on the roof. As the glide car settled to a halt, that laser spat bolts at the guard tower, whose weapon emplacement exploded. And Jason knew Bakiyev was dead.

Then the turret swiveled, turning its rapid-fire laser pulses on them. Carver screamed and went to his knees as the coherent energy grazed his upper left arm. They all fell prone, firing at the glide car. But the light laser carbines couldn't penetrate its armor, and the grenades that McCready and Hazeltine fired were antipersonnel versions, not shaped-charge armor-piercing ones. They exploded harmlessly.

Then, from behind them, came Stoneman's voice.

"Drop your weapons or she dies!"

In a calm corner of his mind, it occurred to Jason to wonder what had brought Stoneman to the slave compound on this particular night. But the question didn't seem terribly important at the moment. Clearly, he must have gotten out of the glide car before it had attacked, and circled around behind them while it had monopolized their attention.

Very slowly, Jason turned around. Stoneman had surprised Rojas, grasping her from behind, and now held her with both arms pinned to her side, with a gauss needle pistol to her head.

"Do as he says," Jason ordered in a dead voice.

Weapons were lowered to the ground, and the glide car's other three occupants emerged, holding laser carbines.

"Very good, Commander," said Stoneman. "We could, of course, kill all of you. But I prefer to wait. It won't be long before this disturbance is quelled. Our fighters should be overhead any time. Afterwards, I will deal with you at my leisure. Oh yes, I'll take my time—"

Rojas suddenly went limp in Stoneman's grasp, causing that grasp to momentarily loosen. Which freed her left arm just enough to get an overhand grip on the hilt of the combat knife in her belt. With a convulsive movement, she stabbed backwards with it, into Stoneman's belly just above the crotch. Then, as he released her with a cry of pain, she yanked upward using hysterical strength, slicing his midriff open almost to the solar plexus.

There was nothing human in Stoneman's scream as he sank to the ground.

His men's moment of stunned immobility gave Jason and the others their chance. They scooped up their weapons and opened fire. The lasers were infinitesimally faster, but the battle rifles' hypervelocity slugs tore the Transhumanists apart in a shower of blood.

Jason and Bermudez, the commando squad's collateral-duty medic went to Carver. "He'll be all right, Commander," said Bermudez after a brief examination.

"Good," said Jason. He picked up Carver's battle rifle, and walked over to where Stoneman was still squalling as he thrashed about in a tangle of his own guts while Rojas stood over him with her dripping knife. He put one foot on the Transhumanist's chest to hold him still, placed his weapon's muzzle against his forehead, and squeezed the firing stud. The top of Stoneman's head blew out with massive hydrostatic shock, in a gusher of brains and blood, leaving what was left of the skull holding an empty cavity.

"*This* time, I'm pretty sure he's dead," Jason remarked.

"Sir, we'd better get going," said Mondrago. "Remember what he said about the fighters."

Jason nodded. He turned to McCready and Hazeltine and, with a sudden inspiration for which he despised himself, pointed at Carver. "You and your men stay here and take care of him. We'll bring the shuttle back here for you."

"Right," said McCready, although his eyes held a puzzled look. Jason could not meet them.

The first hint of light, behind the mountains, was starting to turn the eastern horizon pale as Jason, Mondrago, Rojas, Armasova and Bermudez left the compound behind and headed east. Jason raised the shuttle pilot on his communicator and spoke in Teloi. "We're on the way. I'll leave this communicator on. Home in on it."

The long-range communicator had a tiny vision

screen. The pilot's face wore the standard *Tuova'Zhonglu* expression as he said, "Acknowledged."

Presently, the shuttle appeared over the low ridge to the east, visible against the half-light. As it approached, Rojas stared. "Jason, what—?"

"It's a Teloi surface-to-orbit shuttle." As her mouth fell open, he hastened on. "I *told* you it's a long story. For now, suffice it to say that we've got an arrangement of sorts with a warship of the Teloi. They're going to destroy the Transhumanist colony for us, and this shuttle will get us up to orbit. Our next problem is going to be getting you aboard *De Ruyter* so I can activate the TRDs. That's going to take some improvisation."

As he spoke, the shuttle drifted down on grav repulsion and hovered just high enough to allow its lowered landing ramp to touch the ground. Weak with relief, they staggered toward it.

It continued to hover. Nothing happened.

"Go ahead!" Jason snapped into his communicator to the pilot. "Lower the ramp! Let us aboard!"

There was no response. The ramp remained sealed.

Then the shuttle rose, swung about, and swooped away. The apertures of its photon thrusters came alight and it accelerated rapidly, seeking the sky.

"*Stop!*" yelled Jason. Silence answered him.

They stood staring as the glow of the reaction drive dwindled overhead and vanished.

"Sir . . ." said Mondrago. He pointed behind them.

From where they stood, the lights of the Transhumanist settlement and its spacefield were visible in the distance to the northwest. The fighters were rising aloft.

CHAPTER TWENTY-NINE

The Teloi ship and *De Ruyter* were above this hemisphere in their common orbit—it had been one factor in the timing of the raid—and Jason was frantically trying to raise Odin when the formation of fighters came overhead. Ignoring the small group on the ground, they rose at a steep angle of attack and soared spaceward.

"That's one small favor," said Rojas. "They spotted the shuttle and are pursuing it."

Jason was in no mood to be encouraged. "They'll be back," he predicted. Ceasing his futile efforts to reach the Teloi, he switched frequencies and raised *De Ruyter*.

Palanivel appeared in the communicator's vision screen, with Chantal behind him. "What's happening up there?" Jason demanded.

"Why, nothing, Commander," the young captain replied. "They're still tractoring us, and—"

The image and the voice vanished, replaced by snow and a screech of static. Then, after a moment, an image came back into focus . . . but it was the face of Odin, against the backdrop of his bridge. *Some kind of override feature,* Jason told himself. The Teloi face wore an expression that caused Jason to recall a snatch of poetry: "sneer of cold command."

"Send your shuttle back down here!" Jason snapped. "For some reason the pilot—"

"Silence, you presumptuous ape! Do not attempt to deceive a higher form of life, your creators and natural masters! Our shuttle pilot saw that your group consisted only of humans. So obviously you either lied about Teloi prisoners or failed in your efforts to rescue them. Either way, you are of no further moment to us. The pilot was, of course, under instructions to leave you and return to orbit in this not entirely unforeseen event. The fighters pursuing the shuttle are even now coming into range of our antishipping weapons . . ."

Mondrago touched Jason's arm and pointed up toward the sky, where a number of stars still shone. All at once those stars were joined by a cluster of fireflies that immediately winked out of existence. The fighters, Jason thought, must have vanished like moths in a flame at the touch of that ship's gigawatt laser beams.

"And now," Odin's relentless voice continued, "I will deal with the Transhumanist colony here. Since this world may turn out to be of use later, I will not use nuclear weapons. Nor will they be necessary. Kinetic energy weapons should suffice." Then, as an afterthought: "But first I will rid myself of the nuisance of having to spare your ship a certain amount of attention." And then, abruptly, Odin cut the connection.

It took some fraction of a second for what Odin had said to register on Jason. Then, with trembling fingers, he raised *De Ruyter*.

"Commander, I'm glad to see you again." Palanivel's face looked troubled, as did Chantal's, looking over his shoulder. Beyond them, the bridge's viewscreen was visible. The Teloi ship, too near to require magnification but tiny despite its size, floated in it. "Something's going on up here. They just fired on some small craft coming up from the planet, and now their ship is precessing as if it's turning toward us, and—"

"Go to full boost with your photon thrusters!" yelled Jason, horribly aware of the futility of what he was ordering. "Break free of that tractor beam if you possibly can!"

Palanivel opened his mouth to reply. As he did, something flashed on the flank of the Teloi ship.

The image in the vision screen shuddered sickeningly, and through the audio came a deafening roar, and the indescribable sound of tearing metal. As Jason watch in horror-stricken helplessness, the bridge filled with smoke and showers of sparks from cut, flailing electrical lines. A structural member collapsed with a crash behind Palanivel and he fell forward and collapsed atop the pickup, so nothing could be seen of Chantal.

"Chantal!" shouted Mondrago desolately.

Then the snow and the static returned, followed by the image of Odin. The Teloi did not gloat, any more than a man would gloat for having squashed an insect.

"I have disabled your ship," he stated, "so I no longer need expend any energy on a tractor beam to hold it."

Mondrago shoved past Jason's shoulder, grasping the communicator. "You goddamned soulless butcher!"

Odin ignored him. "I will now proceed with the elimination of the human presence on this planet. Afterwards, we will examine the wreckage of your ship for any information it may yield. And then I believe I will continue on to Earth. It is evident that your species has advanced to the point where it can pose a significant inconvenience to us. It should therefore be cut off at its source. This ship will undoubtedly be insufficient in itself to deal with the problem. But we can reconnoiter, and subsequently an adequate force can be dispatched." All at once madness flickered in the strange alien eye and quivered in the disturbing alien voice. "Creating you was a mistake of those decadent fools of the *Oratioi'Zhonglu*. Now we of the *Tuova'Zhonglu* will correct that mistake." And with that the screen went black.

Jason started to try to reestablish the connection, but then halted. *What's the point?* He turned and met the stunned faces of his companions. Mondrago's eyes had glazed over; he had gone beyond fury into shock.

With nothing better to do, they looked back the way they had come. Downslope to the northwest, the fire-illuminated slave compound was like a disturbed hive as the escapees swarmed away, seeking places to hide. Some of them went in the grav carriers, doubtless driven by twenty-fourth-century people. Still further northwest, visible by virtue of their somewhat higher elevation, were the lights of the spacefield and the Transhumanist town.

For several moments, nothing happened.

Then, overhead in the slowly lightening sky, Jason glimpsed a rapidly descending star.

He only had time for that glimpse before it became a straight, eye-dazzling lightning bar that impaled the town.

Kinetic energy weapon, he thought automatically, recalling Odin's words. *Once referred to, four hundred years ago when the idea was first thought of, as a flying crowbar.*

A small object of super-dense metal, descending at orbital velocity and blazing with air friction, resembled what late-twentieth-century people had thought, mistakenly, a laser weapon would look like when it hit a planetary surface. And at that velocity, an explosive warhead would have been superfluous.

"Another one!" said Rojas, pointing upward. Instead of following her gesture, Jason put his goggles back on and set them for maximum magnification. He focused on the town just in time to see one of the weapon emplacements consumed by the strike. Another was burning.

Precision strikes, he thought. As he watched, he saw the Transhumanists' slave transport lift off in an attempt to get away. It was barely aloft when a line of unbearably intense light speared it and it erupted in a holocaust of flame, its debris showering the field in a rain of fire.

Staring at the death agonies of the Transhumanist colony, Jason barely noticed when the communicator beeped for attention.

What the hell does Odin want now? he wondered as he pressed "Receive."

But the face that looked out of the vision screen was

the soot-smudged, blood-streaked one of Chantal Frey, against the backdrop of *De Ruyter*'s bridge, half-ruined but with its viewscreen still showing the Teloi ship.

"Chantal!" Jason yelped. At that sound, Modrago practically leapt from despairing lethargy to sudden wild hope, rushing to Jason's side and looking over one of his shoulders as Rojas looked over the other one. All three of them started to speak, but she cut them off.

"Listen! There isn't much time. Palanivel is dead, as is almost all the crew. Life support is going fast. The drive is wrecked, and the weapons are inoperable. *But*," she added, her eyes flashing with a strange light, "somebody is still alive back in the engineering spaces. And he says he can give me power in the photon thrusters. And remember, I've learned the rudiments of piloting this ship."

Afterwards, Jason was always certain that at first he genuinely didn't understand. "Chantal, what are you talking about? You can't possibly get away on photon thrusters. Where would you go? And besides, the Teloi would blast you apart before you could get—"

Then, with almost physical force, understanding crashed home. And from the stiffening of the bodies to right and left of him, he knew Mondrago and Rojas also understood.

"Chantal," he resumed in a voice charged with urgency, "you mustn't to this. There's no point—it can't work. Their weapons can—"

"Maybe not." She was strapping herself into the pilot's couch and punching buttons even as she spoke. "They think they've totally crippled this ship, so they're probably not paying any attention to it. This will be so unexpected that there'll be a delay before they fire. Hopefully, the element of surprise will be enough." She paused in her preparations and turned to face the pickup directly. "And besides, I *have* to do it. This Teloi ship can't be allowed to get away. Now that they know what we humans are capable of, they won't stop here. They'll continue on to Earth. And if they report that Earth is a potential threat, God knows what the *Tuova'Zhonglu* will do."

She wasn't listening to Odin, when he said the same thing, Jason thought. *And she knows they won't attack Earth now, in the nineteenth century—the Observer Effect prohibits that. But it doesn't preclude a reconnaissance that nobody on 1897 Earth notices and records. And it also won't stop the* Tuova'Zhonglu *from subsequently sending an expedition, on their centuries-long movement schedules, that arrives at Earth after our time. She figured it all out on her own. Why am I not surprised?*

Mondrago leaned forward, as though to power the sheer force of his will into and through the communicator. "Chantal, *no!* Don't try it—just lay low!"

To Jason's astonishment, Rojas added her voice. "Chantal, *please* don't! We'll—"

"You'll what?" asked Chantal, wiping the blood from a scalp cut out of her eyes. "You have no way to come up here and get me. And my TRD and the ship's are out of range of Jason's control function. Anyway, as I said, the life support won't last much longer." Her expression changed, and she spoke to Mondrago alone. "So you see, Alexandre dear, I'm already dead. Think of me that way. And remember that I loved you."

And with that she turned away from the communicator to the control board and punched more buttons. All at once, her small frail body was visibly pressed back into her chair by acceleration. *The inertial compensators must be dead,* thought Jason in the midst of his swirling maelstrom of emotions. And in the viewscreen in front of her, the Teloi ship swung into line, dead ahead.

She'll never make it, Jason thought desolately. *She'll be vaporized by their defenses first. She'll have died for nothing.*

Unless . . . maybe a brief distraction . . .

Yes. That might offer her a chance.

I must give her that chance.

These thoughts flashed through his mind in an instant. In appreciably the same instant, he cut her off.

"What?" Mondrago blurted into his ear. Before the Corsican could say or do anything more, he raised Odin.

He had feared the Teloi would simply disdain to answer. But the arrogant alien face appeared on the screen, wearing a look of exasperated irritation.

"There's something you need to know," said Jason without preamble.

"What could an animal such as yourself possibly have to say that I need to know?"

Behind Odin, across the control center, Jason could see another Teloi gesturing for his captain's attention. Odin, facing the comm screen, didn't see the gestures.

"There's . . . there's another Transhumanist installation on the other side of the planet," Jason desperately improvised. "It holds most of their military capability. You can expect retaliation from it shortly."

The lower-ranking Teloi's gestures had now grown frantic. But he was behind and to the right of Odin, who of course had no peripheral vision in that direction.

"Why are you telling me this?" Odin seemed amused.

"If you'll agree to pick us up, I'll tell you where it is."

Odin sank back into his chair, exuding complacent contempt. "This is a pathetic lie. And at any rate, why would you—"

But now the subordinate was committing what had to be a major breach of discipline by shouting, and pointing at what must be a vision screen outside the comm pickup. Odin, his attention finally engaged, turned, and his gaze followed that pointing finger. He froze with stunned realization, and swung back to face Jason. His look of horror was almost human.

Jason laughed in his face.

"Die, you miserable piece of filth!" he snarled, and with a savage gesture switched Odin off and Chantal back on. In *De Ruyter*'s viewscreen, the Teloi ship was swelling with soul-shaking rapidity.

Mondrago snatched the communicator from Jason's hands. *"No, Chantal!"* he screamed.

For the barest instant, as the Teloi ship expanded to fill the viewscreen, Chantal turned her head with an effort and glanced over her shoulder. Her eyes and Mondrago's met. And then the communicator's screen went black.

"No!" Mondrago repeated, shaking the communicator frantically.

Did the ship's communicator give out? Jason wondered. *Or did she switch it off, not wanting Alexandre to see?*

He was still wondering when a light overhead caught his eye. An intensely bright new star appeared in the sky, instantly growing into a dazzling mini-sun, and a glowing halo of superheated gas and debris expanded swiftly outward from it before dissipating into nothingness. Then the new celestial intruder guttered and went out.

With a barely human wail, Mondrago sank to the ground, a heap of despair and grief, heaving convulsively. Rojas and the commandos knelt around him. Rojas' face was wet with tears.

Was she still conscious at the end? Jason asked himself. *Or had she already passed out from the G forces? I will never know. So I will believe the latter.*

I must believe it.

CHAPTER THIRTY

Dawn was laying salmon-colored streaks across the pale blue sky when they stumbled back into the wrecked, largely abandoned slave compound and sought out the British and Sikhs. As Bermudez tended Carver, the others confronted Jason.

"What's happening?" McCready demanded. "First those lightning bolts, or whatever they were, started coming down, and then we saw that bloody great blaze of light in the sky, and then the bolts stopped, and . . . well, anyway, where's the shuttle?"

Jason felt drained of everything, including the capacity to lie. "It's been destroyed," he said in a dull voice. "So has our ship. So has the Teloi ship. I'll tell you the details later."

Their reactions varied. Carver, in his pain, blinked with bewilderment. McCready frowned intensely as the implications of what Jason had said slowly sank home. Hazeltine already grasped those implications, judging from the look of grave comprehension with which he met Jason's eyes. Gurdev Singh was unreadable.

Before any of them could speak, a grav carrier approached and came to a halt. Ari Kamen got out, looking relieved.

"Commander Thanou! I'm glad I found you. What's happened? What were those . . . missiles from space? Did your ship fire them?"

Kamen, Jason recalled, was no military man. "They were kinetic projectiles. And no, it wasn't our ship that carried out the strike. It was the Teloi."

Kamen's jaw fell. "The *Teloi*? But . . . but . . . I've heard of them, of course, but I thought they were long since—"

"No. I'll tell you—I'll tell everyone—all about it later. But right now we don't have time."

"That's right," said Rojas, stepping up to Kamen. "Give us a sitrep . . . that is, tell us what the situation is here."

Kamen seemed to stand up a trifle straighter. "Well, the Transhumanists' fighters flew away and never came back. And those, uh, kinetic projectiles destroyed all the weapon emplacements and other military targets— barracks and so forth. But they had only destroyed a few other targets before they stopped falling."

"That makes sense," Jason said to Rojas. "The late Odin's precision strike hit the high-priority targets first. After that, had they been allowed to, they would have proceeded to systematically obliterate the town, and then every trace of human presence on this planet."

"Yes," said Rojas, almost too softly to be heard. "Chantal stopped that." She turned brisk again. "So the Transhumanist survivors must be mostly unarmed civilian types."

"That's the impression we've gotten. We gathered up weapons from the dead guards here, and are getting organized to take the town." Kamen looked pointedly at the group's weapons.

Carver waved Bermudez aside and got unsteadily to his feet. "Just give me one of those pistols, mate," he said to Jason with his old raffish smile. "I've still got one good arm."

Jason looked around at the faces of humans from two different centuries—the soldiers of Queen Victoria and the soldiers of the Confederate Republic of Earth—and saw nothing to discourage him. Even Mondrago was functioning—maybe as a robot for now, but, Jason was certain, a deadly robot.

He shook off his physical and emotional exhaustion and hefted his battle rifle. "What are we waiting for?"

Evening had fallen by the time the fighting was over. As expected, resistance had been light, for few armed and trained Transhumanist soldier-caste types had survived the orbital strikes. For the most part, it had been more a matter of trying to prevent the unarmed ones from escaping into the countryside. In this, they hadn't been altogether successful. But now the town was theirs, and the ex-slaves wandered the now-quiet streets in a daze, still adjusting to the fact that they really were *ex*-slaves.

A large building in the town's center must have been

the governmental headquarters, for it held a conference room whose wall featured the symbol of the Transhuman Dispensation: a hand holding aloft a sword whose blade impaled the DNA double helix. Or rather it *had* featured it, for the rampaging liberated slaves had smashed the bas-relief into unrecognizability. The entire chamber was pockmarked by laser burns and marred by bloodstains but it was still usable. And now an *ad hoc* organizing committee met there. Besides Jason and Rojas, the three British sergeants were present, and so was Ari Kamen and two assistants—a twenty-fourth-century archaeologist and an 1880s North American rancher—he had co-opted to help him now in the absence of Captain Southwick, who had been his right-hand man.

Mondrago was also there. He was, to all appearances, functioning normally. Indeed, anyone who knew him less well than Jason did would not have noticed that there was anything missing in his eyes. The wiseass was dead.

By now, Jason had related the entire story, and explained everything. He came to the end, hoarse and in need of Scotch. At first, there was silence around the table.

"So," Kamen finally said, "now that you and all your people—all the surviving ones, that is—are together here, you can flick your group back to the twenty-fourth century at any time?"

"Just by *thinking* it," muttered Carver to no one in particular, shaking his head.

"Right. As I've told you, my original intention had been to get you and as many of your people as possible aboard our ship, which had its own TRD." *Although God knows how we would have made the selection,* Jason reflected. "But now, of course, with the ship gone . . ."

"And by the same token," said Hazeltine, "you can't get us back to Earth." It was a statement, not a question.

"And not us, neither," added the rancher.

"No, I can't. In addition to our ship, the Transhumanist slave transport was destroyed. They were the only deep-space vessels here." *And therefore,* Jason thought drearily, *they had to be destroyed, because history does not include any people returning to late nineteenth-century Earth with the knowledge you now possess. As always, reality protects itself—no matter who has to get hurt or die in the process.* "So you people from the nineteenth century are also here for good. And . . ." Before he could stop himself, his eyes went to Rojas, and instantly slid away.

But she smiled. "Don't look embarrassed, Jason. I understand. I know you tried—*how* you tried!—but my fate was sealed the moment Stoneman brought me back to this time without a TRD. I know I'm stranded here. But that's all right. In fact . . ." She turned to Kamen. "We're all stuck here on this planet together. We have to start our own colony. I'll do all I can to help. And thanks to Chantal we've got something left here to work with."

"That's true," said Kamen, nodding. "The utilities here are still more or less functioning—we've got drinking water, and electric power in most areas, and I think it can be restored in the others. And the mines and the agricultural fields are untouched."

"And we have something more important than that. We have a purpose!" Rojas' voice grew vibrant. "We know what the Transhumanists intended to do by planting this colony: create an ally that would seem to appear out of nowhere from beyond the frontier sometime shortly in the future that we came from. Well, we can do exactly the same thing!" She turned to Jason, her dark eyes blazing. "So sometime after your time in the linear present, Jason—it has to be afterwards, the Observer Effect requires that—a new civilization is indeed going to appear. But that civilization—the whole culture that we and our descendants build here—will have a tradition of hatred for the Transhumanists! Its foundation-myth will tell it that it is descended from people enslaved by them. It will be an ally for the true humans of Earth." She turned back to Kamen and the others. "We can lay the foundation for that. The Transhumanists planted the seeds of their own destruction by bringing us here. We can do it!"

Yes, I believe you can do it, thought Jason, staring at her. *And I think I have a pretty good idea who is going to end up as leader here.*

McCready spoke up. "You're going to need a militia. We and our men can help with that."

"Right," Carver put in brightly. "We'll get 'em on parade!" But then he and his two fellow sergeants gave Rojas a slightly odd look, as though they still found something just a bit incongruous about a woman in a leadership role who was not the Queen.

You'll get used to it, Jason thought with an inner chuckle. *You'd better!*

Through it all, Jason's brain implant had continued with *idiot savant* single-mindedness to keep the time on

Zirankhu for him to summon up at will. So he knew it was now daylight at the longitude of the outdoor displacer stage there, allowing them to arrive there without the psychic disorientation of materialization in darkness. There was no further need for delay.

Jason, Mondrago, Armasova and Bermudez stood in the glare of the lights (this was one of the areas where the electricity worked) and said their final goodbyes. When Jason came to the trio of British sergeants he gave particularly firm handshakes. "Good luck with that militia of yours. You should be kept busy by the surviving Transhumanists who got away. They'll be skulking up there in the hills. And remember, they're stranded here too; Stoneman said they were displaced without TRDs."

Kamen overheard him, and frowned. "That reminds me of something, Commander. I haven't mentioned it before, but it's something you might want to know. The colonists here are fanatics who voluntarily stranded themselves in the past. But they told us that it isn't *always* voluntary."

"What do you mean?"

"A standard punishment for disloyal or incompetent members of the Transhumanist underground is temporal exile. They're sent back to some particularly dangerous and unpleasant time and place in Earth's history with no TRD, to survive as best they can with no preparation, orientation, equipment, or anything except period clothes, and with whatever bionics they possess deactivated."

"*What?*" Jason stared at him. "You mean the Transhumanists are so irresponsible that they—"

"Their feeling is that the Observer Effect will prevent these exiles from changing history, so there's no danger."

"Maybe there's something to that. But still . . .!" *My God, if I'm this shocked, how will Rutherford react when I tell him these exiles are scattered through the past?*

Mondrago spoke thoughtfully. "It must be a very effective threat to hold over their underlings. The idea of having to live under primitive conditions, on the same footing as the Pugs around them, with no advantages except those that their genetic upgrades give them, has to be horrifying. And I can just imagine some of the milieus they get dropped into. Nanking just before the Japanese took it, maybe."

"I can think of a few myself. Remember, I've seen the Thirty Years' War and the Fourth Crusade's sack of Constantinople." Jason turned to Kamen. "This is something whose implications we're going to have to think about long and hard. Ari, thank you for the information." Jason shook hands with him, and finally turned to Rojas. "Elena, I don't suppose I'll ever be able to look at the night sky without thinking of your descendants here on Drakar."

"No!" she said sharply. "Not 'Drakar.' Don't ever call it that."

"You're right," he said contritely. "You people will have to come up with a new name for this planet."

"Yes." She turned to face Kamen and the other former slaves. "And I intend to urge—as strongly as possible— that we name it 'Frey.'"

Is this something you need to do—a way of making amends for having unfairly distrusted her? Jason wondered. *I don't know. You probably don't know yourself. But it doesn't matter. Your motives are irrelevant. The point is, it's totally right.*

"I think that's very appropriate," he said aloud. "I also think she'll figure prominently in that 'foundation-myth' you mentioned." He took one last look around at the people he was leaving behind, then took his position with Mondrago and the two commandos. "Farewell."

He composed his mind to the state of concentration required to give a mental command.

"Hey," the irrepressible Bermudez suddenly piped up, "you'll also need a name for this town. How about naming it after that water-carrier? What *was* his name, anyway?"

McCready opened his mouth to reply. But by then the neural command Jason had given was irreversible. Reality dissolved like a dream and, after an interval that could have been either eternity or instantaneity, reformed. And the four of them stood on a great displacer-circle with HC-4 9701 shining overhead. The Xinkhan Desert of Zirankhu stretched away to the horizon in all directions.

CHAPTER THIRTY-ONE

"So Mario McGillicuddy is still on Earth, eh?" asked Jason, taking a swig of *dugugkh* and handing the bottle back to Lizh'Ku with a shudder.

"Yes," said the aged Zirankh'shi. "He told me he would be there in rehabilitation for a while after his arm was regrown. But he also assured me he'd be back."

"He told me that too. I'm afraid he was probably telling the truth." Jason shook his head and chuckled.

There was a delay while Narendra Patel arranged transportation back to Earth for him and Mondrago. Jason had decided to make use of the enforced wait to keep a certain promise. So he had made his way to Lizh'Ku's shack, carefully avoiding bumping his head as he entered. And now Lizh'Ku reminded him of that promise.

"But surely you have a marvelous tale to tell me, of your adventures since we last saw each other," he prompted, his tapering whitish-furred snout twitching with curiosity and his huge old eyes bright. Behind him, Luzho'Yuzho sat with writing materials at the ready.

"That's right. I promised that you'd be the first to hear the story if I lived through it. I also told you that it would put a strain on your ability to believe strange yarns." Jason retrieved the bottle, pleasurably imagining the stroke Rutherford would have if he knew some of the things that he, Jason, was about to reveal. *To hell with him. I owe this being.* He launched into the story, sometimes resorting to awkward circumlocutions in order to get certain concepts across. At first Lizh'Ku passed things on in translation to Luzho'Yuzho, but eventually he stopped and just listened.

By the time Jason was finished, night had fallen on Khankhazh and he was beginning to think one might get used to drinking *dugugkh*. Eventually. Maybe. As for Lizh'Ku, he sat silently for so long that Jason began to wonder if he had gone to sleep. But then his nictitating membranes shuttered open and his eyes held a twinkle.

"Thank you for the wonders you have shared with me. There's only one problem: when Luzho'Yuzho writes this narrative, no one will believe him!"

Jason grinned. "There's an individual named Rutherford who would be very relieved to hear you say that."

He was still thinking of that exchange three weeks later, as he and Mondrago faced Rutherford across the desk in his Australian office.

The full report of the expedition, including the audio and video record of Jason's implant, had been delivered and studied. It had given the Authority a great deal to think about, and Rutherford was still trying to assimilate its implications. When he spoke, he took refuge in the immediate and the concrete.

"You'll be pleased to learn, Jason, that on the basis of your report the idea of disbanding the Special Operations Section has been dropped. Indeed, Councilor Kung has been going about declaring that he has *always* been strongly in favor of the Section, and that its successes—including that of this latest expedition—have always been due to the inspiration he has provided with his unswerving support and charismatic leadership."

"Of course," said Jason tonelessly. Mondrago's face was absolutely expressionless.

Rutherford cleared his throat. "The Section may be more essential than ever, now that we know of the Transhumanists' nefarious practice of exiling their transgressing personnel in the past. Of course, they can't do this with any of the obvious cyborgs—only with those that are, to all outward appearances, human. And I gather that any internal bionics are removed or neutralized. But the fact remains that there are—or, rather, were—interlopers in the past with various genetic upgrades. Stronger, quicker . . ." His voice trailed off and his expression grew stricken as he contemplated the possibilities.

"As Ari Kamen told me, they're counting on the Observer Effect to prevent any unintended consequences," Jason reminded him. "Of course, we consider it irresponsible to rely on it that way. But if there's any truth to our theories, anything these exiles do

in the past has *always* been part of the past." A thought
occurred to him. "It might be worthwhile investigating
some exceptional individuals known to history, especially
those whose origins are mysterious."

Rutherford's eyes went wide, for he immediately
grasped what Jason was driving at.

Mondrago spoke up, for the first time. "If we can
locate any of these people in the past, they might be
turned into sources of intel for us. After all, they can't be
too favorably disposed toward the Underground, after
what it's done to them."

"The idea has distinct possibilities, and will be taken
under consideration," Rutherford approved, still looking
shaken. Then he resumed in his earlier desperately
matter-of-fact vein. "And now I suppose we can tell the
IDRF—and the Deep-Space Fleet, if necessary—that it
is all right to go ahead and destroy the Transhumanists'
temporal displacer installation on Planet A, as we're
calling it."

Jason leaned forward and spoke sharply. "I strongly
advise against that."

"I beg your pardon?"

"Don't you see, Kyle? Stoneman told me that his slave-
catching expedition in 1897 was their last visit to the
Drakar colony, and that it was a one-way trip, made
without TRDs. In other words, the Transhumanists in our
era aren't expecting him back. So they have no way of
knowing that their colony came to grief. Hell, they don't
even have any way of knowing that we were there—or, for
that matter that we know about the colony, or about their
displacer.

"But if we destroy the displacer, they'll know that at the very least we know about it. And they'll have to wonder how much more we know—and how much we may have done.

"No. Let's leave their displacer alone and let them think they've gotten away with planting their colony. They'll just continue to leave that planet alone, for the reasons Stoneman gave me."

"Hmm. Yes, I see your point. Let them keep expecting to have the support of a highly developed colony of Drakar on *The Day*, when in reality . . ." Rutherford's eyes took on a faraway look. "To think, the colony of Frey is out there, not quite fourteen light-years beyond our frontier, and has been there since just before the turn of the twentieth century without our knowing it! One can't help wondering what sort of cultural amalgamation has evolved there. To take just one example, they're descended from nineteenth-century Christians, Hindus, Sikhs and Muslims, plus the full range of twenty-fourth-century beliefs. What kind of religious fusion—or fusions—will they have developed in the course of almost five centuries?"

"That time-span brings up something else," said Jason grimly. "Think about it. The Teloi battlestation was destroyed in the Solar System in 1669. Two hundred and twenty-eight years later Odin's warship, following its course and trying to find out what had happened to it, came to the system of Drakar, or rather Frey—and then *it* was destroyed. As you've pointed out, that was almost five hundred years ago."

"Are you saying—?"

"Yes. Even on their time-scale the *Tuova'Zhonglu* have had time to mount yet another search, this time for Odin's ship."

"If they've wanted to," Modrago said suddenly. "Maybe they simply cut their losses and gave up on that particular route as bad luck. Oh, yes, I know: *we* wouldn't, in their position. We'd keep on trying to find out what was eating our ships. But the Teloi don't think like us. In fact, by our lights they're madder than the March Hare."

"Here's another possibility," said Jason. "At some point they *did* send another ship, and it got as far as Frey. But by then the Freyans, as I suppose we have to call them, were strong enough to deal with it."

"Well," said Rutherford, "the one thing of which we can be reasonably certain is that no Teloi warships have appeared here in the Solar System. So presumably one of your two theories is correct, and the problem has been halted, at least for now."

"Thanks to Chantal," said Mondrago bleakly.

"Ah, yes." Rutherford suddenly turned solemn. "I understand how you feel, Superintendent, and we all share your loss. Dr. Frey's act of heroism will be remembered."

"It certainly will," said Jason. "Especially by the Special Operations Section, as we deal with the Transhumanists."

"As *you* deal with them? I remind you that you are an instrument of the Authority, and that your function is to carry out its policies, formulated by older and wiser heads." Rutherford drew himself up rather huffily and spoke with an organization man's prim disapproval. "Am

I to understand, Jason, that the Special Operations Section has now taken it upon itself to unilaterally declare war on the Transhumanist underground?"

"War? No." Jason turned to face Mondrago, and the two shared a moment of perfect though unspoken understanding. Then he turned back to Rutherford, and met the older man's eyes unflinchingly. "No, we're not declaring war. We're declaring vendetta."

The air of the room seemed to freeze into silence, and Rutherford could not quite suppress a shiver as he looked into the two men's eyes and knew that this was not his rite, and that it was out of his hands. After a few meaningless words, he dismissed them.

By unspoken mutual consent, Jason and Mondrago stepped outside. It was a moonless night, and the desert air was chilly, for it was July—mid-winter in the southern hemisphere. It was also the time of year when Serpens, though a northern constellation, was visible even in these southern latitudes.

They looked up into the sky, so clear that the lights of the installation could not altogether banish the stars. Their eyes turned toward the northern horizon.

Jason had never had any interest in descriptive astronomy, least of all from the vantage point of Earth. But since his return he had learned how to pick out Serpens, that strange bifurcated constellation. He had also learned where, relative to the constellation's stars in that region of the sky, HC+31 8213 lay.

Of course a mere G3v star was not a naked-eye object at a distance of 63.7 light-years. But Jason liked to fancy that if he stared at that particular spot of velvet blackness long enough, and squinted hard enough, his sight could penetrate that unthinkable gulf and discern a tiny yellowish gleam.

He mentioned the absurd thought to Mondrago. The Corsican didn't laugh. He nodded, never taking his eyes off the sky. "I know what you mean. I've tried it too, but every time I do my eyes sort of blur." He was silent for a moment. "I wonder how they've fared? I wonder what they've built there, in almost five hundred years, with no one here even guessing they existed?"

"We'll find out. And I don't think we have long to wait." Jason drew a deep breath and released it. "Buy you a drink?"

"Sure."

They went inside, leaving the night to the stars and their mysteries.

AUTHOR'S NOTE

For the interested reader, Charles Miller's *Khyber* is a lively history of the North-West Frontier of British India. (The subtitle, *The Story of an Imperial Migraine*, pretty much sets the tone.) And Captain H. L. Nevill's *Campaigns on the North-West Frontier* will tell you at least as much as you will ever want to know about the military details, while unconsciously providing insights into the mindset of British officers at the time of its publication (1904). Speaking of mindsets, Byron Farwell's *Armies of the Raj* is a fascinating social history of that unique organization, the Indian Army.

I wouldn't *dare* make up Brigadier General Sir Bindon Blood's expedition into the Swat Valley against Sadullah the Mad Mullah. It occurred as described herein, and the commanders and units I have named actually participated. And it was in fact accompanied and reported on by the young Winston Churchill, who the following year wrote a book about the campaign, *The Story of the Malakand Field Force*, which today is required reading for American and British officers on the ground in Afghanistan. There is no evidence that he got separated from General Jeffreys' brigade on August 19, 1897, much less that he encountered an isolated unit led by my (of course) entirely fictitious three sergeants. But neither is there any proof that he didn't.

I have used traditional words like "Pathan" and "Pushtu" rather than the politically correct modern versions ("Pakhtun," "Pashto") because of their greater familiarity and the fact that they better reflect the flavor of the nineteenth-century period. Incidentally, "Pathan" is pronounced "p'*tahn*," not "*pay*-than."

At this writing almost seventeen hundred extrasolar planets (for which the neologism "exoplanets" has been coined) have been discovered. By the time this novel sees print, the total will undoubtedly be far higher. The debate about the frequency of planets (freakish cosmic accidents versus normal side-effects of the formation of stars) is over. Robert Heinlein was right: planets are as common in the galaxy as eggs in a hen yard. I have therefore felt at liberty to give the stars I have used—all of them actual stars, by the way—whatever planets I choose, within the limits of astrophysical reasonableness. In other words, none of these planets are impossible, but that doesn't mean they will turn out to actually exist. In fact, by the time anyone reads this they may have already been consigned to the realm of might-have-been, where they will be in good company alongside the Mars of Burroughs and Brackett and Bradbury.

To Rudyard Kipling, and to everyone connected with the production of the movie *Gunga Din* (including and especially the actors who brought to life Sergeants McChesney, Cutter and Ballantyne), my acknowledgments, and my most heartfelt thanks for inspiration. And finally, to Barry Hughart, wherever you are, my humble apologies. And please, please give us more wondrous tales of Master Li and Number Ten Ox.

THE MANY WORLDS OF DAVID DRAKE